Growing Up Tough

A Novel by

Roderick Saxey, MD

Written about 2017
Copyright 2023 by Roderick Saxey, MD
Selah, WA
ISBN 978-0997018134
LCCN 2023916019

For the children of immigrants.
That means everyone.

Contents

Foreword

The 1920s saw dramatic changes in everyday American life. Not only were there new inventions and services, but basic human interactions were transformed as the country became more urban than rural and more industrial than agrarian, and as people learned to deal with the aftermath of World War I, the energy of the "Jazz Age," and the assimilation of immigrants from many nations.

Price, Utah, was a microcosm of these changes. Originally founded as a Mormon settlement to support the farms and ranches of the region, by the twenties it had grown to be much more than that. The population was mostly Greek and Italian, with a smattering of other ethnicities, come to work in the coal mines of eastern Utah or to serve the miners and their families. Anti-immigrant feeling was increasing in the country, leading to legislation to limit the influx, and to the brief rise of the Ku Klux Klan.

Like so many nicknames for ethnic, racial, or religious groups, "Mormon" originated as a slur and was meant as an insult. It refers to the acceptance by church members of the Book of Mormon as a book of scripture like the Bible. Although the label was accepted by church members as a nickname and during this period was commonly used by them, nevertheless, the correct name of the church is The Church of Jesus Christ of Latter-day Saints and members are referred to as Latter-day Saints or LDS.

Growing Up Tough is a work of fiction. Any resemblance between the characters in the book and real persons, living or dead, is purely coincidental. Some of the characters in the book are historical, Matt Warner and J. Golden Kimball, for instance. Any resemblance between them and the real persons by those names is not only purely coincidental, but highly gratifying. Whenever possible I quote them directly or paraphrase stories from their biographies or other writings. See the **Notes** on pages 308-309. Those interested in more details are encouraged to consult these texts as well as the many other histories of Carbon County, Price, and the early decades of 20th century America.

Thanks go to my beloved wife, Mellisa Saxey, whose helpful comments and edits were instrumental in shaping the final version. Although this book is a novel, nearly all the major events recounted here actually happened; they are based on stories my father told about growing up in Price during the 1920s and 1930s. Portions of our family history are included, though altered and fictionalized. I discovered in my research that the events Dad talked about were even more tumultuous than he described.

Roderick Saxey, MD

5 December 2017

CHAPTER 1

1922, June 14. Eddie's First Mob

Eddie giggled as he nudged the big horse forward. Mother stood in front of him, head up and very straight and stern, but took a tiny step backward.

"Shirley Edwin Taylor," she said, "You come down from there this instant!"

Eddie had found the horse wandering around the alley behind their lot. He walked up to him carefully, speaking softly and quietly until he could stroke his neck, being careful not to look him in the eye, not to spook him. He then pushed him over next to a trash can he could climb on, and from there slid over to his back and rode him over toward the house.

He hugged his new animal friend, buried his face in his thick neck and mane, and breathed deeply. There was that good smell of life. Eddie loved life. And this horse was a wonderful living creature.

Now that wonderful living creature towered over his little mother, who was less than five feet, even when she pulled herself up as straight and tall as she could.

He laughed more loudly. "Uh-uh."

The horse took another step forward and Mother stepped back again, one hand patting the hair that strayed from where it was gathered in a bun on top of her head.

She shook her finger at him. "I mean it. You are too small to be on such a big horse. You could fall off and break your neck. Come down!"

Eddie considered her demand. He loved Mother and tried to be a good boy, but he knew her fear of horses. This was just too much fun to resist. The horse snorted, flicked its ears, and pawed the ground a little.

"Uh-uh."

Before she could stamp her feet and speak again, Father came out the back door, suppressing a smile. He strode over to the horse, reached up, and pulled the five-year-old down. "Come along young man. I want you to go with me. And stop teasing your mother."

He looked at the horse, made a clicking sound, and said, "Go home." The horse ambled away toward the alley.

He then swatted Eddie on the bottom, squeezed Mother's arm, and said, "I'm going over to Anderson's office to watch the strike. Taking Johnny and Junior too. We'll be home in time for supper."

"He deserves more than a swat for that. He could have been hurt."

"I'll take care of it," Father said as he headed around the side of the house to the front yard.

Mother shook her head as they left. She had heard that reply before and knew nothing would come of it. Not that Father did not discipline his children. He could be very strict at times, like most fathers in those days, but Eddie was the youngest, and sometimes it seemed he just didn't have it in him to be as stern with him as he had been with the others.

Eddie's older brothers were waiting for them. They shared the prominent nose, sharp features, and natural spunk that were typical of the Taylors.

"Follow me, boys. We're going the back way."

They struggled to keep up with their father, who always walked briskly. As they crossed the side streets they peeked to the south where in the distance they could glimpse Main Street. It was filled with people. Some carried signs, some stood, others milled about. There were loud voices, but Eddie could not make out what they were saying.

From Sixth Street they went east past the construction site of the new Roman Catholic Church, around the back of the Mormon Tabernacle, across the gravel play yards, behind the City Office Building, to the back entrance of the Carbon County Courthouse, a big double door beneath a portico with square pillars.

Eddie's eyes widened. A soldier with rifle and bayonet stood guard by each pillar; they stiffened a little as the man and his sons approached. Behind them a sheriff's deputy leaned against the door frame. He tipped his hat and waved them on, saying to the guards, "It's okay, boys. They're friends of Judge Anderson."

"Hi there, Carl. 'Come to see what happens, huh. Go on up, there's a crowd gathering."

They hurried up the back staircase, avoiding the county staff and officials and reporters milling in the foyer to hear what was going on.

The second-floor judge's office had a large window that looked out on Main Street. About a dozen people were in the room, alternately looking out at the street or going back and forth through the hall to the other offices. The transom window was open so they could hear the voices outside.

Judge Anderson was older than Father, with a sprinkling of grey in his hair and cheery smile wrinkles around his eyes. He stuck out his hand and shook Father's. "I am glad you could join us, Carl, and I see you brought your boys."

"Yes. These are Junior, Johnny, and Shirl."

"Call me Eddie," piped up the youngest.

"Mind your manners! He prefers Eddie, from his middle name. I thought it would be good for them to see a little history in action. They might remember it later."

The judge laughed. The man next to him snorted and said, "History! Bunch of nonsense by a bunch of troublemakers. They did the same thing in '03."

Judge Anderson introduced them. "Carl, you probably haven't met Fred yet; he's County Clerk and Town Cynic. Carl just moved here from Provo." Fred Thomas was short, shorter than Dad, thin, and quite a bit older. His skin was tanned and leathery. Anderson added, "Fred is a rancher when he's not clerking. He has a spread out north of Castle Gate. 'Doesn't think much of miners."

"Oh, nice country," said Father. "I go out that way for customers."

"Carl is in the wholesale grocery business. He also manages the old Scowcroft warehouse over on the southside," the Judge added. "Karl Karlson works for him."

"Carl and Karl. Nice to keep things simple."

"Yeah. He's Karl with a K. I'm Carl with a C."

"Ah, I suppose that makes it easier."

"My territory goes out to the Ute reservation and Roosevelt; I cover much of the eastern and northeastern parts of the state."

"Must be a lot of travel."

"At times. Life's a lot easier now with telephones, when people have 'em. Unfortunately, a lot of my customers do not. I spend a lot of time in town at the warehouse too."

Loud voices from Main Street interrupted the conversation. Eddie stretched to see.

Similar to other old Utah towns, Price was laid out with very wide streets, large blocks, and large lots. Main Street ran from east to west with crossing numbered streets from the train tracks in the west eastward. Now that large Main Street in front of the Carbon County Courthouse was filled with people for as far as Eddie could see.

Most were men in work clothes, the coal dust permanently staining them. Like nearly all men in 1922, they wore hats–homburgs, bowlers, newsboy caps. Eddie could not see any fedoras like Father's, and no cowboy hats, which was disappointing for Eddie, who had understood they were moving to "cowboy country" when they left Provo. Then again, these were mostly foreigners. They looked foreign.

Shirts were buttoned right up to the top and had long sleeves. There were very few ties. Grown men usually wore ties, but these miners did not. Almost all had dark hair, with mustaches and a few beards. They all looked angry.

One authoritative voice rose above the others. "I want to assure you, we are giving every consideration to each of the complaints we have received. The governor and the mine owners are meeting with leading individuals in the mining community. But nothing will be accomplished by marching around here this afternoon."

Eddie craned his neck to see where the voice was coming from. It belonged to a man standing beneath the portico in front of the courthouse to the right of Judge Anderson's window. He had a large round belly and wore a black suit with black top hat. A dozen other officials stood behind him. They all wore suits and top hats too, except for an officer in a fine-looking uniform.

"You must disperse," continued the speaker. "Go back to work. Go back to your homes. Let the discussions continue and go."

About this time the steam whistle blew; it was one o'clock. The whistle was at the Chinese laundry and blew every day at 8 am, noon, 1 pm, and 5 pm. This helped the townspeople keep track of time and stay on schedule. Coming now like punctuation for the speaker, the miners in the crowd only muttered and shifted their weight and shook their heads.

It was then that Eddie noticed the machine guns.

CHAPTER 2

1922, June 14.
Eddie Meets A Real Cowboy

Thirty or more soldiers with rifles and bayonets were on either side of the portico. In front of the right and left pillars were machine guns secured behind sandbags, with soldiers manning them, hands on handles. They looked grim, and nervous.

Looking back to the crowd in the street, Eddie saw that most of the men, if they weren't carrying a sign, they were carrying rifles or shotguns. Looking more closely, it looked like those with signs had pistols tucked into their pockets or waistbands.

"Old windbag," muttered Fred with a scowl, nodding toward the speaker in front. "It's all the Italians' fault. 'Bunch of Bolsheviks. Anarchists. They ought 'a just clear 'em out."

"Well," added Anderson, "it did start with them, but now the Greeks have joined in, which is a bit of a surprise and a disappointment to me. I didn't think they would."

"They're troublemakers too. The refuse of Europe. And it's not the miners I mind, at least not as such. It's the blasted immigrants." Fred thought a moment. "Well, not immigrants really. Mother's family came over from Ireland not so long ago. It's just this lot, they're full of communists. They want to do the same thing here they did in Russia."

"That's a bit of a stretch, Fred," replied the judge.

"Listen, if they can take down a czar, they can take down a president too."

"Getting carried away, Fred."

Fred sighed and muttered something.

"What's that?" asked Anderson.

"I said 'Aw, horsefeathers!'" He continued, "Now see here, judge. You know the problem. They're coming too fast. It takes time to turn 'em into Americans. 'Takes time for the stuff in the pot to melt."

"Huh?"

"You know, the 'melting pot'. It takes time for them to not be foreigners anymore and start thinking like Americans."

"You have a point there, Fred."

Father asked, "What are they striking about?"

"Wages, mostly. They were cut when the price of coal fell after the war. And working conditions—they are bad, especially living conditions in the camps. They want improvements in the company houses—but I don't see how they can be made any better without a lot more money than the companies can spare. And they want a union, the UMWA." He looked over at Father. "Have you been in the mining camps?"

"Drove past. 'Didn't see much. I don't have many customers there."

"The companies own it all. They rent the houses to the miners and their families and sell them everything they need at the company stores. Oh, and don't get me wrong, there are a lot of good things about the camps— ball fields, dance halls, theaters, schools, churches. Lot's to do to keep people happy. It's just the homes that need improvement, especially in winter."

"That's where it started," said Fred. "That guy right there." He pointed a bony finger at a young man in the front row of the crowd just below the portico. "Frank Bonnaci. The union sent him here as an 'organizer'. More like Italian immigrant troublemaker."

"Well, talk is one thing," added Anderson. "Problem is, now there have been casualties on both sides. There were demonstrations in the camps and at the mines, the management locked them out, some hotheads got carried away. That led to gunfire. Some Italians were wounded, and Greeks shot a company guard and a sheriff's deputy."

"Yes. I read about it in the paper," said Father.

"We have several in jail, but whether they are really the culprits—who knows? No one admits anything."

Fred's face brightened. "Did you say your name is Taylor? Are you the son of Alfred Taylor?"

Father nodded.

"I knew your father. A good judge. Straight shooter." He looked out at the crowd again. "He would have known what to do with a mob like this. He spent most of the Civil War chasing Quantrill in Kansas, you know."

"Yes, I know." Being the son of Judge Alfred Taylor meant automatic acceptance into the social and political leadership circles of the state, at least those that were Republican. It had counted for a lot in Provo, but not so much in Price, where Democrats were the majority.

Another man ambled into the office, square jaw, straight shoulders, and sandy brown hair, about Fred's age. He wore a fedora like father's only a lighter shade of tan. There was a silver star on his shirt.

"Matt Warner," said Anderson, "good to see you." They exchanged pleasantries and introductions.

"Matt is a justice of the peace and deputy sheriff. He usually hears civil disputes and juvenile cases." He cast an eye at Eddie and his brothers. "Stay out of trouble!" The boys looked solemn. The judge turned away to smile. "But it wouldn't hurt to get acquainted with him in any case. He spins a great yarn."

"Nothin' but the truth," insisted the deputy.

The adults turned back to politics, but Eddie kept glancing at Warner. There was something about him that was interesting. Eddie was not sure what it was. He seemed a little different from the other men in the room, jovial, yet at heart very serious, and a little sad. Eddie thought he had a rough edge to him. Finally, it occurred to him that Warner reminded him of the cowboys he had seen at the movies. Sort of like, what's his name in *The Great Train Robbery*? Tom Mix. Neat name thought Eddie.

Warner surveyed the street for a few minutes and grew quiet. "Mobs give me the willies. Maybe 'cause most of the ones I've seen were after me. These fellas' look a lot like that bunch that surrounded me in Ellensburg. Only *they* had ropes."

Anderson chuckled, "I recall your telling me about that. If I remember right, you talked your way out of it."

"Yeah. I was pretty darn lucky. Problem with a mob, you can't predict what it will do, except it's usually nothin' any good. It has a lot of emotion, but no brain." He stared out the window a minute or two more, then added, "'Looks like the mayor has plenty of help. I think I'll go home."

After he left, Anderson said quietly, "Matt is quite a character. A real cowboy. He's a reformed bandit, you know, partner of Butch Cassidy. One of the more interesting people you will meet in our little town."

"Aha!" thought Eddie. He was right. He looked over to where Warner had just left. Mobs had been after him—what did that mean? He looked a little harder at the crowd outside and marveled that so many people could get so upset. "A lot of emotion, but no brain"—that sounded important. Eddie tried hard to remember it.

There were only a few women, all thin, with prominent cheekbones, hardly any muscle on their arms, and no fat. There were some boys—no girls—standing close to men Eddie supposed were their fathers. One of the boys caught his eye, a boy about his age with jet black hair.

The boy was staring right at him.

CHAPTER 3

1922, June 15. Gus

"So, did they settle anything?" asked Mother over dinner that night.

"No. The miners demand higher wages and better housing. The governor and mayor and company men stalled them off. Told them they would negotiate some more, but not if there was any more violence. Eventually they dispersed."

Mother and Father sat at the heads of the table, with the older children, Lizzie and Junior, on one side, and the younger ones, Johnny and Eddie, on the other. Dinner that night consisted of a small roast with potatoes, stewed carrots, and apple pie for dessert.

Father reached for the carrots. "They also want to join a union, as if that would ever happen here. It didn't seem like much was accomplished."

Eddie piped in, "There were guns everywhere. Machine guns too."

Mother looked worried.

"That's enough, Shirl," said Father to Eddie. "Yes, the Guard is out, and a lot of the miners were armed. But cooler heads prevailed." He cast a reassuring smile to Mother.

Carl Junior looked over at Johnny. "Good thing nobody set off a firecracker," he muttered. "Wow!" He threw his hands into the air.

Mother looked worried again and Father scowled. "Cooler heads," he repeated.

The Taylor family was settling into their new home in Price. City lots in old Utah were designed for family living, with room for a garden, a few domestic animals, and a wood-lined irrigation ditch in back (indispensable in the summer). The streets all had large gutters for the spring runoff, which near the mountains could be brisk.

Eddie's home was typical for nicer houses of the time, with a large front porch with four square pillars. It led into a front room, a parlor, and a dining room off a very busy kitchen with coal cookstove, and icebox. Four small bedrooms were upstairs. The basement was for storage and the coal-fired furnace. A small back porch looked onto the back yard, which held the garden, a shed, and a pen for animals. The Taylors were lucky to have indoor plumbing with a bathroom next to the kitchen.

A graveled driveway was marked off at the street by a large rock on either side. This led to a narrow, detached garage with workshop, then continued as a path to the back alley. Electric transmission lines had recently been installed in Price, so the home was well lit without messy gaslights.

Next morning dawned a clear and warm June day. Mother woke Eddie with one of her favorite songs, "Over the mountains the sun is now shining, and all of the world is so bright and refreshed." Then she turned to Eddie and said, "Time to be up, so brighten your mind, awaken your senses and see what you find."

After breakfast and Mother's daily admonition to be good, Eddie went into the back to explore his new neighborhood. He hoped to find that stray horse waiting for him, but no such luck. Instead, he wandered toward the alley, leaving his leather shoes behind so his feet could enjoy the soft dirt and new grass along the way.

Looking to the west he could see where the land dipped down toward the river at the west end of Main, curving around to exit the town beneath a railroad trestle. Mesas and tablelands dotted the scene, leading to the mountains in the distance. His view to the south was obscured by buildings, but he knew already that beyond the fairgrounds were flatlands with bare, rolling hills, more desert than anything else. Most of the town was to the east.

To the north a couple blocks was Wood Hill, stretching diagonally away. Eddie thought it was the most interesting feature around, with vertical cliffs, some of which had rounded fronts that looked like columns. High school students had painted a large *C* there for Carbon High.

An old man was working in the garden on the other side of the alley two doors down, slump shouldered and with a coarse, grey beard. He and Eddie exchanged waves. No one was out in the neighbor yards to right or left, so he continued to the street, crossing to the next alley north. One or two trashcans stood at each lot along the alley; Eddie peaked in each one as he went. "You never know what somebody might throw out," he thought.

"Hey, you," came a voice from Eddie's right. "What do you think you're doin'?"

It was the dark-haired boy from the mob. He strode up to Eddie.

"Nothin'. Just out for a walk."

"Well, those are our trashcans. Why are you lookin' in 'em?"

" 'Cause I can. What's it to you?"

"Well, you can't. Our trashcans. Our alleyway."

"It's a free country," insisted Eddie.

The two boys had been sizing each other up. They were about the same age and height, both dressed in shirts and coveralls, with straw hats and bare feet. The boy unexpectedly shoved Eddie's chest hard with both hands.

Eddie shoved back and soon the pair were rolling around in the alley, letting fly with mostly ineffective punches and incomplete invectives. It was not long before they tired and sat on the grass panting.

"You're new, aren't you?" asked the boy.

"Yeah. How about you?"

"We've been here for years. Where 'you from?"

"Provo. You?"

"I was born in Greece. But we moved here when I was two, so I don't remember it."

"I saw you in the street yesterday."

"Yeah?" The boy wrinkled his forehead. "Are you the kid that was up in the courthouse window?"

"That was me," replied Eddie. "Is your father a coal miner?"

The boy smiled, "Pop? Nah. He has a shop over on Main Street."

"Why were you out in the street then?"

"Pop took me. My cousin works in the mine at Castle Gate, so we went for him. Anyway, Pop said it was history and I should see it up close. "

"Huh. My father said the same thing." The boys sat quietly for awhile, contemplating their common experience.

Then Eddie asked, "What's your name?"

"Argus Constantine Pappas, but I go by Gus. What's yours?"

"Eddie. Eddie Taylor," came the reply. The boys stuck out their hands and shook.

Eddie pointed down the alley and said, "Let's go see what's in the cans."

"Why? What's so interesting about people's trash?"

"Oh, you never know what people might throw away. One time I found a little bag with three marbles in it. Why would somebody throw them away? It didn't matter to me if they had chips in them."

The two boys picked up their straw hats, dusted themselves off, and started along the alley, chatting as they went.

"My ancestor invented history," said Gus, straightening proudly.

"Invented? How can you invent history?"

"Pop told me all about it. He's always telling me about what our ancestors did."

"But isn't history just stuff that's happened? How can you invent that?"

Gus wrinkled his brow for a moment. "I don't know. But it was our ancestor. I think Pop said his name was Herodotus. Pop says a lot of stuff."

"I don't know too much about our ancestors or history. Father tells us stories sometimes. Usually to explain what he reads in the paper."

They had finished with the trashcans in Gus's block and the next, not finding much except for a nice piece of rubber and a broken screwdriver. How could someone break a screwdriver? They turned east and thought the alley on Eighth Street looked promising. No sooner had they looked in the first pair of cans than a small rock zinged between them and struck one of the cans with a loud clang.

CHAPTER 4

1922, June 15.
The Youngest Gangsters. Lambie

The boys looked quickly around to see where the rock had come from. A boy stood in the adjacent yard with a slingshot in his hands and another rock ready to shoot. Two other boys stood behind him.

"What are you kids doing here?" he demanded. He and the other boys were a little older than Eddie and Gus, with jet black hair like Gus's and wearing soft leather caps pulled down in front.

Gus gave the new boy the same answer Eddie had given him not so long earlier. "Nothin'. Just out for a walk. It's a free country." The comment was not well received.

"Well, get outta' here! This is our neighborhood."

Outnumbered and with no slingshots to return fire, Eddie and Gus ran back the way they had come, small rocks peppering their backsides as they ran. The boys in the caps laughed loudly as they ran.

Safely out of range, they stopped to catch their breath and rub their wounds.

Gus shook his head. "I knew not to go there. My brother warned me."

"What do you mean?"

"My brother warned me. That's Little Italy. That block and the next. We always walk the long way around. The big kids think they're mafia or something and always pick on us."

"What's 'mafia'?"

"It's like a gang. A gang of bad guys."

"Huh." Eddie thought for a moment. "We should make our own gang."

"Why do that?"

"We'll be a gang of good guys."

"Like the cops?"

"Yeah."

The two new gangsters spit in their palms, shook hands, and formed the youngest gang in town.

Eddie said goodbye to Gus and headed home for lunch. He found the stray horse waiting in the alley, watching him approach and lowering his head.

Eddie had just given him a rub on the neck when the old neighbor who had waved at Eddie earlier came up and said, "There you are, you old nag." He looked at Eddie. "Don't mind her. Mousey, she likes to go a' wanderin'."

"Oh, I don't mind, Mister. She's a good horse."

The old man smiled. "Yes. Yes, that she is. If she ever is in your way, just tell her to go home and swat her on the rump. She'll mosey back to the barn. What's your name, young man?"

"Eddie."

"I'm Mr. Frandsen. You live over yonder?" He pointed toward the Taylor home.

Eddie nodded, and Mr. Frandsen nodded in reply.

The two parted in different directions, then Mr. Frandsen turned to add, "And welcome to the neighborhood!"

"Thanks, mister."

Mother looked with dismay at her youngest child, disheveled and covered in dirt. She noticed a tear on his bottom where one of the rocks had hit. "How in the world did you do that?"

"I guess I sat down hard," was his excuse.

She hustled him to the kitchen sink and helped him wash, reminding him how important it was to remain clean and neat. "Cleanliness is next to godliness. Don't forget it."

Johnny and Junior watched from the dining room and smirked, careful that Mother did not see their expressions.

Father was home for lunch that day. "Where's Lizzie?" he asked.

"She's having lunch at a friend's, Dear. A girl named Dorothy, likes to be called Dot. I think she's the bishop's daughter."

After lunch came a nap; despite his protests, Eddie fell asleep quickly.

When he awoke, rather than go back out to play with Gus, Mother had him sit at the kitchen table with a book, pencil, and writing paper.

"You will be starting school next year," she said. "That is too long to wait, so I will teach you to read this summer."

His dismay showed.

"Don't worry. There will still be plenty of time for play. And you will enjoy this. Reading will open up a whole new world for you. Worlds and worlds."

Eddie was skeptical and thought the new world of Price was enough for the moment, but he knew there was no point in arguing. Mother could be very stubborn.

"Besides," she continued, "Father has a surprise for you afterward. You will love it." He brightened up at that.

After reading lesson, Eddie hurried into the backyard and down the alley, but neither horse nor Gus was anywhere to be found. He returned slowly, making his way around to the front yard to wait for Father.

Most of the families on his block had a car, often a Ford Model T sedan or touring car, uniformly black. There were a few others, Studebaker, Chevrolet, Davis, and others, which sported the occasional blue or maroon.

Not many trucks on this town block, though they were more common in the country, and only an occasional horse with carriage or wagon. He was particularly fond of those and always looked for the horse-drawn wagon that delivered ice for the icebox.

He watched now for Father's Ford, but his attention was diverted by the progress of a caterpillar crossing the sidewalk next to the front steps, so he did not actually see Father drive up until he was in the driveway.

Father extinguished his cigar and left it on the dash—Mother had made smoking off limits in the house. Eddie ran up and hugged him as he came around the fender.

"Well. By your enthusiasm I see Mother must have let the cat out of the bag."

"Cat? Did you bring me a cat?"

"Much better than that."

Father opened the back door of the car and reached in. When he turned around, he had a little lamb in his arms.

"This is for you, Shirl."

The boy took a deep breath, then squealed for joy. The lamb bleated.

"Now don't startle him." Father leaned over to hand the lamb to his son, who took him gently and caressed his shoulder.

"He's a bummer lamb and will need a lot of care."

"Oh, I will take very good care of him. What's a 'bummer'?"

"That means the mother sheep, the ewe, could not take care of him, usually because there were twins, and she could only take care of one. Without you, Eddie, the lamb would die."

The boy's eyes grew wide and his voice solemn. "I will take very good care of you," he said to the lamb. "I will be your ewe."

"Will you teach me what to do?" he asked his father.

"Of course."

They walked around the side of the house to the pen in the backyard. The lamb was soft and warm in Eddie's arms. His wool was all white, including his face, except for a small spot of black wool on his right cheek, like a beauty mark. He pressed his face into the wool and smelled again the good clean smell of life. It was like Mousey, the horse, but cleaner. Mother had been right, it was only his first day learning to read and a whole new world was already opening up for him.

"I will name you 'Lambie'," he said.

CHAPTER 5

1922, June-July.
Ti Kanis. New Routines.

Eddie was up before breakfast to check on Lambie. His lamb was at the gate of the pen, bleating anxiously and flicking his tail. He took him up in his arms and hugged him. "Don't worry Lambie, breakfast is coming."

In a few minutes Mother came out with a baby bottle of warm goat's milk. Lizzie, Junior, and Johnny followed along to watch.

Mother showed Eddie how to shelter the lamb with one arm while holding the bottle upright so he could suck the milk and not get too much air.

"You have to stop every little while to let air in the bottle," she explained. "Lambie won't like that, but he will get used to it. Just like a human baby, he will get awful gas if you don't give him a chance to burp in between. And the bottle won't give milk after a bit when the pressure gets too high."

"Why is that?" Eddie loved to ask why and to figure out how things work.

"Sucking makes a vacuum. That means the pressure outside becomes greater than inside and the rubber nipple collapses. When you stop for a moment, air goes back into the bottle, and it will work again."

Eddie pulled the bottle back when the sucking seemed hard. Lambie objected but made up for lost time when the flow of milk returned. Some of it dribbled out the sides of his mouth and onto Eddie's arm and leg.

"You will need to feed him several times a day until we can get him weaned."

"What's 'weaned'?"

"That means changed over to regular sheep food—grain and hay. It won't be long, but in the meantime, we must make sure he is fed well. Now is the most important time to make sure he survives."

Eddie petted Lambie as he fed him. He also thought about Mother's last comment. Survives. It had not occurred to him how fragile a little lamb like this must be, and how much it would have to grow before it could handle the regular life of a sheep.

After his own breakfast he checked again on Lambie, then hurried over to see Gus, who came back with him.

"He's beautiful," said Gus. They both stood admiring Lambie's innocent face and white wool, then crouched down next to him to stroke his shoulders and back. "Pop took me to the mountains once to see the flocks and sheepherders and newborn lambs. It was real swell."

"Are there a lot of sheep in the mountains?"

"Oh, scads and scads."

They talked more of lambs and sheep, then calves and cattle, eventually leaving the lamb in his pen and wandering off to play the morning away.

They stopped at Gus's house to pick up a ball. He introduced Eddie to his mother, who was in the kitchen as they entered. She was short, like Mother, with a wide smile that wrinkled her whole face. She wore a white apron over her black dress, and her hair was pulled back in a yellow kerchief.

"*Ti kanis?*" she said in a strong Greek accent. "Is good, meet Argus friend."

Eddie smiled back.

"Say '*kala*'," whispered Gus.

"*Kala!*"

Gus's mother smiled even wider. "Ah! Eddie. You learn a little Greek." She reached out and pinched his cheek, laughed, and turned to the kitchen counter where she picked up two flakey, sticky pastries and handed them to the boys.

"Baklava. You eat."

And eat they did, one of the most exquisite treats Eddie had ever tasted. The rest of the morning was spent tossing Gus's ball back and forth, enjoying the beautiful spring weather. Gus's little sister, Athena, joined them. She was a year younger and often inserted herself into her brother's games. She was, complained Gus, a tagalong, and he ended up being a tagalong's babysitter.

"So, Gus," asked Eddie, " What does *ti kanis* mean?"

"It means 'how are you', but most of the time it is more like 'hello'."

"And *kala*?"

"That's harder. I guess it means 'I'm okay', but it's bigger than that. 'Goodness', 'beauty', 'beautiful'. Pop says one of our ancestors wrote a lot about it. Wrote about things that are good, true, and beautiful. Guy named Aristotle."

"Your pop knows a lot."

Gus grinned. "Yeah. He talks a lot too."

After lunch, nap, and reading lesson, Mother herded Eddie along with his brothers and sister into the parlor. "I have a surprise for you," she said.

She turned to the Victrola and held up a record. "Enrico Caruso. You will love it." She placed the record, turned the crank, and sat in the armchair to listen with the children. Lizzie moaned, but not loud enough for Mother to hear.

Mother loved music. She had a fine singing voice and was often in demand for church choirs and recitals. Eddie loved to hear her sing as she went about the household chores each day. Now she could be heard softly humming along with *La Donna e Mobile*.

As the song ended, she looked dreamily into the distance, sighed deeply, then turned to the children. "You know, Caruso died last year. It was a great loss and very sad. But just this morning I heard that his accompanist is touring the country to raise money for the Catholics and will be here in Price next month! We are all going. It will be a wonderful concert."

But first came work.

They had moved to town a little late in the season for putting in a garden, but Father plowed one anyway, and all the boys helped plant tomatoes, squash, corn, and beans, using starts from the Farmers' Co-op rather than planting from seed as he normally would have.

One of the appealing things about this house was the nice double row of fruit trees in back. "A little orchard!" Father exclaimed when he first saw it. There were cherries, apples, plums, pears, and peaches—everything anyone could want.

Planting finished late in the day as twilight was coming on and the sky overhead was pink and gold and violet. Father leaned against his hoe, looked down the rows of little plants, then at his three sons. "Always remember this, sons," he said softly. "Remember how good it is to work the soil, to smell the good smells of life, to be a gardener in this beautiful world, to help things grow."

The smells of gardening were not always so good. "Oh!" cried Eddie as he pulled weeds one day in the far corner by the radishes, "What's that awful smell?" Father came over to see. He separated the thick weeds by the irrigation ditch with a spade. There they found a rotting trout that had unwisely swum into the ditch from the canal and jumped out of the ditch onto the ground beside it.

"Well," said Father. "Free fertilizer." He scooped up the fish with his shovel and, allowing it to fall apart in pieces, tossed it around the base of the tomato plants. "Animals live, die, then return to the earth they are made of, and provide nourishment for others. All things are useful. All things are here for a reason."

Eddie decided he would let someone else weed around the tomatoes for awhile.

Early summer slipped quickly by. The Taylor children were first responsible for chores around the house and in the garden, then enjoyed the companionship of new friends, exploring the town and looking forward to the next event on the calendar. Each day and each week had its own rhythm; chores, meals, play, lessons. Mother always seemed busiest, with cooking, cleaning, washing, sewing, and mending.

Father left in the morning and returned for lunch, then again for dinner, except when he was travelling. His favorite chore was working in the garden, which included instructing the children in the details of weeding, watering, and trimming. Most evenings were for visiting with family friends, telling stories, and sometimes singing together around the upright piano in the parlor.

Some evenings during the week were diverted with church meetings–Primary for Eddie, Scouts for the older boys, the youth Mutual Improvement Association for Lizzie, and Relief Society for Mother. Saturday was the day to bring the week to a close, take baths, and prepare clothes for Sunday, when Mother and the children went to church. Father went occasionally, when Mother was singing or one of the children had a recitation to give or program to participate in. Then they all enjoyed a quiet day at home and visits with friends and fellow church members. Small town life moved elegantly from one social event to another.

July promised to be especially eventful, and the town looked forward to hearing Caruso's accompanist. Before the concert came Independence Day. Father hung a flag on either side of the front porch. Most other houses had a flag or banner out, and banners and flags lined Main Street.

Father was always indulgent of his children and their love of things that went "bang," giving each a daily allotment of firecrackers. For Eddie there were ladyfingers and for his older brothers two-inchers and cherry bombs. Lizzie expressed little interest in having any of her own. Bottle rockets, cannons, and salutes were saved for the evenings.

The afternoon of July third, Eddie was comfortably seated in his wagon in the front yard with a lap full of lady fingers. He picked them up carefully, one at a time, lighting them with a punk, and throwing them into the yard, laughing at each little explosion. Somehow as he was looking away, the punk fell into his lap onto the remaining ladyfingers resulting in sudden explosions in his lap! He jumped to safety, brushing his coveralls frantically, which now had black marks in front and smelled of gunpowder. Johnny and Junior, sitting on the porch, burst into laughter and rolled back holding their stomachs.

CHAPTER 6

1922, July. The Best Month Ever

Next day the family walked to Main Street to watch the 4th of July parade. It started with welcoming comments by several dignitaries and a speech by Mayor Watson, who reviewed the sacrifices of previous generations of Americans, the need for loyalty to the Constitution, and appreciation for all who worked to prepare this celebration. Eddie listened and tried hard to pay attention. Every once in a while, he pulled on Father's trousers and asked, "When will he stop?"

"Soon," came the reply.

Eddie was not the only one who was relieved when the Honor Guard next to the mayor's stand finally fired the cannon to signal the parade to begin.

Veterans of the Great War carried flags, followed by veterans of the Spanish-American, Indian, and Civil Wars. Bands from Price, Helper, Castle Gate, and other area towns played rousing songs like *Yankee Doodle* and *Stars and Stripes Forever*. There were decorated floats on trucks and cars and horse-drawn wagons, made by towns, schools, clubs, and the Greek and Italian societies, portraying scenes from American history. Altogether a fine parade.

Afterwards the crowd broke up, most going to the playing fields for baseball between the various town teams. They greeted friends and acquaintances along the way. Judge Anderson was there with his wife and their daughter, Angela. Their son was playing on the Price City team. Mrs. Anderson had become a close friend of Mother and they often walked to church together.

From the playing fields the center of attention shifted to the county fairgrounds, on the south of town across the railroad tracks near the Price River, where various patriotic displays were arranged under pavilions. As the Taylors entered the fairgrounds, they passed a display of new rifles and pistols in a booth sponsored by Carson's Guns and Ammo, a store just off Main near the tracks. A sign announced a contest.

"Enter to win," shouted the man behind the booth. "Show everyone you're the marksman to beat!"

"What's the prize?" asked Father.

"This right here," the man said holding up a beautiful new Winchester 30-30 model 94.

Father thought a moment, then said, "I could use a new hunting rifle. When's the shoot?"

"You're in luck, Mister. Just about half an hour. Over there." He pointed toward a field behind the booth where a target was set against a stack of hay bales.

"Okay. Sign me up."

"That'll be one dollar, entry fee."

Eddie's eyes widened—a whole dollar!

When the time came for the shoot, there were twenty-two men lined up to try their skills. Father commented that meant the booth must have doubled their money on the gun. One by one, each shot three rounds with the new rifle. Eliminating the first fifteen men was easy, but the remaining seven all had nearly the same score.

They had a second series of shoots, this time one shot each. Now only three contestants were left.

The final round came, with only one shot each. Each was just into the bullseye. Then Father shot. The judges retrieved his target. Not only was it in the bullseye, it was the exact center!

Cheers went up as Father received his new rifle. He held it over his head in triumph. The crowd at the range slowly dispersed to the other attractions. Eddie stood very straight and tall as he walked along with his father, a big smile on his face. Father was the best.

Next to the shooting contest, Eddie thought the best part of the day were the barbecues. The Greek and Italian community pits were largest, with whole mutton, pork, goat, and beef roasted over hot coals and seasoned with various herbs. The French shepherds, actually Basque, also had a smaller barbecue with mutton. They were all different, but each was delicious. Eddie thought they were wonderful.

Gus waved from the Greek tent. "Can I go around with Gus?" he asked.

Father consented and gave him three dimes. "That should get you plenty to eat," he said, and the boys ran off toward the serving booths.

"Meet us at the bandstand before dark," Mother called after them. The other boys and Lizzie had already joined groups of their friends.

"I guess it's just you and me, Mother," Father said, his new rifle cradled in one arm and the other around his sweetheart's waist.

For Eddie and Gus, the afternoon consisted of walking from one event to another. Along with other children, they occasionally pulled a firecracker from their pockets and tossed it. This was usually followed by some adult shouting, "Not around here. Beat it, kid."

First, they watched a tug of war with ten men on each side pulling a large rope until one side or the other was dragged into a mud puddle between them. Then there was a girls' footrace across a grassy field. Before each event an official would announce, "Please, no fireworks until the contest is completed." Eddie and Gus lost interest quickly and wandered back to the food tents, which they thought were the best part of the day anyway.

Eddie was last to join the family at their rendezvous site near the bandstand, He held up a small paper bag with round pieces of dark meat in it. "Everything was really great, especially the Greek mutton and the Italian beef. And as I was leaving, the man gave me this for free."

"That was nice of him."

"Yeah. They taste good, but different. They squeak when you bite down on them."

"Really?"

"Yeah. He called them Rocky Mountain oysters. I thought oysters came from the ocean. Isn't that right, Father?"

"Yes, Son. The name is sort of a joke." He glanced over at Mother and said quietly, "They are actually sheep testicles."

"Huh?"

Now he leaned over and whispered in Eddie's ear. His eyes grew wide, and he started to gag. Johnny and Junior were holding their sides and doubling over; they seemed to do that a lot, thought Eddie. Mother and Lizzie looked away.

"I need something to drink." Eddie handed the bag to Father and went in search of water. He began to think his brothers had had enough laughter at his expense.

That night was the town fireworks display. Families spread out blankets on the grass and gazed in delight as rocket after rocket exploded overhead. When the show ended, they gathered themselves together and strolled back to their homes, commenting on the excellence of the food and the beauty of the display, enjoying the summer air and the cool of late evening.

The concert by Caruso's accompanist was the next major social event in Price. Besides the whole Taylor family were the Andersons, Thomases, Warners, Pappases, and many others Eddie and his family had met, as well as many they had not, all crowded into the Price Theater. Mother's long hair was gathered into a large mound on the top of her head, crowned with an elegant black hat with small sewn beads that glistened like jewels. Eddie was proud of how she looked with the other fine ladies of the town.

He pulled at his collar and settled back in his seat. He enjoyed music, especially the songs his mother sang or hummed, but the concert was long for a young boy, and he was soon fast asleep, dreaming of musicians, recordings, and his mother's voice. Even the applause at the end did not wake him. Father carried him home.

Eddie woke up next morning to the aroma of bacon coming up from the kitchen. Eddie loved to eat, not as an over-eater, but as one who appreciated the wonderful variety of flavor and texture a good cook could create. And Mother was a very good cook, the undisputed boss of a kitchen that produced a steady stream of tasty, hearty food.

One of the family favorites was *mochshe*. "We learned it from the Arabs," Mother said, emphasizing the first long A. Father ground pieces of mutton shoulder, then Mother combined it with rice, tomatoes and tomato paste, garlic, onions, salt and pepper, and spices.

"Cinnamon, nutmeg, cloves, and allspice." Eddie could recite it like a song.

Eddie's assignment was to go to the grape vines with scissors and cut grape leaves, making sure to pick ones big enough to use, but young enough to be still tender. The meaty mixture was wrapped in steamed cabbage and grape leaves, and stuffed in hollowed out zucchini and green peppers, cooked in a pot for several hours until it was done, then served with a tomato sauce.

"It is just warmed up ketchup," Father whispered. "Don't tell anyone." To which he added, "The Greeks make something like this, but it's not nearly as good. Don't tell them that either."

The high point of every summer in Utah was Pioneer Day, celebrated each July 24th. That was the day in

1847 when Brigham Young, reaching the mouth of a canyon overlooking Salt Lake Valley, sat up in his wagon, surveyed the scene, and announced, "This is the right place. Drive on."

Pioneer Day started with another parade, this one celebrating the courage and determination of the early settlers, some of whom, children at the time, were still alive and now were aged honorees. Many children took part in the Pioneer Day parades, even Eddie, riding as a passenger on Fred Thomas's wagon, holding Lambie and stroking him to keep him calm.

There were games in the afternoon, including footraces and wrestling as well as baseball. In the evening were square dances and other country dances, followed by another fireworks display, this one even larger than the one on the Fourth.

Eddie was very tired as Mother tucked him into bed that night. After his prayers he asked her, "Is every July as great as this one has been?"

"This was especially good, wasn't it?" she replied. "The people in Price have welcomed us and we have made many friends."

She thought for a moment. "No, Shirl, not every July is as great as this one. Not every month is the same as another," she said truthfully. "But every month, every day, is as great as we make it. God sent us here to have many different experiences, some good, some bad. We can learn and grow from all of them. And they are all good if we learn from them. Do you understand?"

"I think so."

Mother smiled, kissed him on the forehead, and turned out the light as she left the room.

"I still think this July was the best month possible," said Eddie to himself as he drifted off to sleep. "At least, so far."

He could not have imagined all that was yet to come.

CHAPTER 7

1922, November.
The Grandparents

The train squealed to a halt, great puffs of steam exhaling on either side of the engine. Eddie heard a voice inside the train call out, "Price Station". The Taylors were all gathered on the platform, craning their necks to see the passengers exit the car doors.

"*Gruess di', Mutti,*" Mother called out as she saw Grandma and Grandpa Mueller step off the train.

Grandma was little, even shorter than Mother, and still spoke only broken English. Her face was wrinkled, and her mouth was a perpetual smile.

After hugging Mother, she turned to Lizzie, "*Ach, Liz',* you grew!"

Turning to Mother, she said, "Such a young lady she is!"

After being away from them for nearly six months, Eddie realized that Grandpa looked different from other men. Not his full black beard speckled with grey, nor his straight, almost military posture; those were typical. It was the hat! Grandpa always wore a small, red, conical hat that was flat on top and had a black tassel that swayed when he walked.

After hugs all around, Grandpa hoisted Eddie into his left arm, his right arm around Junior while Father took his satchel.

"I missed you, Grandpa," Eddie said.

"I missed you, too, Shirl."

"I had forgotten your hat."

"My fez?" He laughed. "It is a habit for me, from old country. Everyone in the Ottoman East wears one, except the Arabs. They wear the keffiyeh. And Jews wear the kippah. And Greeks wear . . ." He thought for a moment, "Little caps with visors. Businessmen like I was, who go everywhere, important people wear the fez."

"How was the train?" asked Father.

"Very good. We left Provo this morning, stopped at Spanish Fork, Soldier Summit, Castle Gate, Sunnyside, and Helper, and now we are here. All in comfort and safety—a wonderful thing to travel so fast! A little snow at the summit, but not enough to slow us down."

"Excellent. I am glad they finished the repairs. Maybe this new company can keep things running on time."

"Let's not get our hopes up too high," laughed Grandpa.

They all climbed into the touring car and headed for home. The hills were barren and brown now, except in little crevices and at higher elevations where junipers and other small trees grew. There was a dusting of snow on the hills. The breeze blew cold. It was the last week in November and time for Thanksgiving.

Before anyone could get settled at the house, Eddie pulled his grandparents' arms to show them into the backyard. "You've got to see my lamb," he exclaimed.

Lambie came running up to him as he approached the gate, bleating loudly. He was much larger now, his tail long since docked, and he had a winter coat of thick wool. He nuzzled Eddie's leg, then his face when he knelt down.

"A fine lamb is that," said Grandma.

"You are doing a good job raising him," added Grandpa.

"He follows me everywhere, when I let him."

"Animals know good people. They know people who love them and will take care of them."

"That's right," added Father. "It's good to be close to the creatures and learn to communicate with them." He looked over at his father-in-law. "We hope to add a dog to the family but have not found the right one yet. Perhaps in the spring. There is a cat who lives in the shed and keeps down the mice, but she is not terribly affectionate."

"Ah," said Grandpa, "cats are often, what's the word? Aloof." He then added in a lower voice, "It may be wise to have another pet before summer. Before this little one is a yearling."

Father only smiled and nodded.

As the family returned inside Father turned on the light switch in the parlor only to see a flash, and then darkness. The boys followed him to the fuse box where he saw that the fuse was burned out.

"My buddy, Hal, says you can put a penny in the place of the fuse, and it will work swell," suggested Junior.

Father shook his head. "Uh huh. That would work but run the risk of the wires getting hot and melting or even catching fire. The fuse would not have blown if there weren't a problem in the circuit, a short somewhere. No. We will have to sit in darkness tonight. Or in a different room. I will call the electrician tomorrow."

So that night they enjoyed the warmth of the dining room where they sat exchanging stories and catching up on news of family and gossip of neighbors. Eddie and the other children listened attentively and answered questions, but generally remained quiet while the grownups talked. Inevitably the conversation turned to politics. At that point Mother and Grandma and Lizzie moved to the kitchen to continue with more personal topics.

"I read the coal miners' strike is over," said Grandpa.

"Yes, finally. It dragged on forever it seemed. In the end the miners got a raise. No union though. It was very painful."

"Especially for the dead and wounded. The rioters, they are in jail?"

"Fourteen Greeks and one Italian."

"So, there will be justice for the deputy who was killed and the others who were hurt."

"Perhaps. But don't believe the newspapers; they are full of lies. People I've talked to say the ones in jail were picked at random. Most of them weren't even there during the riot. Meanwhile, whole camps . . . Well, it is hard enough on the men. There are women and children in the camps too. It was very hard on them with no income during the strike."

The room fell silent.

Grandpa cleared his throat. "The Greeks I knew overseas were very good people. Confused politics, but very faithful Orthodox. Dependable. Italians too, most of them. How are things, now the strike is over?"

"They are working and being paid, and the company stores have supplies. The aid societies are helping out with food and clothing. A lot of Greeks live here in town, shopkeepers, tailors, craftsmen, and they help out their relatives who work in the mines or live in the mining camps. Lots of Italians there, and others, Bohemians and Austrians."

"Austrians?"

"Yes, mostly from the south and east—the Balkans. *Bohunks.*"

"My best friend is Greek," interjected Eddie. "His name is Gus." Everyone looked at him and smiled.

"Ah," said Grandpa, "Has his family been here long?"

"I guess. He doesn't remember Greece at all."

Grandpa turned to Father. "Such a mess in Greece. Have you read about it in the papers?"

"A little. What have you heard?"

"Well, the Turks beat them bad in the war, the king abdicated, and the royal family is in exile. Several ministers are in prison. No government, whole country in turmoil. The British have been trying to work something out. Last I heard there's a big conference going on, but who knows what will come of it?"

The men nodded knowingly.

"The Italians seem to be doing better, in Italy. This new guy, Mussolini. Do you know anything about him?"

"No," said Grandpa. "I think he may just be another puffed up 'big man'. Time will tell. The pictures of him. He looks . . . arrogant."

Grandpa sighed. He wanted to change the subject, looked around at Father, Johnny, Junior, and Eddie. He fixed his eyes on Eddie.

CHAPTER 8

1922, November. Family History and Thanksgiving

"Do you know my family story, how I ended up in the Holy Land, and then here?" he asked. Eddie shook his head. Grandpa smiled. He loved telling a good story.

"My ancestors lived in a village near Stuttgart in Germany. Great Grandpa was forced into the army to fight Napoleon. He was killed somewhere in France. Great Grandma decided to go with her brother and join other family in Russia, where Catherine, the empress, had opened up empty land for German settlers. On the way down the Danube was terrible fever. Many died, including Great Grandma and two of the children.

"So, by the time they reached Neudorff in Russia, near Odessa, Grandpa and his other brothers and sisters were orphans. The family and the German community there helped, but Grandpa had to hurry and become head of house, even though he was just a young teenager. I remember him. He was very strong. Quiet, strong man.

"I grew up there and learned wagon making from my father. And from Cousin Ivan I learned herbs and how to pick them and use them to heal sickness. I also learned languages—I had to, everyone spoke something different—German, Russian, Turkish, Greek, Arabic, a little French. Finally English when I came here.

"As young man I wanted to do more than build wagons, so tried being a merchant. That was how I travelled all over the Black Sea and eastern Mediterranean, among the Ottomans, to Egypt, to Greece, and, of course, to Jerusalem, the Holy City, where I met your grandmother."

Eddie waved his hand. "Was her family Arabs?"

Everyone laughed.

"No," said Grandpa. "Her family was also from near Stuttgart. They believed Christ would return soon and wanted to help the Jews rebuild temple in Jerusalem, so when her father was warned by a friend that her brother was going to be forced into the army, he sold a cow and used the money to buy passage to a colony of German Christians in Jerusalem. He left in the middle of the night and next day when the soldiers came for him, he was gone. Then the family saved and sold all they could so they could join him a few months later."

Grandpa sat back and sighed. "I first saw your grandmother at the Joppa Gate. She was carrying water. I was in love with her from that first moment, for all she was so young. I followed her home so I could meet her father."

Just then the ladies came in from the kitchen with a tray of herbal tea.

"What stories you tell?" asked Grandma.

"Only how the stars shine in your eyes, how your skin has heaven's glow, and how music flows from your voice."

She swatted him on the shoulder. "*Ach, du Gans!* My eyes are dull and my skin is wrinkled from much work. Like an ox I am." She did not comment on her voice. Mother had learned to sing from her. When she was young, Grandma had wanted to be a singer, but life's path did not lead that way.

"So how did you end up in Utah?" asked Johnny.

"The Mormon missionaries needed a place to stay, so they rented a room from us. We did not think much of a new religion, but then. . . It was the fire in their eyes. It was the Spirit that spoke to our hearts when they taught. And," he smiled, "it was the book. The Book of Mormon. It testifies of Christ in such a way. Well, we knew it was true. So, we were baptized in 1887 in the Mediterranean at Joppa, then gathered here to Utah."

"It was so beautiful, our baptism," said Grandma. "The water, the sky, the curious Arabs. And then the move. *Ach*, the move, it was hard." She looked over at Grandpa. "Only my sister. . ."

He put his arm around her. "Only her sister came to the ship to see us off. All the rest, big family, all the rest would not come. Even to say 'goodbye'."

"But here you are now," interjected Mother. "Think of all that has happened since. So many wonderful things. Children and grandchildren and many friends."

Both the grandparents nodded. "Yes," said Grandpa. "We have much to be thankful for. Life is good."

Grandpa looked around the room. "I had many friends with the Jews. Not many Jews in Holy Land, but quite a few in Russia. They have a toast when they get together, especially for weddings, family things. They say, *l'chaim*. It means 'to life'. I think is good toast."

He lifted up his cup of tea. "To Life!"

They all lifted their cups to join his. "To Life!"

Next day was the day before Thanksgiving. The electrician, Nick Fulcher, arrived a little after noon. He was about Father's height, stocky, with a crooked nose and a noticeable limp. He carried a toolbox as he made his way first to the fuse box, then the light switch, then back again. Eddie followed along and watched closely.

First, he disconnected the light switch and replaced the fuse, then returned to the switch. Glancing at Eddie he said, "See these two wires? We call one positive and the other negative. If they touch each other, they complete the circuit. I know if they have electricity running through them like this."

He then touched both wires with his finger. Eddie heard a small sound.

"There. I could feel the shock on my finger tip." A black spot was on his finger where he had checked many previous circuits. "You wanna try?"

Eddie shook his head. It just didn't seem safe.

"Suit 'erself," Nick shrugged. He replaced the light switch, gathered up his tools, and headed for the door.

Grandma called out to Mother. They began talking in German about dinner plans.

The electrician glanced back over his shoulder, then noticed Grandpa's fez on the side table. He stopped, snorted, then continued toward the door. "Foreigners," he muttered.

Thanksgiving Day saw the kitchen come alive with preparations. Eddie decided that it was best to stay out of the way until dinner, so he went over to see what Gus was doing. He found him sitting on his back porch, also staying out of the way.

"Wanna' play marbles?" asked Gus, pulling a small bag out of his pocket.

They took turns shooting marbles from a makeshift circle in the dirt at the bottom of the steps. After awhile Gus asked if Eddie wanted a cookie. Eddie, of course, was always ready for that. Soon Gus returned from the kitchen with a small plate holding several small round objects covered with powdered sugar.

"They're called *kourabiethes*," he said. "For Thanksgiving. Made with almonds and a lot of butter."

They were very sweet, with a nutty flavor and delectable crunch. Eddie complimented Gus on his mother's cooking as Gus reviewed their Thanksgiving menu. Mutton roast with *spanakopita*, which he explained was made with spinach, and *moussaka*, made from eggplant and potatoes. And some sort of pie for dessert, called *melopita*, made from honey and custard.

Eddie said it sounded really good (the fragrance of roast coming from the kitchen may have influenced him) but was not anything like what they were going to have: turkey, dressing, cranberries, mashed potatoes, pumpkin and mincemeat pies.

A cold rain began to fall from the thick grey skies overhead. Eddie thanked Gus for the cookies and ran home, hoping to not get too wet. He was dripping and shivering as he came in the back door.

"Don't move," said Mother when she saw him. "Goodness, boy! You'll catch your death."

She hastily took a kitchen towel and began wiping off the wettest parts of him. Steam rose from him in the warm kitchen. "Now go upstairs and change into something dry and warm."

He did not need coaxing.

Soon dinner was on the table, and all were gathered 'round. Father asked Grandpa to say grace, then he carved the turkey as food was passed from one to the next.

"I love Thanksgiving," Eddie exclaimed, and the family agreed. "Gus's family is having meat with spinach and stuff. It sounds really good, and smells good too, but not the same."

"Well," said Mother, "they are enjoying food that is familiar to them and we are enjoying food that is familiar to us. The important part is to be thankful for all God's blessings."

Eddie thought for a moment. "I suppose so."

Then he turned toward Father. "Father, if Mother and her parents came to America in 1887, when did you come?"

Father chuckled. "I was born in Kansas, Son. My father came with his parents from England in the 1850s. My mother was a Tilden and her people had been here from the beginning. Nathaniel Tilden was a Pilgrim who came on the boat right after the Mayflower. He had aunts and uncles at the first Thanksgiving."

The children uttered a collective "Wow".

"So that's why we have turkey and everything, like our ancestors did," said Junior.

"That's right."

"Nah," countered Johnny. "We have it 'cause it tastes good."

As the late afternoon turned into evening Eddie began to feel fully recovered from the chill of his earlier drenching. He sat in the parlor with his stomach comfortably full and a slowly increasing warm glow overall. In a couple of hours, the glow became a dull ache.

Mother was chatting with Grandma when she glanced his way and noticed Eddie's changed expression. She came over to him, put her hand on his forehead and neck.

"Carl," she called out, "Shirl has a fever. He is burning up."

CHAPTER 9

1922, *November-December.*
Sick For the Holidays

Soon all the adults in the household had looked Eddie over, felt his forehead, and stroked his neck. Yes, he felt aches and pains. Yes, a little sick to his stomach. Yes, he had a sore throat which was increasing every time someone asked. Now his right ear hurt.

Like most families in 1922, they did not worry much about sniffles, congestion, scrapes and scratches, or the odd pain. But throw a fever into the mix and the level of concern was greatly elevated, ever since the Great Influenza Epidemic of 1918. The Taylors had been spared that year, but the follow-up flu epidemic of 1919 was almost as bad nationally and much worse for them. Eddie had only a vague memory of a sister who died.

Mother helped Eddie up the stairs to his room as Grandma went to the kitchen to brew tea and Grandpa went to his suitcase. He reappeared shortly with a black enameled device and a small bottle of yellow liquid. "The *Lebenswecker* will help," he said, "*und Baunscheidt* oil, named for Dr. Baunscheidt."

"Will it hurt?" asked Eddie.

"Only a little. Then you feel better."

Eddie was not so sure. Grandpa had him roll onto his side, then wiped clean an area just behind and below his right ear and along the back of the neck. He placed the device on the skin and released a spring mechanism the drove thirty tiny needles a short distance beneath the surface.

"Ow!"

"Sorry."

"That was more than a little!"

"Just one more."

"Ow!"

"Sorry. Now the oil." Grandpa rubbed a thin layer of the oil onto the puncture sites where tiny spots of red had appeared.

"It stings!"

"Only a little. Almost done." Grandpa then placed clean bandages on Eddie and taped them into place.

"Why does it sting so much, Grandpa?"

"That means the medicine is working. Is made from pepper, mustard, tansy, and some other herbs, in oil solution. The oil irritates the skin."

"But if I'm sick, I'm already irritated."

Grandpa chuckled. "Yes, but this tells the body to hurry and bring the healing to these spots. Over the next couple days, we will see little drops of pus, then you heal. Don't you remember the *Lebenswecker*?"

She smiled. "He's still little, Papa. He doesn't remember when everyone was sick."

"I see. Then I teach you some medicine. First lesson: body heals itself. Everything we do is just help it along. That's what the *Lebenswecker* does. Same with soup. Same with good herb tea. Same with all medicines. God filled the world with useful things we can use to make life more comfortable and teach us to live good, useful lives."

Eddie spoke up, "Mother taught me to read."

"Really? Very good. What you read?"

"McGuffey's Readers. I've almost finished the first book."

Grandma came in the room with a cup of tea that smelled strong and earthy. It was yarrow and peppermint with a little honey. Eddie did not finish it before his eyelids drooped.

He did not wake up later that night when Judge Anderson and one of the other elders from church came by, anointed his head with a couple drops of consecrated olive oil, and pronounced a blessing on him. He slept very well that night.

Next day Dr. Williams came shortly before lunch. He was a tall, thin man, with thick glasses that he removed when looking closely at something. He looked closely at Eddie's throat and eyes and ears. He snorted a little when he examined the *Lebenswecker* sites with their tiny red spots. Taking a gold watch from his vest, he stared intently at it while feeling Eddie's pulse, then returned it to its pocket.

"Well," he said with a slow Midwestern accent, "I suppose it won't hurt. The folk medicine, that is."

He looked over at Mother. "Keep doing what you are doing. Plenty of fluids. Water is best, and soup. Clear soup. Bed rest. Keep track of the fever and let me know if anything changes for the worse."

He smiled at Eddie. "We just opened a new hospital. It's a good little hospital, but I don't want you to have to go there, so just take it easy now, okay? And get plenty of rest."

"Okay."

Mother cringed to hear the word *hospital*. For most people it still meant the place where the very ill go to die.

That day passed slowly for Eddie. Mother tended to him and would not let anyone else come any further than the door to wave and say "hello". Between feverish naps, bowls of soup, and glasses of water, he managed to continue his reading, but could not do anything else. After a time, he was more than a little bored.

He also felt deprived when he was not able to go to the train station to see the grandparents off, or play with Gus when he came to the door to say the first snow was on Wood Hill and would he like to go make snowballs, or when he could smell *Lebkuchen* baking and knew he could not be in the kitchen to watch them bake and then sneak some.

It was, after all, the run-up to Christmas, now that Thanksgiving was past. That meant Christmas cookies— *Lebkuchen, Springerle*, and *Butterkuchen*. And all he could do was wait. Time passed. The fever was usually gone in the morning, returning in the afternoon and evening, but each day it seemed a little less intense. The pain in his ear was subsiding. For a short time, his hearing seemed muffled, but that too passed and he began to feel back to normal. After nearly two weeks, Mother pronounced him well and he was able to re-join the family.

The highlight of the pre-Christmas celebrations that year was the church party. Judge Anderson was there with Sister Anderson and their children, Angela and Gene. Also the Thomases, the Smiths, even the Warners.

Children performed a much rehearsed version of the Nativity, complete with shepherds, three kings, and Mary and Joseph with a china doll baby Jesus. Eddie was a shepherd boy, with Lambie on a leash, occasionally bleating. He worried the whole time that Lambie might leave a deposit on the stage floor, so he carried a rag in his pocket to clean it up, just in case, but he did not need to use it.

Mother sang *O, Holy Night*. Then all joined together singing Christmas carols.

Carols were still ringing in Eddie's mind next day when Father bundled everyone into the car to drive into the hills to find a Christmas tree. Johnny and Junior grabbed the seats behind Mother and Lizzie, which left Eddie unhappily placed on the left. They were not underway long before Father lit his cigar and the smoke went out his window and came back in behind him, right in Eddie's face. At least Father was not chewing—that presented an even greater hazard. Eddie concentrated on the carols.

Following a dirt path up Nine Mile Canyon, they found a clump of trees. Going from one to the next and admiring the shapes and sweet smells, the family finally agreed on a nice pine which was only a little lopsided. Mother said no one would notice if they placed it against the parlor corner. Father let each of the boys have their turns cutting the tree with the hatchet, then completed the job himself. With the tree securely tied to the roof they headed back to town.

That night was a family party, stringing and eating popcorn, hanging pretty little ornaments, and carefully placing tinsel. When it was finished Mother led the family in singing *O Christmas Tree,* first in German, then in English.

"Now do we light the candles?" asked Eddie.

"No," replied Mother. "Not until Christmas eve. It will be special."

"And much safer," added Father. "Always be careful with fire, even with a fresh tree and water in the pan under it."

They did not have long to wait for the candles. Trees were not put up until shortly before Christmas, or sometimes not until Christmas Eve itself, for those following the older tradition. But even one day was a long time for a young boy like Eddie.

He admired the tree again next morning, then went out to find Gus. The smell of coal was in the air from the hundreds of furnaces in town, a slight discoloration was in the air; by evening his clean shirt collar would be dark from the soot. But at his age he did not care much about that. For him the sun was bright, the sky was a cloudless pale blue, and the frozen ground crunched beneath his shoes. The first snow had come and gone, and now there were just small clumps of it here and there on the north sides of houses and other shady spots. No doubt much more would come with the new year.

CHAPTER 10

1923, *Winter-Spring.* *Frank Joins the Gang*

Gus was already in the alley. He had taken up Eddie's habit of checking people's trashcans to see what treasures might be there. "Nothing so far," he said when Eddie inquired if he had had any luck.

"No Athena today?"

"Nah. She has a cold."

Together they wandered along until they reached Second Street, Little Italy. A boy about their age was sitting on a back porch across the intersection, whittling a small stick.

"Watcha' doin'?" called Eddie.

The boy looked up. "Whittling."

"Can we come over and see?"

"Sure."

Soon they were next to the boy and admiring his work. It was a whistle. He put it to his lips and blew a loud, high pitched note. They all agreed it was a fine whistle. The boy's name was Francis. "But my friends call me Frank."

"The last time we came over here there were some older kids who threw rocks at us," said Gus.

Frank snorted. "That was probably my older brother and his buddies. They think they own the place and used to try to keep people out. Sometimes they would try to charge kids a penny to walk down the street."

"Oh," replied Gus, glancing over his shoulder. "They're not around, are they?"

"Nah, 'been gone all day. And since the Greeks joined the strike last summer, they've been a lot nicer."

"Oh."

"Yeah. Besides, Poppa says there are bigger things to worry about than which side of the Mediterranean our ancestors lived in."

"Yeah," said Gus. "Some of my cousins went back to Greece to fight in a war there. They talked about the king and some generals and the Turks and the English. It seems all mixed up. I don't really understand it."

"I don't mean the old country. Poppa says there are big problems here, and not just with the government. Something called a clan."

"What's that?" asked Gus.

"Oh," interjected Eddie, "it's Scotch. Father said some of our ancestors came from Scotland and they had clans."

"I don't know what it is, but it's not Scotch. Some sort of club. But they hate, well, practically everybody—Catholics like you and me," he said, pointing to Gus. "Mormons like you," pointing to Eddie. "You are Mormon, right?"

Eddie nodded.

"Jews. Indians. Negroes. Chinamen. It seems pretty nearly everybody who isn't them."

"Huh. That sounds stupid."

The boys agreed that whatever it was, this clan was something bad, but not knowing anything more about it, there wasn't much more to say.

"What's your Pop do?" asked Gus.

"He has a shop off Main. Other side of the courthouse."

"Yeah? Mine too. On Main around the corner from The Ajax Coffee Shop."

"Hey Gus," said Eddie, "Let's make Frank a member of our gang."

"Okay. What do you say, Frank? Are you with us?"

"Sure. What does the gang do?"

"We don't know yet, but we're a gang of good guys. So, we'll find something to do, 'cause everybody needs good guys."

They soon headed toward their homes; Eddie and Gus were particularly happy that they were welcome in Little Italy, at least by their new friend, Frank. And they were happy that the gang had grown.

Eddie resolved to ask Father about this new club called a clan next chance he had, but soon forgot about it in the joy of Christmas. New toys, new clothes, Christmas cookies and ham, and preparations for New Year's; there was plenty to occupy his attention.

Eddie fell asleep on the sofa on New Year's Eve but woke up when Johnny shook him as the clock struck midnight. Father always saved a few fireworks from July to fire off as a greeting for the New Year. The rockets sailed high above their home and burst with loud bangs and great showers of red, white, and blue sparks. The Taylors were joined by all their neighbors in their front yards shouting, "Happy New Year! Happy 1923!"

The rest of winter passed uneventfully. Eddie spent mornings taking care of Lambie, then playing with Gus and sometimes Frank, enjoying the snow, warming up again in the afternoons by the coal stove in the kitchen, doing chores, reading, and napping.

He enjoyed games with his older brothers, but because they were older, they always won, whether cards or checkers. So as far as his brothers were concerned, Eddie was usually content to watch and listen. Sometimes he heard things that surprised him.

The three of them were sitting on the front steps with two of Johnny's and Junior's school friends, Bill and Hal.

It was early spring when the winds in Price blow steady and strong. Johnny commented that it was good kite-flying weather. Bill and Hal said they had never seen a kite, much less flown one.

"Never flown a kite?" asked Junior. "You gotta be kidding."

"I seen pictures of 'em," offered Bill.

Eddie remained silent. He wasn't sure if he had ever seen a kite either.

"It's great fun," replied Johnny, "and easy." He looked over at his older brother. "Let's make one."

They began assembling old newspapers, wooden dowels, string, tape, and glue on the workbench in the backyard shed. They tied three dowels together in the middle to create a sturdy kite with six edges. An hour later it was resting on the bench while the glue dried. A long tail had bands of paper tied in bows.

"It will be ready tomorrow, when the glue has dried," announced Junior proudly. "This one is just a newspaper kite. We can save up some money and get colored paper to make one that looks better. But this will fly just fine."

Next day the older boys and their friends ran to the Taylor home after school to find Eddie and Gus and Athena waiting impatiently on the front steps. Junior carried the kite out along the alley to the city playfields between the elementary and middle schools. There was a strong, steady breeze. Johnny held the kite while Junior walked a few yards away, unrolling the string as he went.

"Ready?"

"Ready!"

Johnny threw the kite into the air and the wind grabbed it, twirled it around, and promptly put it down to the ground.

"More string," shouted Junior. He played out the string a few more yards.

"Ready?"

"Ready!"

Johnny threw the kite into the air again and Junior ran to keep the string taught, and soon their newspaper kite was sailing high above them, threatening from time to time to fly straight down, but dancing more right and left than up and down. The boys cheered and laughed below.

Other children of all ages began to wander on to the playfields to watch in wonder. Adults too. Bob, the old school groundskeeper, looked up from his raking and exclaimed, "Well! If that don't beat all. I ain't seen one of those in . . . Well! I don't know when."

The other children all wanted to fly, but Junior only let Johnny and Hal and Bill handle the string. "It's too heavy," he said. "And the wind is too strong for little kids. You'll break it."

That caused them to beg all the more. When that failed, they begged for help to make their own kites. Junior stalled at first, then agreed to show everybody who wanted to see the next time he made one. The three brothers shared smiles, not only for the successful kite, but also for the importance they felt from the other children.

It had grown dark by the time the Taylor boys were home, and Mother was not pleased they were late for dinner. The boys were given extra chores the next day. For Eddie that meant spending the morning helping with the laundry, first watching her put clothes one at a time through the wringer washer, then helping her hang them on the clothesline in back. Since he was not tall enough to reach the line, he had to hand her each article of clothing while she pinned it in place.

It was nearly noon by the time he was free to play. He found Gus pacing in the alley. "Have you heard the news?" he asked excitedly.

"What's that?"

"There's been an Injun uprising!"

CHAPTER 11

1923, March.
The Last Indian Uprising

"Injuns? Really?"

"Yeah! The Utes, down south. They shot a deputy and they're riding around on horses and they say they want their land back and they're gonna send in the cavalry and everything."

"Where'd you hear that?"

"Pop. He read about it in the morning paper. Don't you get the paper?"

"Yeah, but in the afternoon. Father reads it when he gets home from work."

"Ask him. You'll see."

The prospect of an Indian War stoked their young imaginations. Soon they were stalking about the alley and backyards in stealthy Indian fashion, then charging imaginary settlers, whooping and chanting and vowing to scalp everyone and burn the towns. When that grew tiresome, they switched sides and became the cavalry, galloping around on pretend horses and waving sticks in the air for swords and rifles.

Gus rolled his eyes when Athena joined in. She was a tomboy. Their mother had given up on keeping her girlie, so her black hair was trimmed short, and her usual outfit was shirt and overalls same as Gus. She even refused to play the role of "settler mother" and galloped around as cavalry company commander instead.

The call of the steam whistle reminded them how late it was. They ran to their respective homes. Fortunately, Eddie was closer to his backdoor than his friends were to theirs, so was only a few minutes late. Out of breath, he closed the back door behind him. Mother raised her eyebrows and sent him to the sink to wash.

He tried hard to sleep at nap time and to concentrate on his reading afterwards, but thoughts of Indians and soldiers kept intruding into his thoughts. When the evening newspaper appeared on the doorstep Eddie brought it into the parlor where he stared carefully at the front page. He had finished McGuffey's Primer and had almost finished the First Eclectic Reader. He recognized many of the words, but he was hard pressed to make sense of what he read.

Later that evening when Father settled in his chair to read the paper, Eddie sat attentively beside him.

"Do you want something, Shirl?" He asked.

"I want to hear about the Indian War."

"Indian War? Oh, you must mean this business here." He pointed at the headline, *Piute Band Declares War on Whites in Blanding!*

"Yes."

"Well, I already read some of this. As usual the papers are making a big to-do out of not much. They would have us believe that this fellow, Chief Posey, is raising a big band of warriors and getting ready to attack the settlers down in Blanding and Bluff. Now, Shirl, don't believe everything you read in the papers. In fact, most of it is wrong, and almost all of it is twisted and puffed up into something it isn't. Look at this article. It runs for two columns, but if you read it carefully, there just is not much there.

"It seems there was some sort of quarrel about a calf that resulted in a fight. The boys responsible were taken to court, but then stole the sheriff's horse and ran off. The chief and some other adults were there for moral support but ended up fleeing with them. Now they are holed up somewhere in Indian Territory. A posse will find them eventually."

Eddie could not help looking disappointed.

"'Sorry there isn't more to it, Son. But I tell you what, as new articles come along with more details, I will be sure to read them with you. It's good to know what's going on."

"Yeah. 'History in the making', right?"

Father smiled. "That's right."

The next evening Eddie was beside Father again, reading over his shoulder and asking for help with unfamiliar words. This time the article claimed that Utes in war paint were riding through the streets of Blanding. Chief Posey was supposed to have formed a "mobile squadron" to rob and pillage the countryside, composed of "sixty men skilled in the art of mountain warfare awaiting the call to service." The San Juan County commissioners had asked the governor for permission to use a military scout plane to bomb and strafe the natives. The governor refused.

"What nonsense," snorted Father.

Eddie did not know what to believe, but until further notice, playing Indian War with Gus and Frank and any of the other neighbor boys they could find was highly satisfying. Details could be added later.

Finally, an evening came when the newspaper reported an end to the hostilities. One report said there had been a shootout near Blanding. Chief Posey and some others had escaped the posse into a canyon where a flash flood washed them out and drowned them. But another account said the chief died of an infected gunshot wound after killing the father of the boy who had stolen the calf in the first place. And another said the Indians believed he died of flour poisoned by the Mormons. Father looked at Eddie and said, "Poppycock. None of us would do that."

It left Eddie feeling confused, not knowing what to believe.

As a wholesale groceryman, Carl Taylor occasionally had to drive or take the train to Provo or Salt Lake City to meet with his boss and with the company's suppliers. He often drove to the small towns and villages of eastern Utah to provide catalogs, maintain business contacts, take orders, and give out samples. Most roads were unpaved, made of beaten dirt or gravel. A can of gas, common repair materials, and tools were kept in a large box in the back of the car. A rifle and a pistol were also taken along for safety's sake.

One Sunday evening he said to Eddie, "Shirl, tomorrow I am traveling up to Roosevelt and would like you to come with me."

"Yeah? Are Johnny and Junior and Lizzie coming too?"

"No. They have school. It will be just you and me. Are you up to it?"

"You bet!"

"Good. I already spoke to your mother and she will pack a bag for you. We will be gone three or four days."

Mother sniffed a little as she helped Eddie into the car next morning. "Be good," she said. "And be careful." She kissed and hugged them both and they were on their way.

They headed out of town on Main Street, the only paved street in town, concrete glistening gray with the dew. From there they drove west, past the little mining towns of Helper and Castle Gate, then north toward Duchesne. Eddie marveled at the Castle Gate, for which the town was named, a beautiful mountain range which narrowed the canyon on each side like walls of a great castle, with cliffs on either side that looked like battlements. He imagined giant knights marching behind the walls.

Spring had renewed the barren hills, which were green with grass, sagebrush, and junipers, called "cedars" by Utahns. Other varieties appeared as they climbed higher, pine and even some aspen. Trees were a special delight for Eddie, who had become accustomed to the more desert countryside around Price. Native trees there were mostly cottonwoods, scrub oaks, and willows along the river and small tributary creeks. He treasured the fruit trees, pines, and oaks planted in town.

They stopped at the side of the road to eat the lunch Mother had packed. The air was clean and crisp, with no trace of the smell of coal smoke. It was so clear, Eddie thought he could see forever. Along the little canyons the white bark of aspen trees gleamed, and their leaves shimmered in the breeze.

After lunch, Father picked up a couple old tin cans someone had left by the road and placed them on a rock. "About time I teach you how to shoot," he said, pulling his six-shooter from the bag next to the driver's seat. He took his son a few paces away and showed him the trigger, hammer, and cylinder.

"Learn to point your hand at what you are looking at. Keep it straight. Keep both eyes open. Then slowly squeeze the trigger—don't jerk it. Watch me first." A loud boom followed, one of the cans went flying, and Eddie clasped his hands over his ears. "Now you try."

Father leaned over his son and helped him hold the revolver, wrapping his large hands around Eddie's. "That's the way, both hands." He took his hands away and crouched behind the boy. "Now look down the barrel at your target, keep your eyes on the target, and squeeze." Another loud boom. This time the can didn't move, but the gun went flying up out of Eddie's hands onto the ground.

Father laughed. "I should have warned you about that. I guess you are a little young for this. Do you want to try again?"

Eddie could not actually hear his father's words because of the ringing in his ears but guessed at the question and nodded. This time he held on as tight as he could and fired again. The can was still safe. Twice more with the same result. The sixth time Father knelt down low behind him, reached around, and held his Eddie's hands firmly in his. Another boom.

This time the can flopped to the ground. He was not sure if he had actually hit it or the can just got tired and jumped down of its own accord. In any case, he was quite proud of himself and accepted Father's praise as they continued on their journey.

"You did fine, son. Just remember a couple rules. First, until you actually look in the breach and know for sure, assume that every gun is loaded. Second, never point a weapon at anything you do not want to shoot. There is a second part to that rule, always expect that anything you shoot at, you will kill. Can you remember that?"

"I'll remember." Eddie felt very satisfied with his first shooting experience, even with the ringing in his ears and the smell of gunpowder in his nose. Eddie smiled as he thought how powerful his father's pistol was and how big and grown up he felt to be allowed to shoot it.

The road narrowed to one lane most of the way, with occasional turnouts. If two cars met, the one going downhill had the right of way and the other had to back up to a turnout to let it pass. Much of the road had not been graded after winter, so there were many ruts. Sometimes if the car could not get past a rough area, Father would back up to where he could turn around and go up the road in reverse. Reverse gear had more power and more dependable gasoline flow to the engine.

It was late in the evening when they arrived in Roosevelt where they found the hotel, a two storey brick building on Main Street. The man behind the desk looked up when they entered. He smiled and said, "Hello, Carl. Nice to see you back again."

"Hi there Jim. Nice to see you too. This is my youngest, Eddie."

"Nice to meet you, Eddie."

Their room contained a double bed with mattress and springs, a dresser with mirror, and a wash basin with a pitcher of water.

CHAPTER 12

1923, April-May. Real Indians

Next morning after a bite of breakfast in the hotel restaurant, Father and Eddie began making their rounds. They visited merchant after merchant in Roosevelt, then made side trips into the surrounding smaller villages. For Eddie it was mostly sight-seeing. He was impressed by how many people his father knew, and how many knew him.

Father would chit-chat a little, then take out a catalog, look through it with the shopkeeper, make a few notes, and write out an order sheet. He always gave a couple samples of candy bars from Startup's, a candy maker in Provo that was one of his best sellers.

Towards evening the two had dinner and spent a couple hours reading in the hotel lounge before going to bed. Father had finished the newspaper and was catching up on his paperwork when he looked over at Eddie and said, "I hope today was not too boring for you, Eddie. Tomorrow will be better. It is the reason I wanted you to come. We are going to the reservation to see the Indians."

"Really? That's swell! No, today wasn't boring." He thought a moment about that and added, "I'm never bored."

Father smiled back. "Me neither."

Next day dawned sunny and warm. They first drove east to Fort Duchesne.

"Not much of a fort now," explained Father. "The army closed it several years ago, but there is a trading post and quite a few people living in the old buildings and surrounding area."

Duchesne was flat and dry with scattered clumps of grass and sage and small trees along the creek beds and multi-colored hills in the distance. At the old fort they found a neat row of houses paralleled by a row of oak trees, with an Indian administrative center, hospital, and other government buildings in the middle. They reached the store about mid-morning. The store-keeper was leaning against the door post, chewing. He spit some black tobacco juice on the ground.

"Howdy," he grunted as they approached.

"Howdy, Jake," answered Father. "The store all yours now?"

"Yep. The old guy retired."

Inside was a single long counter opposite the door. Row upon row of goods lined the walls-food, sewing materials, tools, nearly everything one might need to run a household. Barrels of grain, flour, sugar, and various types of pickles were off to one side.

Father handed Jake a Startup's Opera Bar. He grunted his thanks. As they started looking through the catalog, a stream of Indians quietly entered the store and lined up around the outside of the little room.

Eddie was very curious. Though he knew he should not stare, he could not help it. The first thing he noticed was they were not red, just dark, and he wondered where the term "red-man" had come from. Their skin was rough and leathery from being outdoors, much like the miners and ranchers at home. He thought of Fred Thomas.

There were no feathers. They wore work clothes like everyone else, though a couple were wrapped in blankets, and some wore strands of beads. The men had long black hair in braids that hung down in front on their chests. There was something that seemed a little odd; it took

Eddie a while to figure out what it was. Everyone was stone-faced.

Father finished filling out the order, shook hands with Jake, then turned to the small crowd and smiled. An old man in the middle stepped forward and put out his hand. "Welcome Taylor. You bring magnolias?"

Father chuckled. "Yes, Chief Hank. Of course. I did not forget you. Let's go out to my car."

The two of them strode out to the waiting car, Eddie right behind and the rest following. Jake came last, scratching his head.

Father reached into the backseat and took out a large box, opened it, and let the Chief reach in. He carefully took out a small round pastel candy and popped it in his mouth. His eyes closed briefly, then he exhaled through his nose. "Ah, good."

Magnolias were small sugary candies with liquid centers. They tasted and smelled like flowers. The Taylor kids called them "perfume candies." Father said they were "an acquired taste."

He handed the box around and everyone took one or two. He then handed the box to the Chief. "A present," he said. "My gift to you."

The Chief looked down at Eddie, who had not taken one. "You no like?"

Eddie glanced at Father, then replied, "They're okay. Father says they are an acquired taste."

The Chief handed him one. Eddie hesitated a moment, then popped it into his mouth, which immediately smelled of roses.

"Your son?"

"Yes," answered Father, "my youngest."

"Good. You take him with you and teach your business."

"Yes. And teach him about people."

The Chief looked at Carl a moment and his eyes softened. "Good."

"Mind if I visit the camp?"

"That also good."

As the Indians walked off, Jake ambled over.

"Carl, before you go. Looks like the old guy has a sweet tooth. Are the magnolias his favorite?"

"Yes, though he likes other candies too."

Jake thought a moment. "All right. Let's add half a dozen boxes of magnolias to the order."

"Happy to. Say, Jake, you weren't here last fall, were you?"

"No."

Carl smiled, "Well, wait 'til September. The Indians use hard candy for their sweeteners rather than sugar. They stock up in the fall to last through the winter. If you want, I'll go back through our records and make some suggestion as to how much to order."

Jake looked relieved. He brightened to a genuine smile, his first since they arrived. "Thanks, Carl. I appreciate that."

Father and Eddie climbed back into the car and headed back toward Roosevelt.

"One more stop before we go home," said Father. He cleared his throat, then continued. "The Indians are proud people. They used to own all this land and ranged wherever they wanted. Now our people have most of it— we beat them fair and square, mind you, but they took it hard. Some can't just accept that and move on, so they still feel beat down, not so much physically as in the spirit. But, like the scriptures say, we 'carry them on our shoulders' and try to help them. I first met Chief Hank— his Indian name is *Anape*, means something like 'brave one'—I first met him a few years ago when I came this way with my boss. Anyway, they go in town to Fort Duchesne quite a bit, but their summer camp is down by a creek not far out of the way. I hope I can find it."

Just past the river he turned off the road onto a flat stretch of prairie, making a path between clumps of sagebrush. The tires kicked up a small cloud of dust behind them. Soon they descended into a gulley with a creek in the bottom. An old shack and five teepees were there among a cluster of trees. A thin wisp of smoke rose from a central campfire.

Father stopped the car and they continued on foot. Several Indian men, women, and children of various ages began to assemble to see their visitors. An old woman stepped forward.

"Hello again, my friend," Father said.

"Hello," said the woman in a cracked, dry voice.

"I visited with the Chief back in Duchesne, but wanted to greet you as well." They shook hands. "This is my youngest, Eddie." Hosts and guests nodded their greetings. Eddie was especially interested in a boy about his age who stared back at him, both mutually curious. The boy's clothes were worn and full of holes.

Father retrieved a box of Fruit of Paradise bars from the car. The Fruit of Paradise candy was made of chocolate with raisins and nuts in a pectin filling. "I think you said these were your favorites," he said to the Chief's wife. "I wanted to make sure they got to you."

She smiled broadly and broke into a laugh. "You know us well. Come, have tea."

She and her brother escorted them into the central teepee of the group. Eddie marveled at how large it was inside, much larger than he expected, and filled with piles of blankets, furniture, and trunks. It smelled dusty, but also warm and comforting, a place where people lived and enjoyed each other's company. It reminded him of the good smell of the horse he had found in the alley, when he pressed his face against his neck and breathed deeply.

A small fire was in the center in a fire pit. She made the tea from small green twigs. Father noticed Eddie's perplexed look and said quietly, "It's called 'Brigham Tea'. Made from a plant that grows in the hills along with the sagebrush." The tea was surprisingly refreshing with a gentle, soothing flavor.

After tea they said their farewells and resumed their journey.

It was late in the evening by the time they arrived back in Price. Eddie had long since fallen asleep but woke up when the sound of the tires changed as they went onto the pavement of Main Street.

"Well, Eddie, how did you like it?"

"Great," he replied sleepily. "I was just dreaming about Indians."

"Oh? Cowboys and Indians?"

"No, just Indians." He looked up at his father. "You know, they were not at all how I imagined."

CHAPTER 13

1923, *Summer. Selling Lambie*

"Eddie, Frank," shouted Gus. "Take a look."

The two boys hurried around the corner to catch up with their friend. Main Street seemed to be sprouting a forest.

Some construction or other had been happening along the street since last year. Now tall poles had been placed along either side of the street, with small trees planted between them and, at the far end, electricity lines were being strung overhead.

Gus stuck his head in the shop door. "Hey, Pop, what are they doing?"

A man with slick black hair and a fine handle bar mustache wiped his hands on his white apron. "I tell you before, Argus. It is the lighting. The city is putting lights all along Main."

Gus's father had just arranged candy bars in a neat pyramid next to the cash register of his store. The glass counter and shelves behind him held assorted household goods of many kinds. A teenage girl with long blond hair gathered in a pony tail was working on the other side. "Put a little more on those shelves under the glass, Katy," he said, then joined the boys in front.

"Is fine project, no?"

"It sure is, Mr. Pappas," replied Eddie and Frank, almost in unison.

Eddie thought again what a great summer it was, just like the last one, except he found himself much more efficient at chores than last year. Work in the garden, caring for Lambie, clean-up work, all went quickly, and then he found himself playing with Gus and Frank, wandering around the city and surrounding hills–their range had increased. And now there was this. He loved to watch construction, to see how things were made.

It seemed that there was always something going on, something new being built, or something old that was being changed. Signs that had said "Saloon" had been painted over as "Club" or "Cafe". Several other clubs were there; Eddie had asked about them, but Father said they were not for children, something called "Gentlemen's Clubs." There were two hotels, one just for Italians; a couple restaurants including a Greek restaurant with small outside tables and chairs; two movie theaters; and several clothing, grocery, and sundry shops along Main Street, in addition to the government buildings further to the east.

Leaving Mr. Pappas and the shop behind, the boys walked slowly west, then turned toward Eddie's house.

Lambie was a full-grown sheep. They had kept him in wool rather than have him shorn in the spring, and now it was time to take him to the livestock market.

Eddie took the large brush from its place on a nail in the shed wall and began brushing. Lambie bleated in response and seemed to enjoy the petting by all three boys as they gathered around.

"Are you really going to sell him?" asked Frank.

"Yeah. Father says that is what lambs and sheep are for." He brushed a little softer. Lambie nuzzled his chin.

"He is a beautiful sheep," said Gus. "He always was beautiful, but even more after you took such good care of him."

"Yeah. That's what Father said too." Eddie thought hard about how important it was not to cry in front of Gus and Frank.

"How much do you think you'll get for him?" asked Frank.

Just then Father came out the back door. "Hello boys," he said. "Well, Shirl, uh, Eddie, are you ready?"

"Sure." Eddie led Lambie around the side of the house to the car where he and his friends lifted him up into the backseat, crowding around beside him. Johnny and Junior sat together in the front. Father glanced back in the mirror. He regretted again not having gotten a dog for Eddie, but Mother had vetoed it. She knew a dog would be in the house, and that meant shedding, and it was hard enough keeping up with the dirt without adding dog hair to the mix.

The livestock auction was on the south side, beyond the railroad and the fairgrounds. Dozens of men were milling around and looking, sometimes pointing, at the sheep, goats, cattle, and horses in various pens. The auction house was a low wooden building that stretched along the end of a dirt parking lot filled with small trucks and a few cars and wagons. There was, of course, a lot of dust.

"You boys wait here in the car. I will be right back," said Father after he parked.

He returned a few minutes later with another man, a rancher with darkly tanned and leathery skin, long mustache, and broad-brimmed hat.

"Boys, this is Bill. He has a ranch out north of Castle Gate."

They exchanged greetings and the man leaned over to stroke Lambie. He felt his head, then ran his hands over his back and down his legs.

"Well, Carl, you were right. He is a fine looking rambouillet. Horn buds just coming in."

"Yep, make a good addition to the flock."

Bill thought a little. "Okay, how about ten dollars?"

Father rubbed his chin. "No, a lot of work went into this little fellow. Plus we need to buy a new lamb to raise. I was thinking more like twenty."

"Twenty? No, that is much too much. Tell you what. How about twelve and you get to pick one of the lambs I have waiting for market over there."

"It's a deal," said Father, extending his hand.

Eddie slowly handed Lambie's rope over to his new owner. "You'll take good care of him, won't you?"

"Yes. I will."

Lambie looked back at Eddie as he was led away to Bill's truck, bleating farewell.

When Bill returned, they walked over to a pen filled with older lambs and yearlings. The animals were all on the other side near a water trough. Bill made a high-pitched warbling sound in the back of his throat and the whole flock came running to him.

The boys laughed. "That was neat, Mister," said Junior. "How do you do it?"

"Well, just make a sound back here," he pointed at his neck, "and loosen the back of your throat. Keep pushing air until it sounds right. It's how the Frenchies call their flocks. They say it is like how they make an *R*, of all things. Do it once or twice at feeding time and the sheep figure it out real fast."

Soon all the boys were making various versions of a French *R*. The sheep looked a little confused, starting first one way, then the other, as the different boys finally succeeded in making the correct sound.

One of the lambs with a black face bleated mournfully and stared up at Eddie. "This one. I want this one." They separated out his new lamb, then filed into the auction house to watch.

Individual animals or small groups were sold there. The auctioneer rattled through the numbers quickly in a sing-song sort of voice that made the most mundane transactions exciting. Buyers and sellers wandered in and out as their parts of the business came and went.

About noon the auctioneer left his desk in the building and led the men out to the pens where he sold the larger lots of animals. Father explained, "The sales in the building are generally stock for breeding or show, or to individuals for butchering. These larger sales are for the meat packing houses."

"Well," he added, "I suppose that is enough. Let's take your lamb to see his new home."

Father spoke quietly to Eddie as he settled into the backseat of the car with his new lamb, "Bill will take good care of your sheep. He will become part of a large flock, living in the hills."

"I know. Thanks. All the same, I think I won't name this one. He will just be Sheep."

Father smiled. "Whatever you say."

As they drove back into town they saw that something had changed during the few hours they were gone. Small groups of men and a few women were moving along Main Street, carrying signs that said things like, "No Immigrants", "Go Home", or "Only Real Americans".

"What's going on?" asked Johnny.

"Not sure," answered Father. "Nothing good."

CHAPTER 14

1923, Summer.
The KKK and the Riot

The car came to a halt behind a few others that were stopped by the gathering crowd. Further ahead a man stood on an apple crate and was speaking loudly, accompanied with vigorous gestures and occasional outbursts by his audience in response. Eddie and his friends could not make out the words, but Eddie thought it was the electrician, Nick Fulcher.

It reminded Eddie of the miners' strike when they first moved to Price, but with a different feel. These people looked like everyday pedestrians, the ordinary people of the town; they looked clean. The miners had looked like, well, miners, dirty and sort of tired. And foreign. They were angry and almost everyone had a gun and there were soldiers with machine guns, so it sure looked threatening, but Eddie did not feel any real danger. This time he did not see any guns, but the anger was different, less controlled, more general. More vicious. He shivered.

"I think we need to get out of here," said Father.

He made a U-turn in the wide street, drove back a couple blocks, then headed north to go around Main Street. Arriving home, he said to Gus and Frank, "Boys,

I think you need to go directly home, okay? Do not go over to Main."

"Yes Sir, Mr. Taylor."

Eddie's friends left quickly for their homes while the Taylors settled their new lamb in his pen. Soon they were all standing on the front porch, leaning their ears toward the south. There were muffled sounds of voices and shouting and sometimes crashing glass. Father looked grim. After a time, the sounds diminished and the family went inside for dinner.

"It reminds me of the war, and the dress shop, only worse," said Mother quietly.

Father nodded. The children remained silent, wondering what it meant.

Eddie could not sleep. It was after midnight when he heard the floor boards in his room creak. He sat up and looked. It was Johnny and Junior. When they saw him, they both put their fingers to their mouths, looked at each other, and came over to his bed.

"Don't say anything," whispered Junior. Eddie shook his head.

"We're going over to see what happened," added Johnny, "but don't tell the folks."

"Okay. But I want to come too."

"You're too little."

"No, I'm not. Either I go or I tell Father."

The older boys looked at each other again and grimaced.

"All right. But hurry up. And be quiet."

Soon Eddie was dressed, and the three boys were creeping out the front door and down the street. It was a very dark, moonless night. Every house was dark. Only the numerous stars above glistened with brilliant intensity.

As their eyes adjusted to the scene, they saw a police car to the east near the courthouse, with another to the west near the railroad tracks. There was no sign of life; no one stirred. Along the street were scattered signs and trash. They walked slowly toward the courthouse and became aware of paint splashed on some of the shops, their windows broken, pieces of board or cardboard fitted temporarily to protect the displays.

"And what do you boys think you are doing?" came a stern voice from behind them. They turned abruptly. It was Deputy Warner, his hands on his hips, pushing this coat back so they could see the star on his chest and the six-shooter at his side.

"Nothing, Sir," came their hasty replies. "Nothing. Just looking to see what happened."

"You're the Taylor boys, aren't you?"

"Yes Sir."

"I bet your father doesn't know you're out here, does he?"

They all shook their heads solemnly.

"Hmph. Well, you can see what happened here. 'Bunch of hotheads made fools of themselves, broke windows, roughed up a few of our fellow citizens just because they came from somewhere else." He shook his head. "At least nothing was burned down."

He waved his arms in a slow circle. "Too many to put 'em all in jail, where they belong, so just cleared 'em out, gave a few bruises."

He paused a bit, then added, "You boys should be in bed. I'll walk you home. Over that way, isn't it?"

"Yes Sir."

Soon they were standing in front of the Taylor home. Warner leaned over to them and whispered, "You boys behave yourselves now, go get in bed as quietly as you can, and there's no reason anyone but you and me needs to know where you were tonight. Okay?"

They nodded quickly, "Thanks!"

Eddie searched the alley for Gus next day but could not find him. He knocked on Gus's back door and Mrs. Pappas came, wiping her hands on a dishcloth. Her eyes were red and puffy.

"Oh, Eddie, so good see you. You want Gus? Gus down at shop, help clean up."

"Thanks, Mrs. Pappas." He started to go, then turned and added, "I'm really sorry about what happened."

"I know Eddie. You good boy."

"*Kala!*"

"*Kala!*"

At the shop Gus and Athena were sweeping up glass and debris while their father picked out pieces from the sill. Someone had crudely written "Foreigners" across the door with charcoal. It was misspelled.

"What can I do to help?" asked Eddie. Soon he was picking up pieces and cleaning off store merchandise.

"Big men," grunted Mr. Pappas, spitting the words. "I see big men like this before. What good they do? None! If they steal, I understand thieves. But these, they just shout bad words and break."

He looked at Eddie, "You know what they do, Eddie? First, they walk up and down street telling Katy and other girls working in shops to go home. They should not work for foreigners. What? Is shop work bad? What? They want the girls work down the street in their speakeasies, their 'Gentlemen's Clubs'?"

An embarrassed look crossed his face. "Oh. Sorry. I very sorry." He sat on the chair by the counter, slumped over and held his head in his hands and began to weep.

Gus and Eddie were still at first, not knowing what to do, but Athena went up to him and put her hand on his shoulder, then both boys did the same. "It's okay. It's okay." But they looked at each other and knew it was not really okay.

"Mr. Pappas?" came a voice from the doorway. It was Katy, peeking in around the doorpost.

"Katy," he replied, wiping his nose. "So good to see you."

"I came to help." She walked up to her employer. "I am so sorry. Those men." Her jaw tightened. "They can't tell me who I can work for. May I still work for you?"

"Of course." His voice cracked.

Soon the shop was nearly back to normal. The other shops along Main Street were repaired as well, and the city cleaned the street. The papers called it a demonstration against foreign workers, supporting congressional action to limit immigration. Everyone else called it a riot.

"Hurry or we'll be late," said Father to the whole family a few days later. It was early evening, and the dinner dishes were still on the table, but the Taylors were walking briskly toward on Main.

There they joined the rest of the townspeople in front of the City Office Building. Mayor Watson was on the steps behind a podium with lanterns on either side, top hat in place, hands raised in enthusiastic oratory.

"Our thanks to the many workers who have completed this fine addition to our fair city. Thanks to the supervisors who have kept the project moving forward, especially last winter when the snow slowed our progress. And thanks to you, the good citizens and taxpayers of Price."

He paused for applause.

Fred Thomas came up behind the Taylors and clapped Father on the shoulder. "He's still an old windbag," he said. The men chuckled as they shook hands.

"With this improvement," continued the mayor, "Price joins the ranks of major cities around the world. It will result in greater enjoyment of our downtown, greater appreciation for the arts, and greater safety for all our citizens. The Council and I have named it 'The White Way' of Price, for it is nothing behind the Great White Way of Broadway in New York City itself."

"Except for all the theaters, and the people, and the shops," whispered Fred. "And, oh, a whole lot of money."

"And now, with no further ado, I inaugurate the White Way of Price." With a flourish the mayor flipped a large electrical switch on the podium and lights on the poles lining Main Street from the courthouse to the railway suddenly blazed brightly. The lanterns on the podium faded. It was as if night had turned to day.

The crowd roared its approval. Someone shouted, "Hip hip" and all replied, "Hooray". When the cheering died down and the mayor dismissed the ceremony small groups of people began strolling up and down the now well-lit street.

Fred turned to Father. "Well, for once the old windbag was right. This is a sight."

CHAPTER 15

1923, Summer. Times of Change

Most of the family was exhausted when they arrived back from their train trip to Salt Lake City. They walked through the front door, breathed deeply, and went their separate ways, Mother and Lizzie to bed for naps, Father to the back porch to smoke a cigar, and Johnny and Junior to their rooms to stretch out and daydream. Eddie had slept half the way, so he had more energy than ever.

First, he checked on Sheep. Sheep was happy to see him. The neighbor, Mr. Frandsen, had made sure he was fed and watered. Next, he wanted to find Gus and Frank.

Travelling to Salt Lake had been another of Father's ideas. President Harding was on a tour of the western United States, going all the way to the Alaskan Territory, and had stopped in Utah. This was a rare opportunity to see a president, to see "history in the making" as Father liked to say.

There were large crowds lining the streets, with little children waving small American flags. The president had arrived in Ogden earlier, then made his way to Salt Lake City where he was escorted around the capitol. He attended a concert at Temple Square. The Taylors could not get into the Tabernacle for the concert, but did see the president, the governor, and church leaders up close as they walked by on the temple grounds.

"History in the making," said Eddie triumphantly when he finally found Gus.

Gus's eyes widened. "That is swell. What did he say?"

"He said something, but I don't remember what it was. He has short white hair, bald on top. Didn't smile much except when a little girl came up to him and gave him some roses. There were a lot soldiers, and police on horses."

It was the end of June. They found Frank walking the base of Wood Hill, lighting off firecrackers. He was as attentive an audience for Eddie's story about their trip as Gus had been, especially when it came to police on horses.

"I would love to ride," he said. "Just like Wyatt Earp or Butch Cassidy."

"But Earp was a good guy and Cassidy was a bad guy," replied Gus.

"I guess that's right. So, like Wyatt Earp or Buffalo Bill then."

"How about Annie Oakley or Calamity Jane?" asked Athena, who had followed along.

"They're girls!" Gus laughed.

Frank poked him, and soon the two were tumbling around on the ground, pretending to fight. Eddie let them go for a little, then separated them.

"Okay. Knock it off." Eddie paused for effect. "I know someone who knew Butch Cassidy."

"Really?" Their mouths opened wide with amazement. "Who?"

"Matt Warner, the deputy sheriff."

"No. Really? Could we meet him?"

"Sure." His mind began to race. How could he arrange that? "I'll see what I can do," he added. Eddie suddenly rose higher in their estimation.

Independence Day that year was very much like the year before, with one exception. The parade included a contingent of about thirty men marching in rows and columns, dressed in white sheets and pointed hats that covered their faces. The leaders carried an American flag and a large banner that read, "Carbon County KKK".

Eddie was not in the parade this year. He was standing with Frank and Gus and Athena. He laughed as the Klan marched by, shouting, "You look like ghosts!"

The marchers ignored him. But soon all the children were laughing and pointing their fingers. Then Frank noticed one of the men had a pronounced limp.

"I know you. Hey everybody, it's Nick Fulcher, the electrician!"

With that he ran into the street and pulled off the man's hood. It really was Fulcher.

"Give me that, you little brat." He swung at Frank, missing him by several inches. Now the whole crowd roared as he pulled his hood back on and hurried back to his place in the parade.

Rejoining his family, Eddie found Father and Judge Anderson in animated conversation.

"There's nothing much we can do about them," said the judge. "It's a free country and they can say what they want, demonstrate, even burn crosses, so long as they don't damage other people's property or hurt anybody."

"People have been hurt and things have been damaged," noted Father.

"We haven't been able to identify who did what or make arrests that stick. Or get people to testify."

Father shook his head. "I know what this leads to. My father had a lot to say about them. Remembered them from his time during Reconstruction, after the war, trying to keep order."

"Yes. I remember him talking about it. Chased them during the war, then chased them again afterwards. The Klan figures they can make progress in Carbon County because of all the immigrants; they can stir up people's jealousy and resentment. Turn it towards the newcomers. Then too, the county is mostly Democrat."

"Yes. That is what my father used to say. The Klan is just the street side of the party, the party of slavery, sedition, secession, and segregation."

The judge glanced over quizzically.

"I used to set copy for a paper my father published," explained Father, "when I was a kid before we came to Utah. That was a quote."

"Well. That's a pretty good line, but best not to say it too loudly. We need to just hope our neighbors have the good sense to push back against them."

The two men nodded. Not much else to say.

The remainder of the month slipped by without disturbance. Sheep grew well, as Lambie had, and followed Eddie around if he let him, but Eddie was careful not to hug and pat him as much as Lambie, knowing he was only there for a year. "You are, after all, just a sheep," he said; Sheep said, "Baa."

One day Father came through the front door with a large box. He placed it on the floor and called the family together.

"I have bought a wonderful new device," he announced as he pulled back the top and reached inside. He pulled out a brown box with a lid. Raising the lid revealed knobs, a bulb, and a small handle that dialed a circle of numbers.

"This is the Radiola Senior. We are now fully in the 20th century."

Everyone gathered around to admire the shining black control panel and complex controls.

Father reached back into the box. "It works on a battery, but with this adapter we can use wall power. And this," he reached in again and pulled out a large black object that looked like a flower, "will let everyone hear it without having to hand around an earpiece."

"Oh," added Mother, "like our old gramophone."

"Exactly!"

Soon Father had cleared a space on the side table in the parlor, set up the radio, and was twisting the knobs. The machine emitted a variety of strange crackling sounds and warbling tones that fluctuated from high to low to high pitch. After twenty minutes he sat back in frustration. "Hmph. Doesn't work."

After rubbing his forehead a little he added, "Oh, wait. There is this." He reached into his pocket. "The man at the store said to try this." He peered at the paper as he carefully turned the large lever on the control. Faintly at first, then more clearly, they heard music. It was *Carolina in the Morning*. The family cheered.

Life at home changed with the addition of the radio. They could only hear one station well, the station in Salt Lake City, but that provided new and varied entertainment in the evening, and everyone hurried to complete chores so as to hear each program.

Music, including live performances by orchestras and bands around the country; recitations of great and not so great literature, with dramatic enactments; events such as presidential addresses and church conferences; all these became standard fare in the home for the first time in history.

Plus, there was news, something beside the newspaper. At first radio reports seemed more authoritative, but it did not take long for Father to see through that false impression. Corrections were always forthcoming. And the tone of each report was as authoritative as the one before it. One story proved accurate from the start.

"Katharine," called Father from the parlor, "come quickly."

Mother ran into the room still wiping her hands with a dishcloth.

"President Harding has died. Listen."

The reporter told how the president, thought to be recovering from food poisoning and pneumonia, died suddenly in San Francisco, bringing his western tour to an abrupt close.

"What a shame," said Mother.

"Yes. He was a good man. He wanted a return to normalcy after the war turned everything upside down. Now he's gone."

"So, what about the vice-president? What's his name?"

"Coolidge. I don't know much about him. From New England. Vermont, I think. I guess we'll find out."

Although they found themselves spending more time together listening to the radio, they still spent most evenings with church, club, and friends. And of course, the end of summer also brought the circus. It was not a very large circus, but it came each year and made its way from one town to the next all through the inter-mountain west.

Jugglers, trapeze artists, horseback riders, even an elephant were part of the show, and games of all sorts lined the walk between the gate and the big tent. What fascinated Eddie the most, as well as all the boys his age, was the freak show. The two headed calf and three-legged sheep were old hat for him. The freak show at the County Fair always had those, but here were the oddest people he could imagine.

"Wow," he exclaimed as he watched a contortionist twist herself into a pretzel. Billed as "The Boneless Lady," her unlikely shapes seemed impossible to him. "How does she do that?"

Then there was the midget, not standing much higher than Eddie's hips, and the giant with bulging muscles, the bearded lady, and the tattooed man. They were all pretty amazing, but he and Gus agreed the Boneless Lady was best.

"That was great!" exclaimed Eddie to the ringmaster as they left the circus.

"Glad you liked it. Come back." He paused for a minute, sizing up the young admirer and always eager to create a devoted customer. "Say kid, maybe when you get older, you can come to work for us. Be sure to keep coming back."

"That'd be even greater!" For weeks Eddie's mind imagined the thrill of working in the big top.

CHAPTER 16

1923, Fall. First Grade Fights

The family was in final preparations for dinner one night when Lizzie came home from an overnight stay at Dot's. It was shortly before school was scheduled to start in the fall. Junior was setting the table, Mother bringing potatoes from the kitchen, and Father folding his paper in the parlor. Eddie and Johnny had just come in the back door. It seemed they all saw her together.

"Wow!" exclaimed the irrepressible Junior. The rest were in various stages of amazement with mouths open. Mother felt her cheeks redden.

"What in the world have you done?" asked Father.

"I bobbed my hair," replied Lizzie, patting the side of her head, now covered with loose curls where there previously had been long, nearly black hair gathered in a bun. "It's called a finger curl. Dot and I both did it. All the high school girls are wearing it this way. Isn't it nifty?" She struggled to smile.

There was a moment of silence. Father started to say something, but Mother spoke first. "I think it is very nice, Dear." Father looked perplexed.

"Yes," said Mother. "It looks very stylish, and sensible too. Pretty. The cat's meow, I think." She took a deep breath.

The children did not know what to think. They were sure Lizzie had brought upon herself the wrath of parents with a capital *W*. They looked at one, then the other, finally voicing their approval as well.

Father stammered a little, "I am sure we, well, we. . . It is nice. Yes, . . . nice."

Lizzie smiled self-consciously and sat with the rest of the family as dinner commenced. Conversation reviewed events of the day, weather, more events, more weather. All except Eddie stole furtive glances at the new style in the room. Eddie just stared.

As the children were clearing the table, Father rose to return to his paper. He turned to Lizzie, looked into her worried eyes, and said, "Actually Lizzie, I do like it. It is pretty, and very becoming."

Now Lizzie beamed. "Thank you, Father."

Eddie was excited for the start of school. He waved to Gus and Frank across the playing field behind the Tabernacle as they all approached from different directions and continued to the crowd of students. Each boy had new or freshly cleaned overalls, new or freshly polished shoes, and a satchel with paper, pencils, and lunch.

A tall, official looking woman with her hair in a bun and a clipboard in her hand called out, "First grade here, to my right. Second grade here, to my left." Other women called out for other grades and soon the mass of children had formed into groups by grade. With a surprising degree of precision, they began to file into the school.

And then something wonderful happened.

Angela Anderson was standing with another girl at the door. She was in third grade and was a "Monitor", helping the teachers organize and direct the new students toward their classrooms. Now, her long hair falling in ringlets to her shoulders, her fair skin glowing in the morning sunlight, her sweet smile—Eddie realized that Angela was the most beautiful girl he had ever seen. Maybe the most beautiful girl that had ever been.

As he came next to her, he leaned toward her and kissed her on the cheek, then hurried through the door.

He glanced back to see her puzzled look, followed by embarrassment at the giggling of her companion. Frank poked him in the side. "I saw that."

"Good thing the teachers didn't," added Gus.

Eddie's mind was soon diverted from Angela by the official looking woman with the clipboard. She turned out to be Mrs. Murphy, his teacher.

She welcomed them to her class, explained school rules, and announced, "This is going to be one of the best years of our lives. We are going to have a wonderful time together, learning material that will make you happy, healthy, and successful. But first let's get acquainted."

She picked up the clipboard from her desk and began reading the names of her class.

"Abbott, William Fulbright"

"Here."

"Albino, Nicholas Albert."

"Here."

"Baderitakis, Stefano Constantino."

"Here."

Bjarnson, Magnus."

"Here."

And so, through the list. Although most of the children already knew each other, some sounded unfamiliar, even a little strange.

"Pappas, Argus Constantine."

"Here."

"Rossi, Francis Luigi."

Finally, it was his turn.

"Taylor, Shirley Edwin." A couple of the boys in back laughed.

"It's Eddie."

"Pardon?" asked Mrs. Murphy.

"My name is Eddie."

"I will make a note of it—you want to be called Eddie." She scribbled a little.

"Not just called. Eddie is short for. . . for Edward."

"But it says here," she glanced around the room. Many of the children were snickering now. "Quiet!" said the teacher. There was instant silence.

Mrs. Murphy came over to Eddie's seat in the third row and looked into his eyes. She smiled a soft, gentle smile that belied her otherwise stern, official manner so far that morning. "Yes, I see. Right here." Now she wrote a little longer and more carefully on the sheet before her. "Edward Taylor. The record has been corrected. Thank you, Eddie, for that information."

She returned to the front of the room and continued the roll. As for Eddie, he decided he was going to like his first grade teacher a lot.

Having confirmed that everyone who was supposed to be in the class was actually there, and already having memorized most of the names, Mrs. Murphy continued, "Now children, you may have noticed that we have many and varied names in our class. Some of the names may have sounded strange to you. Let's see something. At home, how many of you speak at least some Greek?"

About a fourth of the class raised their hands.

"Italian?"

Almost as many.

"German?"

A few.

"And if we tried, we would probably find a few other languages as well. That's wonderful. But here at school we will speak only English, understood?"

The class solemnly nodded.

"Our town has a rich heritage of many nations. You have many and varied names. We have all come together in what is called 'The Melting Pot'. No matter what nation your family came from, here we are Americans. And Americans speak English. The next step is to learn to read it. We start with the alphabet."

Mrs. Murphy began pointing to the large letters posted on the walls and having the class recite the name of each letter. Eddie found the next two hours very tedious. Fortunately, he had a good view of the window and ample imagination to occupy his mind.

As the children filed out for recess, he stepped cautiously up to his teacher's desk.

"Yes, Eddie?"

"Mrs. Murphy. Uh. I already know the alphabet. And how to read too."

"I see. Do you read at home?"

"Yes, Ma'am. I'm in the middle of McGuffey's Third Reader."

Mrs. Murphy thought for a minute. "Very well. You of course must read the material we have here in class so that you can know what everyone else knows. But if you want more, when you finish the class work, you may bring whatever other book you are working on and read it quietly too, while the rest of the class catches up. Does that sound good?"

Eddie sighed with relief. He loved reading, but starting over from the beginning seemed such a waste.

Once outside he looked around at the playground and started for the slide when three other boys came up to him.

"There he is," said a redheaded boy with a round face covered with freckles. "He stayed behind because he's the teacher's pet. First day and he's the pet." The other boys laughed.

Eddie's cheeks grew warm.

"And he ain't even a boy. He's really a girl. Shirley. That's a girl's name." The laughter grew louder.

"The name is Eddie," he snarled back.

"Shirley, Shirley, Shirley."

Eddie swung hard and hit the boy in the belly. That was followed by a shower of blows in both directions which continued as both fell to the ground in close combat.

CHAPTER 17

1923, Fall. The Gang Meets Matt Warner

Though he would never admit it, Eddie was relieved when the playground monitor pulled the two boys apart. Fighting this kid with freckles was harder than any of the other fights he had been in. His left shoulder hurt where it had been hit. He could feel a bruise forming.

Soon the two of them stood in front of Mr. Hammond, the Principal.

"I suppose you little ruffians have a good explanation. No doubt you each have a version of who started it and so forth." He peered at them through small, round glasses. "Don't say a word. I don't care what you have to say. There is no excuse. Fighting will not be tolerated. And on the first day of school too."

He stepped behind his desk and took a large paddle from its hook on the wall. It was a wooden paddle with well-worn handle and with holes for greater effect.

"They don't call me 'Hammond the Hammer' for nothing. Now bend over and grab your ankles." Each had one swat on the bottom. Eddie wanted to cry but knew he must not. The boys did not know how lightly the swat had been given—they were only first graders, after all.

"Now back to your class. And don't let this happen again." Mr. Hammond watched as they moved quickly down the hall, rolled his eyes, and thought, "It's going to be a long year."

Eddie looked down and away from his classmates when he returned to class, and supposed the other boy did too. He did not see Mrs. Murphy watching them, tapping her teeth with her pencil. She had heard the stories about how the fight started, thought how the Taylor boy had responded during roll call, and decided she would not tell the parents. In fact, she would ignore the whole thing, except perhaps . . . She reached out to a large book on her shelf to check on something.

"Eddie," she called as the class was leaving. Eddie thought for sure it was more trouble.

"Yes ma'am?"

"Eddie, I understand what the fight was about. You should know, up until recently, Shirley was always a man's name."

"I know. That's what Mother said."

"Well, it means a bright clearing in the forest, a place where men in olden times would gather and decide things. It's really a very good name."

Eddie brightened a little, then said, "But now it's a girl's name."

"True, mostly, but really for both men and women. A famous writer named Charlotte Bronte, have you hear of her?"

"No ma'am."

"Well, she wrote a book, and the heroine was named Shirley. And that was the title, too. It was a popular book and ever since then more girls than boys have had it as a name."

"I like Edward."

Mrs. Murphy could see his mind was made up.

"Yes, Eddie. Edward. I like it too."

He wanted to avoid having to talk about the fight at home, so Eddie brushed himself off and washed before seeing Mother. He enthusiastically praised the teacher who understood him so well and would let him read at his own level. Having pleased his mother and satisfied her curiosity about school, he hurried out to do his chores, take care of Sheep, and rendezvous with Gus and Frank.

They were waiting in front of Gus's father's shop. From there they walked the short distance to the city building, a rectangular building, not so elegant as the county courthouse, but still very imposing with its two stories of stone work and flag display in front. A receptionist directed them down the hall to where a deputy stood guard.

"What do you boys want?" he asked.

"We're friends with Judge Warner," replied Eddie. "Just here to watch."

The deputy raised his eyebrows, then shrugged and said, "Okay. Sit in the back row and be quiet. If I hear a peep, I'll pull you out of there so fast, you'll think it's the bum's rush. Got it?"

"Yes Sir. We'll be as quiet as quiet can be."

They slipped into the small courtroom and sat in the back row near the door. Matt Warner was in the judges' seat, lecturing two teenage boys standing slump shouldered in front of him. Two older men, a court reporter, and another deputy were the only others in the room.

". . . boys oughta know better." Warner was in mid-sentence when they entered. "Stealin' a poor man's flask. Then gettin' in a fight over it." He rubbed his chin. "Did you get into a fight before you drank the whiskey, or after?"

The boys mumbled something.

"Speak up, or I'll get right to sentencing."

"After, Sir. It was after we had drunk some. Still some left, and we were feelin' kinda hot. And . . . "

"That's enough. You know, if you had a' been sober, you might not have had a fight. And if you had not gotten in the fight, you might not a' been caught. Did ya think of that?"

"Yes Sir."

"But you didn't think much at the time, did you?"

"No Sir."

The justice of the peace rubbed his chin again. "Do you know much about me?" he asked.

The boys looked at each other. "No Sir, just that you used to be a bandit, but went straight."

"Well, there's a little more to it than that. I was on the outlaw trail nearly twenty years. That's a long time to be on the wrong side of the law and still be alive. And you know how it all started?" They shook their heads.

"With a fight. I was about your age, walkin' my girl home from a dance at Mutual, you know, a church dance, the Mutual Improvement Association. Well, there was this big bully who tried to take her at the dance even though he knew she was my girl. Then he made fun of me and my girl all the way home. I took it as long as I could, barely holding back 'til she went in her front door, then I took a stave off the picket fence and proceeded to beat the boy senseless.

"I thought I'd killed him, so took off to make my fortune as a cowboy. But one thing led to another, one bad decision and setback to another. All I wanted those days was to raise enough money to buy a little ranch and settle down.

"It turned out, the boy I beat up didn't die. All that runnin' was for nothin'. And in the end, after all those years and robberies and more fights and camping out on the range and hiding and suffering, I still didn't have money for a ranch. In fact, I didn't have anything. If it hadn't been for the kindness of the governor and others to plead my case, I might have died in prison, and that not even for a crime I had committed.

"So, there it is boys. It's not worth it. Don't fight, and don't steal. Not even little things, because little things lead to big things, and pretty soon, there goes your whole life. Crime doesn't pay. I know."

He turned to the adults. "Are you men their fathers?"

The two men stood up. "Yes, your Honor."

"I've done my part. Now it is up to you. If you want these young fella's to grow up to be fine, upstanding men, you have to raise them. Raise 'em right. Teach 'em right. Understood?"

"And how!" came the reply.

Warner turned back toward the boys. "Now about the drinking. You heard about Prohibition, didn't you? No law about the actual drinking of liquor, or of gettin' drunk, so there's not much I can do about that. And far be it from me to lecture you about the evils of demon rum. But it did make you more stupid than you already were, now, didn't it?" They nodded.

"I suppose I have to sentence you to something, so you are to sweep the Main Street sidewalks. Have it done by tomorrow night." He smacked his gavel down. "And you fathers have to supervise them. Make sure they do a good job!"

"Yes, Sir. We will."

"Oh, and about this." He picked up the tin flask on his desk and handed it to the deputy. "See that this gets back to Tom. He's in the drunk tank."

He spoke to the boys. "So, if you do get drunk, do it in private, not in public. You don't want to be in there with him and the others."

The men and their sons filed out of the courtroom. Warner looked over at Eddie and his friends and motioned them to come forward.

"You're Carl Taylor's son, aren't you? We've met before."

"Yes Sir. And these are my friends, Gus and Frank."

"Nice to meet you. Now, what brings you here today?"

Eddie felt a little sheepish. "Well, I told them I knew a real cowboy. So, I brought them here to meet you."

"Really? I hope it wasn't disappointing. With that introduction though, it might a' been better to be near a corral or a barn or on the range. Was this interesting enough?"

They all agreed it was.

Saying their goodbyes, the boys started for the door. Warner called after them, "Come back anytime. Just not as defendants."

They chuckled. "No Sir."

Eddie was a little uncomfortable that the case they heard was about the evils of fighting. He figured he had had about enough of that for one day. Fortunately, aside from seeing the occasional smirking face, he had no more run-ins with Jimmy, the redheaded boy. At least not that fall.

CHAPTER 18

1923, Fall. The Burning Cross

Besides school, fall was also the time for hunting. Each year Father went into the hills for a weekend, sometimes with Junior or a friend, and returned with a deer. If the hunting was especially good, he might go out a second time. The carcasses were already gutted in the field, but then had to be hung in the shed for skinning, cut into quarters for sharing, then cut into smaller pieces for wrapping, storing, and cooking. If the weather had already turned cold, it was left to hang in the shed. Father said it would "cure" there and would taste better.

Sometimes Father had the meat frozen and stored at a commercial locker for rent near the Fairgrounds. Beef and mutton bought right from the ranchers at a discounted price was also stored there. The family ice box in the kitchen was small and did not keep food frozen hard.

Other hunting trips were with the shotgun for birds—ducks, geese, pheasants. One year Father returned with a wild turkey, so they decided to have an early Thanksgiving.

Eddie liked all the meat, but especially beef and mutton. Venison tasted a lot like mutton, only stronger. Mother called it "gamey".

One day in early October he returned home after school to find his mother weeping softly in the parlor.

He put his hand on her shoulder and asked what was the matter.

"It's my father. Grandpa Mueller has died."

Eddie was dumbstruck. Grandpa had always been so strong, so healthy. How could this happen?

"My sister, Vilate, just called. He was experimenting again. You know, he always wanted to find what things were useful for. Since castor oil is a useful medicine, he thought castor beans. . . Well, you know, we all know, castor beans are poisonous. He knew that too but thought if he just had the right dosage."

She wept again. "I called your father. He is on his way home."

The Taylor children were mostly on their own for a few days while their parents attended the funeral in Provo. Sister Anderson and other church members checked in on them to make sure they were all right.

When Mother and Father returned, they described the proceedings. "Provo City Cemetery is on a low hill on the southeast side of town with fine trees interspersed among the rows of headstones," said Father. "Your Grandfather Mueller is buried not far from your other grandparents. Your mother's sisters and brothers were all at the services, as well as a great many townspeople— people from church, but also others. Grandpa was well known, and well loved by many.

"One other thing. Grandma is being looked after by your aunts for now but will come live with us as soon as things are a little more settled. That will mean some re-arranging of the bedrooms."

Eddie wondered why Grandma would leave Provo. She had lived there for so many years, surrounded by friends and family. He looked over at Mother. She had a calm, peaceful expression. "Are you her favorite?" he asked.

Mother was surprised. "Favorite? Heavens! Parents don't have favorites." Then she thought a little longer and smiled ever so slightly. "Perhaps," she said softly. "Perhaps I am."

Father had to make two trips to bring Grandma's things from the train station, not because there was an awful lot, but because it included a large, green trunk that simply would not fit in the car with everything else and the whole family.

"Poppa had it made for me in Stuttgart, before we move to Holy Land. Katharina," she said to Mother. "I want you to have it."

She looked around at the assembled Taylor family in the parlor and her eyes moistened. "I love you all. Frederick loved you all. There is something here for everyone, to remember him." She opened the trunk and began withdrawing her gifts. An old-fashioned tie for Father, a large cameo brooch for Lizzie ("He gave it me many years ago"), Grandpa's much-worn scriptures for Junior, a carved olive wood box from Jerusalem for Johnny. "And for you, Eddie, his hat."

A large smile appeared on Eddie's face as he took the fez from his grandmother and placed it gently on his head. It was large, coming down over his ears. "I love it!" he exclaimed.

"You think of him when you see these things. And remember what he teach—'Be useful. Be useful for good.'" At this she looked down, sniffed, and wiped her eyes. "Sure. I will miss him."

Eddie had not known his grandparents on his father's side and so had not felt the sorrow that he now felt. The family talked of the resurrection and of reunion in the next life, which gave comfort. Eddie was happy to have Grandmother in the home, especially for her cooking. Mother was a very good cook, but after all, she had learned from her mother. Nevertheless, Grandma was sometimes a little hard to understand, and not just because of her accent.

Every afternoon when Eddie returned home from school, Grandma would smile, nod, and say she was ashamed of him. It made no sense to him, but he concluded that now she could see him day by day at close range, he just did not measure up. He soon found himself dreading the daily homecoming and looking for ways to avoid it, or at least shorten his time in the house, hurrying off to chores or play.

One evening after dinner, as the Taylor children were helping with the dishes, there came a knock at the back door.

"Can Eddie come for a little while?" asked Gus anxiously, his cap in his hand, "I have something I want to show him. Tonight."

Mother nodded and soon the two boys were running up the back alley.

"What is it?" asked Eddie as they ran.

"You'll see."

At the intersection they had a clear view of Wood Hill. There they could see a large cross burning on the top, its flames brightening the whole northwest side of town.

"Wow! What is it?"

"A cross."

"I see that. I mean, what's it mean?"

"I dunno, but ain't it swell?"

"And how!"

Eddie and Gus stood admiring the scene. Soon Frank came up to join them. All around town, others stood watching. Most young people just enjoyed the show, like a bonfire in the distance on the hill, only too far away to roast marshmallows.

Older people viewed it differently. Those who did not know what it meant scratched their chins and wondered why anyone would go to so much trouble. A few thought it might be sacrilegious. A few who knew what it meant approved of it. But most only shuddered, shook their heads, and muttered something like, "What's this country coming to?"

For three boys watching the scene from the intersection near their homes, the fiery display was the spark for another great idea.

CHAPTER 19

1923, Fall. The Gang's New Name

"Let's do something like that," exclaimed Eddie. His friends echoed in agreement.

"Yeah," added Gus, "it'll be part of our gang, the thing we do."

"But not a cross. It don't feel right," said Frank.

"Besides, somebody else already has it for their gang." Eddie was very serious now. The three looked at each other as they considered their future. Each had a suggestion.

"How about a big *C*, like the one the High School kids paint on the cliff each year?."

"People will think it's just another High School stunt."

"Maybe *P* for Price?" They shook their heads.

A smile spread across Eddie's face. "I know. How about a big circle? We could call ourselves *The Flaming Circle Gang*."

The three young gangsters nodded in enthusiastic agreement, spit on their palms, and shook hands. Their gang, previously just a thought, was now a reality.

Next day was Saturday, so they spent it gathering materials—used car oil, old rags, tin cans, short pieces of dry wood they could tie together as a torch, shovels—all snitched carefully and quietly from their fathers' garages or sheds. More oil was had from the car repair shop south of Main. The afternoon saw them hauling boxes up Wood Hill to a site across a ravine, opposite from where the cross had burned the night before. The hill had more of a slope there, was less vertical, so the circle could be seen from below.

Gus was afraid that they might be seen setting up the circle and get in trouble, but Frank said not to worry about it. Nobody would think anything about it, if they noticed. It was just kids, fooling around.

Eddie had first wanted to dig a trench so the outline of the circle would be solid flame, but Frank pointed out that there was no way to contain the fuel; it would just leak away. So, they came up with the thought of cans with rags as wicks, like lamps. The circle had to be big, big enough to be easily seen, and a lot bigger than the cross had been, because there was no sense in half measures.

"Glorious!" exclaimed Eddie. "It has to be glorious."

Using their fathers' shovels, they cleared small level spaces where the cans could be placed. They knew it was important for each can to be level so it wouldn't tip over, and there couldn't be any dry grass nearby. There would be awful trouble if they started a brush fire.

After they had placed the cans, Eddie hiked back down to the base of the hill to evaluate their work. "Looks good," he said when he returned, flushed and out of breath. "It's gonna' be wonderful."

"'Glorious'?" asked Frank with a grin.

"Yeah. Glorious."

By now it was early evening. "Alright, guys. Let's go home, wash up, and have dinner, so no one will suspect anything. Then meet back here. Okay?"

They all agreed, hid their remaining materials and boxes behind a clump of sagebrush, and hurried home.

"Where have you been all day?" asked Mother as Eddie entered the back door.

"Just out." He worried they had been seen. "Playing with Gus and Frank."

Mother wiped her hands on her apron. "Well, you didn't finish making your bed this morning. It was only half done. And you didn't take out the trash like I asked you."

"I'm sorry, Mother. I guess I forgot."

She looked at him carefully. "Remember next time, okay? If a task is once begun, never leave it til it's done. . . "

Eddie finished the rhyme, "Be the labor great or small, do it well or not at all."

"Right. So next time, finish making the bed. And don't forget the trash."

"No, ma'am. I mean, yes, ma'am."

Always a polite boy, Eddie was especially courteous during that dinner. He smiled a lot. Mother attributed it to a proper amount of guilt for not having finished his work and to having played hard all day, both healthy things for a child.

It was very dark when Eddie snuck out the back door and made his way down the alley and up Wood Hill. The stars were bright as ever, but the moon was not out, so he stumbled now and then. At their rendezvous point he found Frank already waiting. Gus soon joined them.

"Well. Are we ready?"

"Yeah."

"You bet."

The boys decided it wouldn't be fair for only one person to get to light the circle, so they took turns, each running one third of the way around with the torch, touching each oil can/lantern as he passed, like a relay race. When they were finished, they jammed the torch into the dirt and ran as fast as they could down toward town, glancing back occasionally in admiration.

They walked more casually when they reached the streets, hiding as best they could their breathlessness and the anxiety they felt, lest they be caught. Finally safe in the alley, they turned and watched the wonderful flaming circle light up the night.

"It's beautiful," exclaimed Frank, to which the others agreed. "Even glorious."

As they stood there, they were aware of neighbors craning their necks to see the new marvel.

"*The Flaming Circle Gang* has struck! Now, not a word to anyone, right?"

"Right."

At church the next day Eddie was greatly tempted to say something when he overheard some of the other kids talking about the fire on Wood Hill. Grownups debated the significance of it. Eddie remained silent, though he continued to smile a lot.

Gus and Frank were waiting on the front steps when Mother and the Taylor children returned home. Mother was a little surprised; Sunday was not usually a day for play, certainly not play away from home, so she invited them in for cookies and milk.

Father was waiting in the parlor, the Sunday newspaper spread across his lap. "Katharina," he said, "you know that circle of fire last night?"

"Yes."

"Well, it says here that it must have been a response by the Catholics to the Klan's cross burning. Apparently, there is something called *The Knights of the Flaming Circle*. It's a secret society. Their response to the KKK is a warning that Catholicism is strong and will not be intimidated. "Must be more of 'em than anyone thought."

Eddie's jaw dropped and he started to speak, but then saw Frank shake his head gently, eyes wide.

"Did you say something?" asked Father.

"Uh. No. I, just. Well, that is really interesting—what's in the paper."

Father looked perplexed at his youngest. "Yes. Well, we know how often the reporters are wrong. Still, it does sound sensible." He looked at his son again. "Glad to see you are interested in current events, son."

Safely gathered around the kitchen table with their snacks, Eddie whispered to Frank, "Why not tell him the real story?"

"We all promised. Besides, remember what I told you about the Klan? If people think it was some bunch of Catholics pushing back, well, maybe that's a good thing, but if people think it was just kids . . . And I still think we might get in trouble for it."

"He's right," added Gus. "And you know, it's kinda' nice to have a secret, a big secret, that nobody else knows about."

Eddie wrinkled his forehead for a moment, then smiled again. "Yeah, I guess that's right." And he ate another bite of cookie.

CHAPTER 20

1923-1924. *Preparing For Stake Conference*

They did not hear much more about the KKK in Price that winter, though Father read reports of their marches and cross burnings in Helper and Castle Gate. The Taylors, like most families, were more concerned with the particularly cold weather, the high snow, and the enjoyment of Thanksgiving, Christmas, and New Years.

For Eddie there was the daily routine of school, chores, and playing with his buddies when he could. There was little talk of flaming circles; they decided one display was enough. He continued to have occasional scuffles, especially with Jimmy Curtis, the kid with freckles, but nothing that resulted in swats from the Vice Principal or reports to his parents. It turned out Jimmy was the Stake President's son. "That doesn't make him special," thought Eddie.

It still bothered him that his grandmother was ashamed of him, though he tried to ignore it. Maybe it was because Grandpa died, or the other boys were her favorites, or he didn't look enough like her side of the family. Nearly every day when he returned from school, she would be sitting in the parlor or kitchen, look over at him, and say something like, "What a shame" and shake her head. And smile. That didn't make sense, but he was beginning to realize that a lot of things didn't make sense. He guessed he would just have to live with it.

The calendar soon brought a new item of interest. Stake Conference was coming on the first of March and rumor had it that they would have a General Authority in attendance, and not just any of the brethren. This would be J. Golden Kimball. Eddie did not know exactly what made this speaker special, but clearly, he was special since all the men would smile when his name was mentioned and the ladies would look away. Apparently Elder Kimball was known for saying things some people thought inappropriate.

In preparation, Eddie was given a new Buster Brown suit, store-bought, right out of the Sears and Roebuck catalog. Other suits were cleaned and mended. Lizzie had a new dress with straight lines, very fashionable for the young girls. It was a little short according to Mother and Father, but still came to below the knees and had short puffy sleeves.

Choosing a dress was harder for Mother. She contemplated the contents of her closet. What to wear? There was the stylish new chemise. Not quite right, too young for church. Or the black gown? A little too black. Perhaps the pink floral frock, or the calico. No, also not quite right for church, at least not for this meeting, and besides, it was still winter.

Her eyes lit on the heavy jacket in the corner, and she smiled. She touched the elaborate bead work and black satin and thought how many hours she had spent making it.

"Humph," she muttered. "Above their station."

It still rankled to think about it. Before she was married, she and her sisters had a dress shop on Main Street in Provo. They were good seamstresses, so it was very successful. All the stylish ladies in town patronized them. It was only natural that their best work went into dresses they made for themselves. The newspaper editor—Mother suspected it was actually the editor's wife—was so upset about it that he made it the subject of an editorial: "Certain young ladies in our fair city dress above their station."

"'Above their station,'" she muttered again.

She loved the fashions of those years. Her bustle was neatly folded away somewhere, and she still had the corset, but would not really want to wear it again. On the other hand, the hourglass figure of a Gibson girl was classically beautiful; the gowns hung so elegantly, especially nice when paired with a wide-brimmed hat with feathers. She glanced up at the shelf where her hats, new and old, were stored.

But fashions change with life. Carl whisked her away to married life, and her sisters were not able to keep the shop through the war. The war changed everything. The Mueller's, after all, were German.

She smiled again, touched the beads once more, and sighed. In the end she chose the grey dress with black velvet trim. It went well with her black winter coat. She reached up for a matching cloche hat with jeweled pin securing a small feather.

"This will be nice," she said to herself. "Neither a Gibson girl nor a flapper. Just neat and clean and smart-looking."

The Tabernacle contained a large hall behind the chapel, and when the partition was opened it was perfect for Stake Conference, when attendance exceeded a thousand, with church members from nine wards and branches. This conference was different, though, for word was out that J. Golden Kimball was to be the speaker, so even members who never attended and many curious non-members came. They wanted to hear for themselves what the famous "swearing apostle" would say, especially what he might inadvertently blurt out.

Kimball was not actually an apostle. He was one of the seven presidents of the Seventy, who reported to the apostles and First Presidency, but he was known to cuss, which caused no little embarrassment to the other General Authorities. He was a wiry cowboy, had grown up with coarse language, and struggled mightily to control his natural tendencies.

Now the Tabernacle was filled to overflowing, with many in the congregation standing along the back of the hall and in the hallways. The Taylors arrived early and found convenient seats in the middle to the right a little.

"Sit here beside Grandma," Mother said to Eddie, pointing to a spot on the bench.

He shook his head and dove to a spot on the other side of Father. Mother started to speak again, then turned her head, patted Grandma on the shoulder, and sat down, smoothing her skirt.

Eddie struggled to be patient, pulling now and then at his collar and scratching his low back where the seams of his suit came together. He was between Father to the left and Johnny and Junior to the right. Mother and Grandma were on the other side of Father, with Lizzie on the end. He leaned forward to see them.

Grandma had her usual relaxed smile, what Father called "the smile of reason." Father said it was a quote, something Voltaire had said, but Eddie did not know who Voltaire was, or what made him an expert on smiling.

Mother looked particularly elegant today. And Lizzie, well, Eddie was not quite used to her short hair, make-up, and straight skirt with tassels, coming to just below the knees. He thought she looked like a lampshade. She said it was the fashion. "Fashions are funny," he thought.

The Stake President, Will Curtis, started the meeting by welcoming all who had come, especially the visitors. They all sang *The Morning Breaks*, had an opening prayer, and raised their arms in sustaining votes of church officers. Eddie closed his eyes, knowing that, seated between Father and Junior, there was little else he could do between now and the end.

A recently returned missionary told of his experiences in South America. A new father testified of the joys of family life. One of the stake presidency talked about something or other, but Eddie heard none of it, his body overcome with sleep.

A loud blast from the organ woke him with a start. The whole congregation was standing and singing the rest hymn, *Awake, Ye Saints of God, Awake.* Finally, President Curtis introduced their visiting General Authority.

Eddie craned his neck to see the man so many people were interested in hearing. J. Golden Kimball was tall, thin, and had a grey mustache. He had a small chin and a tall round forehead with very little hair left on top. Eddie thought his head looked like a light bulb. But it was the visiting authority's voice that really surprised him. It was high pitched and crackly. Eddie laughed. He did not sound very authoritative.

CHAPTER 21

1924, Mar 2. J. Golden Kimball, Straight Talker

"My Brothers and Sisters," he began, "I suppose you have all come here today to hear the word of God. I plan to quote plenty of scriptures, so be assured that this desire will be fulfilled. Now, if you came here to hear something else, maybe a good story or something humorous, well, I'll see what I can do on that score as well." He glanced over at President Curtis. "And I will do my best not to cuss."

Eddie saw the congregation settle back for a fine speech.

"When I was a young man I worked as a mule-driver. I enjoyed my work, though it was hard. Stubborn animals, you had to swear hard and loud at 'em to get 'em to move at all. So, I have had to work hard not to swear since my calling, not always successfully. Some nice sister who should have known better once asked me if I wasn't afraid they would cut me off from the Church. I told her, 'They can't excommunicate me, I repent too fast.' Only the original version of that story had an extra word or two in there."

Kimball waited a minute. "My mother wanted me to go on a mission, so to appease her and keep her from bothering me about it anymore, I went to see the president of the Church, John Taylor.

"I figured just seeing me in all my mule-driving glory would convince him I was not missionary material. I swaggered into his office dressed in my old boots, dirty chaps, and stained shirt, with my Bowie knife in my belt and six-shooters at my side. Well, he taught me something about being a prophet. He jumped up from his chair, shook my hand, and said with a big smile, 'So glad to meet you. I just read your mother's letter, and I know, just like your father, you will make a great ambassador for the church. The Lord wants you to serve in the Southern States Mission'. So, I was caught in my own trap. Apparently, he believed Mother's letter more than his own eyes."

There were a few chuckles in the crowd. Kimball went on to talk about the importance of testimony, having faith, studying the scriptures, and personal prayer. Eddie's mind wandered for awhile until near the end.

"Now, Brothers and Sisters," continued J. Golden, "there are several specific items I want to mention, that the Brethren asked me to tell you here in the Carbon County Stake. The only thing I am afraid of is that I will say just what I think, which would be unwise, no doubt, but I will try. First, concerning the Word of Wisdom. You may know that I struggle with this myself. I grew up drinking coffee and frankly have a hard time thinking straight without it from time to time. But I do my best and the Lord expects you to do your best too, that includes tobacco, even those wonderful cigars from Cuba. . . "

Eddie saw Mother glance at Father and kick him in the ankle. He winced.

". . . and black tea and alcohol, including the homemade kind. Oh, I know, Prohibition is supposed to remove that last temptation from our tables, but you and I both know that liquor is easier to get now than ever. Don't touch it and the Lord will bless you.

"Second, and this is something that was a bigger problem out in Wyoming a few years ago than here and now, but still, there it is. I hear there are some young fella's thinking they are tough guys and firing their guns off at dances and parties just to make noise." There was an uncomfortable rustling in the back where the older teenagers were milling around and flying paper airplanes. Kimball spoke up, "I hear some of you have been walking around town with pistols in your hip pockets. Better be careful—'might go off and blow your brains out."

When the laughter died down, he continued, "Finally, we have all heard about the Ku Klux Klan. They had died out until the last few years. Now some ignorant zealots have revived it, mainly in the East, but here too, to push against the immigrants, the Catholics, and us Mormons. I trust no Latter-day Saint would have anything to do with them, but sometimes trust is broken, so I'm telling you, have nothing to do with them. Teach them the Gospel and hope they repent. In the meantime, mind your manners and use your influence with the government to keep them under control. I assume you still have some influence."

He paused a moment, looking into the audience. "I remember my first mission, five years in the Southern States, starting in 1883. They killed the elders in those days, and on more than one occasion I was surrounded by men in white sheets and pointy hats." He paused again. "Waste of a good sheet."

Kimball concluded thoughtfully with his testimony that the Church was true, the Book of Mormon is true, and that Jesus is the Savior. Though the last parts of the talk had caught his attention, Eddie was relieved to stand after the closing song and prayer. He stretched, yawned, and looked around at the people.

He realized the Andersons were just three rows behind them. Angela was as beautiful as ever. His day was made. He still hadn't talked to her other than to say 'hello' when the families passed each other at church or in town. She was in different classes everywhere. "Never mind," he thought. "Someday, when I'm older, I'll talk to you a lot. Then I'll marry you."

"Good meeting," said Father. "Very edifying."

"You just liked all the stories," Mother replied.

"I liked those, but I especially liked how he was so direct. A straight-talker. And a strong testimony too."

Eddie hung on those last words, straight-talker. That's what he wanted to be.

Being a straight-talker was not always as easy as Eddie thought.

Shortly after returning home and changing their clothes, Mother put her hand on his shoulder, guided him into the parlor, and told him to sit. "Alright, young man. I want to know what is going on. You have not been yourself lately."

Eddie's mind flashed to the flaming circle. He suddenly was unable to speak.

"Well, what have you to say for yourself?"

"I, I, gosh, Mother, I can't say. Everything's okay." Denial was the best he could manage. "I didn't do anything. Really."

She leaned into him and spoke quietly. "Why have you been avoiding your grandmother? What is the matter?"

Eddie felt both relieved and concerned. He did not really want to talk about that either. But there was Mother, her face inches from his, eyes gazing intently into his soul.

"Because she's ashamed of me," he sniffed.

Mother sat back. "What?"

"She's ashamed of me. And I don't know why. And I'm sorry I'm not better." He sniffed again more forcefully as his many sins and indiscretions flashed through his mind.

"What in the world makes you think that? She loves you, Eddie. Why do you think she's ashamed?"

"She says so. Every day when I get home from school she looks at me and says, 'Such a shame'."

Mother sat back, perplexed, then her face brightened to a smile, and she began to laugh. Oh, that was too much to bear! First Grandma was ashamed, and now Mother was laughing about it. Eddie began to sob.

"Shirl," she explained, "That's not what she's saying. It's German. She says, *'So Schoen'*. You've heard me say it too, but Grandma has a different accent. Where she's from they pronounce it *'Zo shayn'*. It means 'So beautiful'. She thinks you're beautiful, Eddie. She loves you."

His sniffing slowed to a halt. "Really?"

"Yes, really. Now start being nice to her. Okay?"

"Okay." He wrinkled his brow. "That's all it is? Really?"

"Yes, really. Silly boy." She reached over and hugged him.

"I guess I didn't hear it right. I thought I always heard things right."

"Nobody always hears things right, Shirl. And you couldn't help not understanding her accent."

Eddie thought again. "You know, I think she's beautiful too."

Mother smiled again. "Next time she says that, say, *'Danke. Du auch.'* It means, 'Thanks. You too.' She'll love it."

Eddie left, repeating his newly learned German.

The following week was good for Eddie. He didn't get into any fights. Mrs. Murphy was a delightful teacher, his reading was well ahead of the class, and he was learning about arithmetic, history, and art. Even his writing was beginning to come along. But best of all, each day when Grandma said he was beautiful, he replied, she smiled, and she hugged him. And there was not a word about flaming circles or his gang.

The following Saturday morning was cold, crisp, and clear. Eddie and Gus were walking toward the ball fields when the sirens sounded. They looked around to see the fire but saw nothing at first. Then men could be seen hurrying along the streets, not just firemen and police, but regular guys. The boys felt a low rumble.

"Was that thunder?" wondered Eddie.

There were no clouds in the sky.

"Maybe an earthquake."

"Look," said Gus, pointing toward the west. Toward Castle Gate, twelve miles away, was a plume of black and grey smoke rising above the hills.

They ran to the Greek shop. More men were hurrying along Main.

"What's happening, Pop?" shouted Gus when they arrived.

"Mine explosion at Castle Gate. More I don't know. Big fire."

CHAPTER 22

1924, Mar 8. The Castle Gate Mine Explosion

The boys went back to the ball field and tried to play catch. It was hard to concentrate on the game, their eyes drawn back to the western horizon and the ever larger plume of smoke. Frank joined them, grim-faced. Eddie did not know anyone who worked in the mines, but Gus's cousin and Frank's brother were there, as well as other relatives and family friends.

Father was late when he arrived home. He was dirty, a little pale, and smelled of oily smoke. Mother and Grandma bustled about to get him some supper while the children stood by, eager to hear the news.

He seemed to choose his words carefully. "The explosions were big, three of them they guess. A lot of men trapped inside. Pieces of machinery were thrown across the valley—half a mile at least. Everyone rushed in to help. Those who rushed in first were caught in the second blast. The steel doors to the mine were blown right off the concrete frame."

Mother handed him a wet washcloth to wipe his face and hands.

"Anyway, lots of volunteers. I tried to help, but not much I could do. Mine rescue crews are on their way from all over. They will be more useful. There are fires everywhere, and poison gas. Just picking through the debris is dangerous."

The following days dragged on as attempts to rescue trapped miners quickly became cleanup, collecting bodies, clearing collapsed tunnels, consoling grieving widows and fatherless children. Work continued through the nights, but bitter cold made the grim work even more harsh and difficult.

There was little Eddie could do other than keep Gus and Frank company as they waited for news they knew would be bad. Frank's brother was found first, burned almost beyond recognition, then his cousin, crushed by rock not far away. It was eight days before Gus's cousin was found; he died of poison gas deep in the mine.

One evening as the Taylor family gathered around the table for supper, Lizzie volunteered to tell a story she had heard at school. One of her classmates was a girl from Castle Gate who came in on a bus each day. Her father had been killed in the mine, but prior to the explosion her mother had experienced an unusual dream.

"She said her mother often has dreams that came true. A sort of second sight. About a month ago she dreamt that streams of light came down from heaven and lit one home after another in Castle Gate. She asked the bishop what it meant, but he didn't know. Then when the mine blew up, each home that had a stream of light was where one of the men was killed." Lizzie's eyes were large. "Father, what do you think?"

Father cleared his throat. "Well, people have dreams, and sometimes they come true. Other than that, I don't know." The family sat in silence.

"I suppose," he continued, "I suppose this might have been a sort of reassurance to your friend's mother that everything was going to be all right, that God is in charge and will take care of His children. Reassurance to everyone who hears the story, too. A sort of comfort in the midst of this awful loss."

The dead were buried in several towns, but the greatest number in Price. Some of the early funerals had already taken place, but there were so many that it made sense to wait so services could be performed in groups, more especially since some of the remains could not be clearly identified.

Eddie stood with his friends and his brothers at the edge of the ball field between the Tabernacle and the school. The field was filled with coffins, arranged in rows, with cards stating whose body was inside. 172 men had been killed in the disaster, 50 of them Greeks. A hundred coffins were now assembled in Price. Women in black and children with black armbands walked along the rows, stopped when they came to a husband or brother or cousin, and burst into tears.

It was an impressive sight for anyone, but for a young boy who had never seen even one coffin it was overwhelming. Eddie was very solemn and felt much older than he had a few days earlier.

He wrinkled his nose, "What's that smell?"

Junior was at his side, "That's the smell of death, Eddie. The cold weather delayed it a little, but it's there."

"It smells like that dead fish we found by the garden."

"Yeah."

Roman Catholic and Greek Orthodox priests in flowing black robes moved among the crowd, swinging round metal balls on chains with smoke coming from them.

"That's incense," added Junior. "It smells good and helps a little."

"Not enough. It's awful."

"It's supposed to be awful."

Junior touched Eddie on the shoulder. "Look over there," he whispered, "It's Heber J. Grant. He's the president of the Church, the prophet."

A distinguished looking man with spectacles and a trimmed white beard walked slowly along the row nearest the boys, President Curtis and several other men and women following along. They approached a woman who was sobbing quietly and holding a bundle of white temple clothing.

She looked up and, recognizing the man, said, "Oh, President Grant, my husband, we couldn't dress him for burial because he. . ." She could not continue.

A teenage boy standing next to her put his arm around her and continued softly, "His legs were so badly burned, if we tried to dress him, they would have fallen off."

President Grant thought for a moment, reached out to them both, and touched them gently on the arms, as if they were his children. "It's alright, Sister. Lay his clothes beside him and on resurrection morning he will dress himself."

Funeral services were held in all the churches, cemeteries, and assembly halls. The Knights of Pythias Hall was converted into a temporary mortuary to give relief to the over-worked Price mortuary. Eddie tried to comfort Gus and Frank as best he could for their cousins and brother and friends of their families, but then retreated to the pen in the backyard.

Brushing Sheep was somehow comforting to Eddie, though he could not explain why. He knew it was important not to get too attached to Sheep, not like he did with Lambie, but surely a little nuzzling would not hurt. Again, he put his face into the warm wool and breathed. Ah, that good smell of life. How he loved it.

Despite the best efforts of the clergy and the lay leaders of the community, the atmosphere in Price and in all the mining towns remained somber through the rest of the spring. The state of Utah and the coal companies put together funds to help the families hurt by the disaster, but even then, many widows saw their family income drop from $300 per month to $64. They took on odd jobs and extra work to make ends meet, in addition to the increased responsibility of raising children at home without their husbands. Older children quit school to work wherever they could. The Latter-day Saint Relief Society as well as aid societies in the Greek and Italian communities helped out, especially with food donations.

There was a general sense that this was a time of great trial. Though Eddie did not know anyone who was killed, he saw the loss and sorrow around him, especially among his friends and classmates. But even great sorrow cannot last forever. The early signs of spring reminded Eddie and all the people of Price of the promise of new life, of renewal, and of happier times ahead.

Music helped. Many families found their evenings refreshed by new, cheery songs on the radio, *It Had to Be You, California Here I Come, Hinky Dinky Parlay Voo*, and of course, *The Charleston*. Lizzie especially enjoyed that last one as she practiced dance steps around the corner, out of sight of her parents. More to Mother's taste was Gershwin's new song, *Rhapsody in Blue*, an especially romantic, exotic melody with harmonies that went beyond familiar classics or popular songs.

Work helped too, and spring meant spring cleaning. The Taylor kids were all recruited to take down drapes and gather up rugs. These were hung over the clothes lines and poles and beaten with a carpet whacker made of cane and wicker. Great clouds of dust flew up with each stroke.

While the boys cleaned the drapes and rugs, Mother and Lizzie scrubbed the coal soot from the walls with clay, then thoroughly swept the house, moving furniture to get under and around every piece and into the corners and crevices that were missed the rest of the year. A new broom was purchased each year for spring cleaning. "A new broom sweeps clean," said Mother.

It took a full two days to complete the process and get everything back to normal.

"'Glad we don't have a bigger house," Father commented.

CHAPTER 23

1924, Spring. Lambing in the Hills

Carl Taylor sat back in his easy chair and admired the little parlor around him. He was glad spring cleaning was over, and glad the house was clean. It seemed to go much faster now than it did when he was little.

He reached for a cigar, ran it past his nose appreciatively, then put it back in his shirt pocket. "No smoking in the house" was a hard and fast rule. The rule was not just because his wife said it was stinky and dirty. Keeping the Word of Wisdom, the church's health code, was one of the requirements to go to the temple. For her it was part of being fully active in the church; for him it was a stumbling block.

He was not alone. Most members in those days did not observe it strictly. "I'm just part of the majority," he said to himself. "At least in this." He sighed. "Someday I'll quit. Just not today."

He had not always smoked; it was a habit he picked up in the Philippines. Ah yes, the Philippines. Hard to keep things clean there, not because of coal smoke, cigar smoke, and dust, but because of mud and hard living.

Carl had served there in the army shortly after the Spanish-American War. Fortunately, he had been a clerk for the company commander, so did not have it as hard as some of the other troops. They were forever traipsing through the jungle and being shot at by Aguinaldo and his men, rebels who did not accept American government of the islands.

Still, it was very unpleasant. The food, dysentery, army life. He had asked his father to pull strings to get him sent home early. The judge was friends with Senator Smoot, but that was not enough. The wheels of government and the post office move slowly, and by the time the judge and the senator had exchanged letters, Carl's time overseas was half over. "May as well stick it out," wrote Smoot.

"Oh well," he thought, "it was good experience, I suppose. Toughened me up." He knew, though, his time in the army was not like his father's. Fighting an insurrection in the Pacific was not the same as freeing the slaves and preserving the Union. "Tough enough, anyway."

He glanced over at their wedding picture on the wall and smiled. "Besides, if I had not gone, I might not have met Katharine."

He was heading home from the army when the train stopped in Provo. Katharine was a volunteer, welcoming returning soldiers and handing out cups of coffee or lemonade. He was on his way to Spanish Fork, where his father had settled after retiring as judge. "So beautiful," he whispered to himself. "And such spunk!"

He soon was spending much more time in Provo than at home. Work, marriage, children, all came in quick succession. Life was good. Then came this opportunity with a larger territory, more responsibility, a raise. Price was a rougher town with more than a little touch of the wild west, more like the towns he had grown up in during the '80s, before moving to Utah.

"A little rough here in some ways, but things are turning out well," he mused. Carl Junior and Johnny were bright, hard workers who should do well. Lizzie was much like her mother. Then there was Shirl. He seemed a lot more sensitive than the other children. Carl smiled again. "He is a lot like I was. Well," he thought, "he'll toughen up, just like I did."

One Saturday morning a small truck pulled in front of the house. Frank hopped out of the back and ran to the front door and knocked.

"Can Eddie come?" he asked breathlessly when Father answered. "We're going up to the hills. My cousin has sheep and they're having lambs. We'll be back before dinner."

Permission was granted and Eddie started toward the car.

"Here," called Mother, "take your jacket." It was a warm day, but Eddie knew it was pointless to argue.

Soon he was bouncing along with his friend and one of his brothers as Frank's parents drove them out of town, west past Helper, then north toward the mountains. They quickly ran out of road and found themselves trekking between boulders and rock outcroppings, eventually coming to a broad meadow with new green grass peeking out in clumps, a small stream meandering through, fed by the higher uplands.

Scattered in small groups were two or three hundred sheep, still large with their winter wool. Even at the auction, Eddie had never seen so many sheep in one place. A small shelter was built at the meadow's edge, with a log pole corral holding three horses, calmly surveying their surroundings. Another truck was parked there. A few men could be seen among the sheep, stooping here and there to assist as the ewes delivered their lambs. One of the men waved when Frank's parents drove up. He shouted something in Italian.

"That's Tony," said Frank. "He's my cousin. Good guy. Doesn't speak much English."

Tony was wiping his hands on a large rag. "*Buongiorno!*"

Soon everyone was exchanging hugs. It felt odd to Eddie. The Taylors were loving, but they were English and German. They didn't hug much, certainly not people they had only just met. Besides, the shepherds had been working hard with the flock, not all the smells were pleasant, and there were streaks of blood on their clothes.

The two boys spent the rest of the morning watching the men help deliver one lamb after another, wiping the wet newborns and making sure the placenta was passed. There were many sets of twins. Eddie wondered about that. Why twins? Why didn't people have more twins? He didn't know any families with twins.

There was also the occasional lamb born dead, or that died shortly after birth. Frank and Eddie stood over one for awhile, poking it with a stick.

"I wonder why it died," he wondered.

"I dunno," replied Frank. "Poppa says it's because something didn't grow right, or maybe there was something wrong with the mother."

"It doesn't look any different from the others." He turned it over to see the other side.

"It must be something inside. Do you want to cut it open and see?"

Eddie shook his head slowly. "No. This is enough."

A little after noon there was a pause in the activity in the flock. The breeze was cold, and Eddie appreciated that Mother made him bring his jacket. The men gathered at the shelter where Frank's mother and her sister had been making soup in a large pot over a fire. They rubbed their hands over the fire and thanked the women as each received a bowl. It was unlike other soups Eddie had tasted, a little spicy, with vegetables, a little meat, and a few noodles. Very flavorful. Bread was broken off in chunks, white bread, but hearty and with good crunchy crust, perfect for dipping in the broth.

"It's called *minestrone*," answered Frank when asked what kind of soup it was. "It's different each time. You just put whatever you have in it."

It was late in the afternoon when they drove back into town. Eddie thought how satisfying it was to see so many lambs come into the world. He sorrowed for those who didn't make it, but still, it was a wonderful experience, just to be in the hills with the clear stream, the new grass, and the clean fresh air. Death was there too. He figured it had to be, because it was part of life, and not quite so bad as he had feared, maybe because the rest of life, the good part, the living part, was so much stronger and better.

CHAPTER 24

1924, Spring-Summer.
Gunfight on Main Street

"You shoulda' been here," exclaimed Gus to Eddie and Frank next day, waving his arms. "It was ab-so-lute-ly the greatest thing ever!"

The two boys were defensive. They had had a great day too.

"Nothin' like this. It was real cowboy stuff. I was helping Pop down at the store, and Warner was there and bought something. You know, the justice of the peace who used to be the bandit."

"Yeah, yeah."

"Anyway, he goes out and there's this young guy, maybe a teenager. Pop didn't recognize him but had said to watch out for him 'cause he thought he might steal something and he's wearing his six shooter on his hip like he's somebody, you know. So, this guy comes up to Warner right out there in front of the store and says, 'You Matt Warner?'"

"And Warner just looks him up and down and says, 'Yeah'.

"And the guy says, 'You used to ride with Butch Cassidy?'"

"And he says, 'Yeah, a long time ago.'" Gus was moving back and forth as if playing two different characters.

"They say you were a real fast draw."

"And Warner says real quiet like, 'Fast enough.'

"And the guy says, 'Well, let's see how fast you are now.' So, he draws his gun!"

Gus was breathless by now, and Frank and Eddie's eyes grew large.

"It was like light'nin'. I never seen nothin' like it. Before the guy had his pistol up to fire, Warner pulled out his piece and shot it right outta' his hand. And there's the guy holding his wrist with blood all over the place. And Warner keeps his eyes on him while he picks up the pistol and he says, 'That was a mistake, young fella'. I could just as easily have put that bullet in your belly or your head or anyplace else I wanted.' So he walks him off to jail."

"Wow!"

"And how!"

The three boys decided to walk over to Main Street to Gus's father's store to see where all this action had taken place. Once there, Gus again rehearsed the entire story, now placing the action on site and visualizing every detail. Later, the other two related their experiences in the hills, witnessing the birth of many lambs. Gus had never seen a lamb born and decided that was pretty neat too. It remained undecided who had had the greater day.

That summer was particularly hot. At the base of Wood Hill to the north of town was the city reservoir, near the canal. The water was dirty brown, but it was cool. Johnny and Junior and the other older children were already swimming and laughing, thoroughly enjoying the water, such as it was. Eddie was at first reluctant, never having tried swimming before, but decided that it couldn't be too hard since so many others could do it.

He followed Frank and Gus into the shallow edge of the reservoir, feeling the mud ooze between his toes. He bounced there in the water, first on both feet, then just one. He bounced further and further into the water, then realized he was over his head. Rather than bounce he kicked and paddled. There was much sputtering and gasping between dunkings, but little by little, then more quickly, he found himself swimming around with all the rest.

When the boys tired of that, they lay on the grassy bank and admired the scenery of the town below and the rolling hills and plain beyond. The closest house was the old Games' family log cabin. Games had been one of the early settlers and had moved his cabin to the base of Wood Hill to be in town. Now in the distance they could hear the hammering and sawing of new houses being built to provide for the growing community.

"Hey," said Gus, "Let's go down to the Cafe. Pop said they're making ice cream today." His young friends needed no convincing.

At the Greek Cafe around the corner from Gus's father's shop they found two men operating a large freezer.

"No, no. Not ready yet. First make, then freeze," said the younger man.

"Aw, just a taste?" urged Gus.

"No, first a taste, then a dish. You think it's all free?"

The older man shrugged and said something in Greek. He opened a drawer and took out three large spoons, put them in the top of the freezer, and pulled back portions of the unfrozen vanilla ice cream, handing one to each. He smiled and said, "I think it's best this way. Still soft."

It was a new delight for Eddie, soft, yet firm enough to hold its shape on the spoon. Cold and delicious. He thought, "Someone should just make it and sell it this way."

Keeping things cold had apparently been on his father's mind as well. When Eddie returned home he found a delivery truck parked in front. Two men were hoisting their old icebox into the back of the truck.

"Where are you taking our icebox?" he asked.

"Away, kid. You got a new one."

"A new one? Oh boy!"

He rushed into the kitchen where the whole family was gathered around a gleaming white refrigerator. The door was open and Father was pointing inside.

"See," he was explaining, "it even makes ice. You fill these trays with water and put them in the freezer compartment and it freezes."

Seeing that Eddie had come in, he asked, "How do you like our new refrigerator, Shirl?"

"It's swell! But Father, where do we put the ice block to make everything cold?"

"We don't need a block of ice anymore. This is electric. See? It will make everything inside it much colder and keep food fresh, and even has room for frozen food."

Mother hugged Father and there was praise and admiration all around for the new addition to the kitchen. It occurred to Eddie that the iceman would not be stopping at their house anymore. In fact, if this caught on, the iceman might go out of business all together. He would miss the horse.

Summer passed much as the previous one, with the addition of swimming in the reservoir and in the canal. Eddie noticed that Mother often sighed and sometimes shook her head when he or his brothers came in from working in the garden or playing. Only much later did he realize how dirty he was. Dirt, dust, and mud it seemed, were everywhere. And every tear in their shirts or trousers or coveralls meant more mending, more work for her.

As he became old enough to help, he learned to pick fruit and vegetables; prepare cherries and apricots, plums and apples for drying in large racks in the backyard; and bottle peaches, corn, peas, tomatoes, and beans. The kitchen was a bustling factory all summer and fall. The half-buried vegetable cellar next to the shed was a storehouse. By the end of the season it was filled with burlap bags of home-grown food and large store-bought bags of potatoes and onions; the basement walls were lined with shelves filled with bottles and cans of all sorts, including cans of honey as well as smaller containers of salt, flour, and sugar.

Eddie decided that his brothers were not always as annoying as he had thought. Their kindness to him after the mine disaster and seeing so many coffins and so many mourners had reminded him that they did not always laugh at him or make fun of him. They were, after all, his brothers, and he supposed they had been pretty much like him when they were his age. Then again, it can't have been exactly the same because they did not have older brothers.

One evening at dinner Mother looked across at Father, then at the four children around the table and said, "Children, your father and I have an announcement. We think you will be very happy." She paused for effect, smiling broadly. "You are going to have a baby sister or brother."

There was a moment of silence as that sank in, then all the children started talking at once.

"That's wonderful," said one.

"Neat," said another.

"When?" asked a third, echoed rapidly by others.

Mother raised her arms. "Just a minute. Not all at once." She beamed at her children's faces. "This winter, probably after Christmas, maybe the first of the year."

"Which is it, a sister or brother?" asked Eddie.

"We won't know that until the baby is born."

"I hope it's a boy."

"I don't," countered Lizzie, "there are enough boys around here. I want a sister."

"We will be happy with whatever the Lord sends us," replied Father.

CHAPTER 25

1924, Summer-Fall.
Death at Any Age

Despite the heat of the afternoons, the first touch of fall can usually be felt in early August mornings. This was the first year that Eddie noticed it. There was a chill in the air when he went out to take care of Sheep. It seemed strange to have it change so quickly to sweltering in one day, each day. Cloud formations in Price are varied and beautiful, especially when thunderstorms roll in. High billowing cumulus clouds float side by side with thunderheads and cirrus wisps, all glowing and changing in sunset colors. Local cells of rain can be seen moving across the canyons toward the plain from west to east.

Congress passed the Johnson-Reed Act that year, further limiting immigration. To celebrate, the Ku Klux Klan in Utah burned crosses on hills overlooking Helper and Castle Gate. Their marches remained poorly attended though, and often the focus of laughter and ridicule; these towns were, after all, mostly immigrant and Catholic or Mormon.

Fall weather came in earnest with the start of the school year. Grandma Mueller noted the early cold and how thick the caterpillar hair was and predicted a hard winter. She could not have known how hard. Snow came early and stayed late. The coldest temperature ever recorded to that time was in December, minus 31 degrees. Frost formed on the windows, the outer walls were too cold to be near, the furnace worked overtime to keep up, and the family spent much of their time near the stove. Christmas vacation started early with the schools closing for winter.

It was especially harsh in the camps. Doc Williams commented on it when he came to check up on Mother's pregnancy. "Some of those shacks have no insulation. 'Like living in a tent. I've seen it all this year: pneumonia, frostbite, meningitis. Poor plumbing, frozen pipes; they'll all burst when spring finally comes. Hygiene? Huh. You wouldn't believe it. Poor souls."

He gathered his things together into his bag. "Dr. Dorman is up there mostly, but it's too much even for him this year, so the rest of us have been helping." He looked at Father directly. "I called on one family out near Sunnyside. When they didn't answer I went in and there they were, frozen. Mother and child. The father had died in the mine explosion and there they were. Plenty of coal, but the fire was out, and so were they. Poor souls."

He looked over at Mother, cleared his throat, and smiled. "Everything is normal," he said. "A little large for dates, but should be fine. Get plenty of rest."

It was too cold to play outside during Christmas, so the family stayed in as much as they could, only venturing out to care for Sheep and make sure the yard was secure. Frost formed fast on eyebrows, nose. Fingers and toes turned numb after a few minutes. Better to play games inside, even if it was only with Johnny and Junior and the folks.

The family couldn't help but notice how large Mother was becoming. She had carefully saved her maternity clothes from previous years, but now these were stretched tight. Her movements became more and more methodical, careful, and slow. Everyone pitched in to lighten the load of cooking, cleaning, and washing.

It was sometime after New Year's that she began to hurt. She was lying on the parlor sofa when Eddie noticed her panting. "Get your father," she said.

"Call the doctor," she added when he arrived. "The baby is coming. I'm sure of it."

Father went to the dining room and rang the crank on the phone. "Esther," he said anxiously to the operator. "Call Doc Williams. We need him right away."

It was over an hour before the doctor arrived. By then Father had boiled water, brought in a stack of towels and clean rags, and spread a blanket and sheet over the sofa. He and Grandma Mueller had helped Mother to the bathroom and now were guiding her back onto the sofa.

The doctor washed his hands and leaned over Mother, first feeling her abdomen, then listening with his stethoscope. He looked at his pocket watch as she complained about pain. "Well, well. It looks like we are going to have a baby tonight."

He glanced at the children in the parlor door and waved his hands. "Time for you all to scoot. Go on upstairs for awhile. We'll call you when you can come back."

"Not you, Lizzie. You can help. And you, of course," he added, looking at Father and Grandma.

It seemed like hours for the three boys, exiled upstairs. They tried to play cards, but quickly lost interest and pretended to read their respective books. Occasionally Mother cried out and it was all they could do not to rush back down.

At last, they heard the faint cry of a small baby, but Father did not come to get them. Time passed. Mother cried out more and the boys thought there must be some sort of problem. Then the cry of the baby again, but still they were not called. First Junior, then the others made their way slowly to the top of the stairs to listen more closely.

Father appeared. "Okay boys, you can come down now and look through the parlor door. Stay quiet, though. Your mother needs to rest."

Junior, Johnny, and Eddie nearly tumbled down the stairs to crowd at the door. Doc Williams was buttoning the arms of his shirt. Lizzie stood next to the sofa, looking tired, but cheerful and quite satisfied. Grandma sat in a chair, her "smile of reason" wider than ever.

As for Mother, she was pale and moist with sweat, a faint smile on her lips, and there, cradled in each arm, were two tiny babies.

"Twins!" exclaimed Eddie as his brothers' jaws dropped in amazement. "Just like the sheep."

"Yes," chuckled Father, "Twins. Twin girls. That's why your mother was so large."

"And why they came early," added the doctor, frowning. He started to speak again, but then thought better of it. This was not this mother's first child, and yet . . .

He said goodnight to Mother, then took Father by the arm as he headed for the door and said quietly, "Keep Katharine quiet. Make sure she gets plenty of rest and all the fluids she can tolerate." He paused. "As for the babies, well, they are early and very small. Lizzie can help, but I would keep the boys at a distance for now."

"I understand, Doc. Thanks."

"You know, Carl," he added, "ordinarily I would say we should probably keep a mother and small twin babies in the hospital until they are a little stronger, but just getting from here to there in this weather would be dangerous. And she is an experienced mother. So, just be careful. I'll be back in the morning."

The next few days were a blur for Eddie. He spent most of the time reading, looking out from time to time at the snowdrifts, or warming himself in the kitchen when he tired of his room or wanted to get away from his brothers.

The parlor remained Mother's bedroom and nursery for the time being. Grandma and Lizzie hovered over her and the babies. Ladies from the Relief Society visited to help, bring in meals, and provide moral support. Slowly Mother regained her strength and needed less and less help getting to the bathroom or kitchen. Soon she could join the family for meals.

It was another matter for the twins. The doctor returned every day to check on them and never seemed happy with his findings. Eddie heard him say something about the hospital, but that was followed by slowly shaking heads. Grandma and the ladies who visited spoke in low tones out of earshot. Something was wrong. Their little cries, tiny to begin with, became smaller as the days went by.

One morning as Eddie descended the stairs, he heard Mother weeping softly in the parlor. She held the motionless babies in her arms as she rocked back and forth with Father, Grandma, and Lizzie gathered around her.

He hurried to the backdoor and into the cold January air to sit on the porch steps, bowing his head. "I wanted the twins. Even if they were sisters. We all wanted twins," he thought, his chest feeling heavy within him.

Sheep bleated in his pen. Eddie thought of lambing and all he had seen there. "Why couldn't at least one of them have lived?"

He looked over at Sheep and sniffed. "She would have been a bummer, a bummer sister, like Lambie."

CHAPTER 26

1925, Winter-Spring.
More Reasons to Fight

Mother was quiet at the twins' funeral. Eddie wanted to say something, but he could not think of anything that would do any good. He wondered why God had allowed something like that to happen, especially to Mother, who was always so nice.

It only began to make a little sense when the bishop spoke. He said the little girls wanted so much to come to earth that they came early, and they were so perfect, they didn't need to stay long for testing and learning like the rest of us, but just went right back to heaven, ready for eternity. Life is a school and they had graduated. Eddie looked up at his parents when the bishop said this and they were nodding slowly, Grandma too.

He wasn't so sure. It seemed to him that there was an awfully lot more sadness in life than there needed to be, and if life is like a school, what was it that we were supposed to learn from all the pain and sorrow and death that happen here? Eddie decided he was going to ask God about it when he met Him.

Like everything else in life, the sadness of the twins' death faded as one month melted into another. Things were pretty much back to normal by the time the snow was gone, except for Mother. She seemed older now, and a little more serious. Her smile began to resemble Grandma's even more than before.

It was later that spring when Eddie realized there actually were two sets of twins in Price, the Bernardi brothers, who were Eagle scouts, and the Smith sisters. The Smiths were not identical, but close enough that when they dressed alike Eddie could not tell them apart. "What a neat trick," he thought as his mind wandered to all the possibilities of having a look-alike.

A loud peal of laughter came from the parlor one evening. Father was reading the paper and passing pages to the children, seated all around. He called out to Mother, still in the dining room, "I like our new president more and more."

"Why is that, Dear?"

"They call him 'Silent Cal' because he doesn't talk too much. Not jabbering on like most politicians. That's reason enough. And he is sensible and follows the laws instead of trying to go around them. That's another. But it's his sense of humor that gets me.

"Listen to this." He read a little, then summarized. "There was this state dinner, and some fancy society lady sits next to him and says, 'I bet I can make you say more than two words.' And he looks at her and says, 'You lose.'

"Get it? Two words, 'You lose.'" Father laughed again, now with Mother and the children joining in.

Eddie loved the newspaper. He pulled out the funny pages to follow *Little Orphan Annie, Felix The Cat,* and *Moon Mullins.* He enjoyed *Helpful Henry, Dumb Dora,* and *Flapper Fanny* too, but didn't always get the jokes. Father explained that some of them were a little 'old' for him. A lot of the humor was right out of vaudeville—George Burns, Gracie Allen, and Laurel and Hardy. Eddie didn't know George and Gracie, but Laurel and Hardy were in the movies too, and really funny. It was always funny to see other people doing stupid things, though he thought sometimes they were things he would have done too. Maybe that's why they were funny.

Most Price kids were in the movie theaters on Saturdays. There were two of them, Price Theater and Crown Theater. Admission was a nickel for a double feature. A piano player accompanied the show and the older audience members read the captions for the younger ones, often with their own added commentary. Johnny and Junior were among the most vocal narrators. Eddie usually sat with Gus and Frank or another of his classmates but could pick out his brothers' voices loud and clear.

Glancing over at Athena seated behind Gus, then at his own brothers down front, it dawned on him that he might be regarded as a tagalong, just like her. He shook his head. He was not! After all, he had his own gang, was sort of a leader of the gang, and was not trying to follow his older brothers.

Further to his right was Angela Anderson in the middle of a small group of other giggly girls. He often caught a glimpse of her at the movies or at church or around town. She was still the most beautiful girl in the world. Someday he would tell her so.

Whatever the movie theme of the week, that set the tone for afternoon play; cowboys and Indians after a western, cops and robbers after a crime show, pretend vaudeville after a comedy. Charlie Chaplin was a favorite to imitate. The boys copied his walk with short steps, bobbing from side to side.

Birthdays in the Taylor household were quiet affairs: a family dinner, a cake, a present or two, sometimes with a friend. 1925 was different. Eddie was turning eight, and for Mormons that meant the "age of accountability", time to be baptized. The last Sunday in March Bishop Johnson called him up in front of the whole ward and announced that Shirley Edwin Taylor was going to be baptized the following Wednesday on his birthday, April 1st, 1925.

Eddie was mortified. He could feel the redness sweeping across his face. Not only did the bishop use his full name, the official name on church records, he announced the date of his birthday. Little groups of children all through the chapel could be seen leaning toward each other and laughing. Quietly of course, since their parents were right there, and they were at church—at least one or two little heads were swatted—but laughing just the same. He could hardly wait to get out of there and get home.

Safely changed into play clothes, he wandered toward Eighth Street, past the Catholic church. He had seen how Frank's little brother was baptized while he was still an infant and thought how much easier that would have been. He stood there on the corner awhile, admiring the red brick, square pillars, and stained glass windows. He didn't notice the boys come up behind him.

"There he is, the boy with a girl's name, Shirley," came a familiar voice. Eddie turned.

"Shirley Edwin. Girl name, girl name," said red-headed Jimmy Curtis. Two other boys were with him, all with turned up noses and caps askew.

He didn't know what to say. His muscles tensed, eyes blurred, and his breath grew deep and hard.

"Stop it, Jimmy Curtis!"

"And an April Fool too!" They all laughed. "April fool girl. April fool Shirley."

That was too much. He launched himself full force into Jimmy's chest mid-laugh, pushing him to the ground with Eddie on top, raining blow after blow. The other boys stepped back in surprise.

Eddie stopped hitting only when the blood from Jimmy's nose and face became too slippery.

"Now will you stop?" he cried. "Now will you?"

Jimmy blubbered something, coughed, then more clearly, "Okay, okay. Sorry. Enough. Okay?"

Eddie stood up, trembling. The other boys came forward now, steering clear of him, and helped Jimmy to his feet. He was pinching his nose, glancing at the young victor.

As the trembling passed Eddie felt better. He ached all over, but the sense of having put a bully in his place was immensely satisfying. He walked over to Gus's house to clean up there; he didn't want Mother to see the blood on his hands or how dirty he was. Then again, except right after bath, he was almost always dirty.

The baptism was uneventful. Bishop Johnson was blissfully unaware of his faux pas and performed the simple ceremony gracefully. Jimmy Curtis was there—his parents made him come, along with other children in that age group. He and Eddie didn't speak but looked each other in the eyes with mutual respect.

Newly baptized people are supposed to know the difference between right and wrong, and when there is a grey area, the Holy Ghost is supposed to help decide. This gave Eddie a sense of confidence. Not just another year older, he was more mature, tougher, able to stand up to the challenges of life. He soon learned it was not quite that easy.

CHAPTER 27

1925, June 28. Murder and Frontier Justice

"Another shooting out in the camps," said Father one evening as he read the paper. His three sons looked up from the comics and other pages they were looking at.

"It seems one of the miners had it in for the Castle Gate company agent, who was also town marshal, laid wait for him and shot him. Some Negro by the name of Marshall. Kind of ironic, Marshall killed the marshal. Guy's on the lam now. Lots of people looking for him."

Shootings were not rare events, so they did not think about it again until two days later. Eddie and Frank and Gus were loitering on Main Street, trying to decide whether it was hot enough to go swimming or if they should wander out to the prairie to see what they could find. Several cars drove fast up Main and parked outside the General Store.

"They got him," someone shouted to others on the street. A crowd soon gathered.

"Up near Castle Gate. The posse caught him hiding out in a shack."

Soon after, another half dozen cars arrived, including a police car. They stopped outside the county courthouse and pushed a tall, thin, black man toward the side door that led to the jail. A sheriff's deputy stepped out, drawing his pistol.

"No, you don't," he said. "Sheriff's not here, so I'm in charge." He looked narrowly at the prisoner, hit him with the butt of his gun, knocking out his right eye, and folded his arms. "You ain't puttin' that piece of trash in my jail."

It occurred to Eddie that it wasn't his jail.

One of the men replied, "What are we supposed to do with him?"

"I don't really care."

The crowd murmured. One of the men from the General Store held up a rope. It was Nick Fulcher, the electrician. Why was it always him? "Let's have a necktie party!" he shouted.

Loud shouts followed. The deputy said nothing. Leaders of the posse tried at first to protect their prisoner, but then joined in as Marshall was pushed into a car. The prisoner remained strangely silent, knowing perhaps that protestations would accomplish nothing.

The boys looked around. One of the men nearby had a truck.

"Hey mister," asked Gus, "can we go in the back of your truck?"

"Sure."

The three boys crowded in with other bystanders, the truck bouncing along among dozens of other vehicles, some said a hundred, out of town toward the canyons. The mob grew rapidly as shopkeepers closed their stores to join. There was the feeling of a spring outing, a celebration.

About three miles out of town stood a tall cottonwood tree, one of a grove along a small creek on a nice ranch that belonged to one of the townspeople. Fulcher and ten others hanged the prisoner there while perhaps as many as a thousand looked on. He was in the tree only a few minutes before two more cars arrived containing other deputies, not the one who had barred the way to the jail.

They pushed their way to the tree, cut the prisoner down, and chastised the crowd for taking the law into their own hands.

"He's still alive!" someone shouted. Marshall was coughing up a little blood.

Then the mob surged forward despite the deputies' calls for calm. Soon he was back in the tree, shaking at first, then still.

Eddie looked around. It seemed right that a murderer had met justice, and he thought it must be right when so many people were there to watch. Not just the handful that actually did the lynching, but hundreds of men, women, and children, all regular people.

The article in the *Price Sun* agreed. It said the mob consisted of "your neighbors, your friends, the tradespeople with whom you are wont to barter day by day, public employees, folks prominent in church and social circles, and your real conception of a 'mob' might have undergone a radical turnover. . . No attempt at concealment was made by any member of the lynching party. . . Quite a sprinkling of women—the wives and mothers of the good folks of the town. And, too, there were even some children."

Father disagreed. He shook his head and muttered as he read. "Fools! That's just not how we do things anymore."

Judge Anderson came to visit soon afterwards. Eddie listened as the judge and Father met in the parlor. "You know," said the judge, "Sheriff Deming is just appalled at what happened. He was rushing out to the ranch to stop it when he ran off the road. Broke an axle. Anyway, the Governor is upset and wants us to make sure the leaders of this mob are brought to justice. Says it's not the wild west anymore and 'lynching is a crime and a disgrace to the state'. Those were his exact words. He said to use 'all proper measures'."

"What can I do to help?"

"Well. We've made the arrests. The problem now is to impanel a jury. Half the town was there, so they can't serve, so we are asking responsible men who were not there to serve on the jury. I noticed your name on the clerk's list. Will you?"

"Of course."

The judge smiled. "Good. I knew we could depend on you. And that you will be fair and follow the law." He glanced into the dining room where Eddie was pretending to read. "And good to see you, Eddie. If you were old enough, I would ask you too. You are dependable too, aren't you?"

"Yes, Sir."

Actually, he was not sure. He had been there. He thought at the time it was the right thing, but if being there meant you could not serve on the jury, maybe it wasn't. Deciding right and wrong was not as easy as he thought it should be.

The trial against the eleven who had been arrested for the lynching dragged on through the summer. Father was gone day after day. Witness after witness was called. In all, there were 134 witnesses. Every one of them testified that they did not know who actually performed the lynching. Eddie sat in as a member of the audience for some of it, but it became monotonous.

"Were you present when Mr. Marshall was hanged?" asked the prosecutor.

"Yes, Sir," replied the witness.

"Was the defendant, Nick Fulcher, or any of the other defendants, present?"

"I don't remember."

"Did the defendant, one or any of them, help hang the victim?"

"I don't know."

At first Eddie was puzzled. He remembered it all very clearly, so clearly, he was having bad dreams because of it. He remembered nearly everybody who was there, especially Fulcher and the rest who helped him. Why couldn't any of these grownups remember?

It could only mean that they were lying. Adults lying. Not just a little lie, but a big one, after swearing to tell the truth. Did they like Fulcher and the rest? Were they afraid? Afraid of what? To be a part of all this perhaps, but that didn't make sense; they had acknowledged they were there and were witnesses, so they were part of it.

Only gradually did it dawn on him that Fulcher was part of the Klan and each of the other ten defendants also likely Klan members—not Mormon, not Catholic, not immigrant. Certainly not Jewish; Eddie knew only one Jew, Mr. Gordon, the scrap metal dealer.

His stomach hurt when he thought about so many men and women lying in court. His stomach wasn't the only one. There were a lot of sour faces around town, not angry, just sad. The world seemed more gray, dark despite the brilliant summer sun, sort of like after the mine explosion. Only this wasn't sadness about death. It was deeper. It was guilt.

One day he and Gus were sitting on the courthouse steps when the clerk, Fred Thomas, stopped next to them and said, "Boys, my nephew is visiting here from Montana. How would you like to come out to the ranch for a few days and keep him and my two sons company?"

The Thomas brothers were a year older, and Eddie did not know them well, but he jumped at the chance to go out to a ranch. Plus, he felt relieved to be out of town for awhile.

"Okay. You go ask your mothers and make sure it is all right with them, pack a bag, and I will pick you up after work today.

"I don't know where you live," he added, looking at Gus, "but if you are over at the Taylors, I can take you too."

Effusive in their thanks, the boys hurried home. Fred watched them go and thought, "Good. That will help everybody, all the way around."

CHAPTER 28

1925, Summer. Cowboy Life

The Thomas ranch was several miles outside of town toward the mountains, situated in a grassy meadow with rocky cliffs and narrow canyons all around. A small stream ran through the middle of the meadow, fed by smaller creeks from the canyons and a little spring near a high cliff face. A couple dozen horses and a few hundred cattle grazed here and there, many standing in the shade of scattered clumps of trees. There were separate small ranch and bunk houses, as well as barn and cattle sheds. A large canvas tent was set up for the summer as a cook and chow hall.

Eddie and Gus found Bill and Jim Thomas to be kindred spirits. Their cousin, Tom, was equally agreeable.

"Tom Thomas?" smiled Eddie when they were introduced. His own experience had taught him to appreciate funny names.

Tom was a good-natured boy with blond hair and deep blue eyes. He ignored the joke. "No, Tom Jenkins. My Mom is their father's sister."

"Ah."

Bill and Jim normally slept in the ranch house in a room next to their parents' room, but now they slept in the bunkhouse to be close to Tom and the other boys. This consisted of one large room lined with bunk beds. Two hired hands were there, older cowboys who viewed their young visitors warily, knowing they belonged to the boss.

Each morning started with face washing in the stream, a visit to the outhouse, and a big breakfast in the tent. A long table there was filled with bacon, eggs, sausage, pancakes, and potatoes. Then came chores—feeding and brushing horses, making sure all the animals are well and accounted for, and for Eddie the more familiar chores of watering and weeding the garden, fenced off in a sunny spot away from the corral, arena, and barn. Afternoons found the boys practicing their riding skills and exploring the meadow and canyons.

One afternoon as they were resting in the shade of the house and watching the billowing clouds pass overhead, one of the cowboys came around the corner and said, "Hey boys, we'll be breaking some young horses in the corral. 'Wanna come see?"

"You bet!" The boys came running.

"Will they buck a lot?" asked Gus. He was thinking of rodeos he had attended at the fair.

The hand didn't say anything, but Bill volunteered, "Nah. We don't want 'em to buck. These are workhorses. 'Breaking' just means teaching them to take a saddle and rider. Not buck. That's different."

They lined up along the fence, feet on the bottom pole and holding on to the top. Mr. Thomas was there in the middle of the corral standing next to a tall post in the ground. Eddie supposed he didn't have to work as a clerk today. His favorite riding horse was there, a sorrel gelding with four white stockings, a beautiful horse called Mac. Tied to him was a young paint Eddie had noticed in the herd, with a high arched neck. The two hands took their places, one on each side, and Thomas slowly led the horses in a circle around the post.

The paint objected a little at first but could not move from Mac's side. The three men in the corral spoke softly and he quieted down. They continued going round and round for what seemed the longest time. Then they stopped and Thomas brought out a horse blanket and rubbed the pony all over with it. Eddie figured that probably felt pretty good after walking around in a circle for an hour.

"What's he doin' now?" Eddie whispered.

"Getting it used to being touched," answered Bill. "He's getting a little tired after walking, but now he knows to follow the horse next to him. Watch this."

One of the ranch hands took Bill's father's place. While he was positioning the blanket on the pony's back, Mr. Thomas climbed into the older horse's saddle. The cowboy stepped away as Thomas pulled the rope on the paint, keeping him close up against Mac's side. Now they continued to walk in a circle without a leader in front.

"Dad says it's important for a young horse to never learn to buck. If you don't let 'em buck, they won't," said Bill. Then he chuckled, "unless you want to train 'em for the shows. Those you can teach to buck—it's pretty easy—but then they're not good for anything else."

Another hour passed before the horses stopped again. The paint received another rubbing, his blanket was adjusted, then ever so carefully and slowly a saddle was put into place and cinched down. He didn't like this and tried to move away, eyes wide, tail swishing hard. More reassuring words. A little tighter with the rope. More walking in a circle. Finally, as the afternoon wore on, one of the hands came out with a sack of grain and put it on the saddle.

The boys had long since moved from their places hanging from the top rail of the fence to the ground where they took advantage of a small shade tree, chewed on grass stems, and watched. Time passed in an unhurried, pleasant way; Eddie thought he could really enjoy cowboy life.

"Watch this," said Bill.

The cowboy who had put the sack of grain on the saddle now took it away, placed his foot in the stirrup, and eased himself up into the spot where it had been. This time the horse did not move his feet, only swished his tail and glanced back. They continued to walk in a circle, but the rope binding the paint to Mac was slowly loosened.

That was enough for one day. Tomorrow would be the next lesson in becoming a good range horse.

"Well, boys," said Mr. Thomas next morning at breakfast, "I need to take you back to your families tonight."

Eddie and Gus could not hide their disappointment.

"I think maybe you lost track of what day it is. Yesterday was Saturday. Today is Sunday. I already apologized the other day to your parents for not getting you back in time for church, but you do need to be back for the new week. School will be starting soon and there will be things to do." He glanced around the table at all the boys.

"I tell you what, though. It's been a real pleasure having you here, and you've been a good help. Anytime you want to come up and visit, so long as it is okay with your parents, you are welcome. Is that a deal?"

The boys eagerly accepted.

"In the meantime, has anybody seen Dempsey lately?"

The others shook their heads, but Eddie asked, "Who's Dempsey? You mean the fighter?"

Mr. Thomas laughed. "No. Dempsey is my prize bull. Named after the fighter. He stayed here years ago. In the old days Jack Dempsey wandered from town to town fighting in the saloons and brothels." Thomas looked down and cleared his throat. "Well, wherever he could get a fight going. He fought for pocket change, wasn't famous yet, hadn't won the title, but he stayed here when he fought Charlie Gibbons, the local champ in Price. It was an all-comers fight and everyone bet on Gibbons except me, 'cause I had seen Dempsey fight before. 'Made eight bucks that night."

"What's a brothel?" asked Gus. Mrs. Thomas cast a stern glance at her husband.

"Oh, just a slip of the tongue. I meant, uh, brotherhood. 'Came out funny, brotherhood. Yes, the clubs, fraternal organizations like the Elks Club." He smiled broadly.

"Well, let's go find our Dempsey, and you will see why we named him that."

CHAPTER 29

1925, Summer-Fall. Back To School

Soon Mr. Thomas and the boys were on horseback, exploring the more remote corners of the meadow. Every now and then Thomas rang a bell. After awhile a grunting sound came from a patch of cattails near the lower reaches of the stream. Soon the bulk of a large bull emerged, growing ever larger as he approached the riders.

When the bull came up alongside Mr. Thomas he reached out and patted him on the head. Dempsey had a white face and chest, large white horns, and glistening red body. He mooed deep and low.

"He looks pretty ferocious with the horns and bein' so big and all, but he is really the gentlest, sweetest animal you could ever know."

Thomas glanced over at the boys. "Not like that bull you saw penned up t'other side of the corral. Good bull, but nasty. You stay away from him, or he'll poke holes in you with his horns. Might not be much left when he's done."

"Mr. Thomas," said Eddie. "Even the cows have horns. Why is that?"

"Well. A lot of people cut 'em off when they're still calves. But I figure, God made them with horns, and out here with coyotes and cougars and others that might want to turn 'em into critter dinner, they may just come in handy. Besides," he chuckled, "I like 'em. They look good."

He kicked Dempsey in the rump and added, "Go on home! Git!" Dempsey moved a couple steps, then continued a slow steady course toward the barn with the rancher and boys following along.

A full week on the ranch had passed without Eddie realizing it. The cycle of washing in the ice-cold stream, eating, working at all sorts of chores, and exploring, filled him up. No room for other thoughts. Time seemed to move differently there.

Mother and Father checked in on him when he went to bed that night. Junior and Johnny were reading in their bunks, and he was just settling into his smaller bed set at right angles to theirs, his hands behind his head. He was thinking of Dempsey and of Mac and of the cowboys.

Father handed him a magazine. "The new issue of Popular Science arrived. I thought you would like to see it."

"Thanks Father. That's swell." He looked at the cover, a painting of a great two engine airplane flying over a cruise ship and put it down on his chest.

"So, you enjoyed your time at the ranch?" asked Father.

"Yeah. It was great."

"I thought you would. Fred said you and Gus were very helpful, did a lot of chores, and kept his boys company."

"Yeah. They were nice. So were the cowboys, but they didn't talk much."

"Most cowboys don't. That's one of the reasons we like 'em. Not too many words, just the right ones."

Mother tucked him in and added, "I'm sure you will have a chance to go out there again."

"I hope so."

Summer had ended. Routines changed again. Every spare moment was spent harvesting the garden and orchard and preparing the fruits and vegetables for storage. Mother made new shirts and trousers for each of the boys, and helped Lizzie make a stylish new dress for school.

Eddie did not see Lizzie as much as in the past. She spent much of her time with Dot, studying, practicing for band, talking about whatever teenage girls talk about, going to dances. And when there was not a dance at the school, there were the dance halls in town.

Father called it a fad, but all the young people spent their spare time dancing, especially the Charleston. They even had contests for best dancer, best couple, and longest dance. Lizzie wanted to try for an endurance record, but Mother and Father would not approve of staying out all night dancing. Their children had to be home by bedtime.

For Eddie, any spare time meant time for play, and play was best with playmates. Eddie couldn't find Gus after school for a few days. He finally caught up with him on Friday and asked where he had been.

"Greek school," said Gus.

"Greek school? What's that?"

"Over at the church. We have our school after school to teach us Greek and about our history and stuff."

"You mean you go to school after school? Wow!"

"Yeah. I tried to get out of it, said we don't need that here, but Pop says we do, so . . . Anyway, it's only an hour or so, four days a week. And it's interesting."

In practice, that hour or so was enough to sorely limit possibilities during the week for play. Plus, third grade had more homework, and there was always a lot for Eddie to read about and do on his own. Even his brothers became interesting, at times.

Junior sent away for a crystal radio set. It consisted of thin copper wire, a small clear stone crystal, a second smaller wire with a handle, a set of headphones, and a battery. Eddie and Johnny watched with fascination as Junior wrapped the wire around an old oatmeal box and attached it to the crystal. He put on the headphones and carefully moved the handle, causing the smaller wire to scratch along the crystal.

At first, he only heard static. The boys all held their breaths. "Is that all there is to it? Maybe there're more pieces for it to work," suggested Eddie.

"No. That's it. Just hold your horses."

Junior listened more intently, the other boys leaning their ears against his. "Ah! Did you hear that?"

"I didn't hear nothin'."

Junior turned one of the earpieces toward Johnny. "Yeah. Somebody's talking."

"What's he saying?"

"I . . . It's . . . It's a preacher. Something about heaven and hell and sin and stuff."

"What's he say about it?"

"Well . . . He's against sin. And . . . He's for heaven." Junior frowned a little. "I guess that's it." He put down the headphones and sighed, then beamed triumphantly. "Anyway, it works. Let's try again later. When something else is on."

Regardless of content or lack thereof, Eddie was fascinated. With just a little wire, a rock, and an oatmeal box, they could hear words and music from far away, through the air. It was not nearly so clear and nice and fancy as Father's radio in the parlor, but even more amazing.

Eddie decided he wanted to build his own project. He hunted through issues of *Popular Science* for something interesting and found instructions to build your own electric arc furnace. Using a wire coil, an electric plug, two pieces of graphite he borrowed from Father's workshop, and a hollowed-out brick, he was able to fashion it with only minor changes from the original. A brilliant spark arose between the tips of graphite when he plugged it in and moved the rods together. To his delight, the little furnace was able to melt small pieces of glass.

A few weeks later Father announced at dinner that they were all getting up early next day, Saturday, for a surprise outing. They were meeting Judge Anderson and his family out at the Thomas's ranch to celebrate, or perhaps mourn, the conclusion of the trial. They, along with everyone else in town, were relieved that it was over.

It was most unsatisfactory from Father's and the judge's perspective. Despite having so many witnesses, not one admitted being able to remember who committed the crime or whether the defendants were involved in any way. So, they had to be acquitted, even though everyone knew they were guilty.

"The galling part was Nick Fulcher's smirk when the verdict was read," said Father. "Plus," he added. "They were all or nearly all in the Klan, not that that was relevant as far as the court was concerned, or whether they were guilty, but still."

He held up the evening paper. "At least something good came of it. Now several towns have passed laws against wearing masks, including Salt Lake and Ogden. Fat chance of getting that passed here." He thought for a moment. "Of course, in our little town it's pretty easy to tell who is in the Klan, or at least, who is not—no Mormons, Catholics, or immigrants. Not many others left."

CHAPTER 30

1925-1926. Back to the Ranch

The Taylors climbed eagerly into the car early Saturday morning. Everyone loved an outing and Eddie was particularly excited to go back to the ranch. He hurried to claim a spot on the passenger side but lost out when Johnny jostled him out of the way, toward the left. He was behind Father and his cigar again.

Road trips were a time for family sing-along. They were not long underway before Mother or Father struck up a popular song and soon everyone joined in. This time it was Father who started with *Let Me Call You Sweetheart*, followed by *Alexander's Ragtime Band*. Then Mother soloed with a German song, *Das Wandern*. Before the parents could sing another, Lizzie began with *Yes, Sir! That's My Baby*, quickly blending into *If You Knew Susie*. That led to wordless singing of *Charleston*, which clearly established big sister as the expert on current tunes.

The family continued in silence for a time, enjoying the clear air as they moved higher into the mountains of eastern Utah. Mother smiled and she began to sing her favorite, softly at first, then louder for all to hear and join in:

For the beauty of the earth,
For the beauty of the skies,
For the love which from our birth,

Over and around us lies,
Lord of all, to thee we raise,
This, our hymn of grateful praise.

The Thomas ranch was much as Eddie remembered, only now the aspen and cottonwood leaves were yellow and gold and the air was cool. The Andersons were already there. Eddie felt his heart beat a little faster when he caught sight of Angela. Fortunately, Bill and Jim called out to him and his brothers to come riding with them.

Soon the boys were riding out to the canyon southwest of the meadow, leading toward Castle Gate and the mines. The land became more and more rugged, with seams and layers of rock rising at odd angles, the layers ranging in color from brown to golden, red, and black.

"The black stuff is coal," said Bill. "Not good coal, though, just junk. I suppose it would burn, but not good enough for the miners to want it."

There were scattered old camps, tumble-down shacks, fire pits with circles of charred rock. No people, but sure signs they had been there.

Eddie was youngest in the group. The older boys tended to wander off together, laughing and telling stories from school. That suited Eddie fine. The rocks were beautiful and every now and then he would stop, get off his horse, and put a small pebble in the cloth bag he had brought for saving any treasures he collected.

Besides the rocks, he wanted to see what might be lying around the camps, just like looking in neighbors' trashcans. You never know what you might find. It was mostly piles of tin cans, rusty nails, broken boards, and boxes. Then the glint of something shiny caught his eye. He hopped down from his horse again and pushed aside some pieces of cardboard. There on the ground was a narrow copper cylinder. As he picked it up, he saw there were more, covered in dirt. He dug around, dusted them off, and stuffed them into the cloth bag, counting out loud, "eleven, twelve . . . twenty, twenty-one . . . twenty-eight, twenty-nine."

"Wow, twenty-nine pieces of copper!" he thought. "I can melt them down into a bar and sell it to Goldman. They must be worth a lot of money."

He turned over the other boxes and boards in the camp to make sure nothing was missed, then remounted his horse.

"Hey kid," said Junior when the older boys returned from higher in the canyon, "what'cha been doin'?"

"Just lookin' around this old camp."

"Your bag is bigger. Wha'd ya find?"

"Just rocks. I got a rock of each color. Want to see?"

"Nah." He looked over at Bill and Jim and snickered. "What a goofy kid!"

As they left the canyon they could hear a bell ringing in the distance.

"That's Mom," shouted Bill, "We better beat it." With that he kicked his horse into a gallop with the other boys close behind.

Eddie did not want to gallop; he had never gone faster than a walk, but the horses were accustomed to riding together, so when the others took off, so did his.

He held on tight, lowering his head down to the horse's neck and trying to say 'whoa', but the word never came out. It was all he could do to hold on, bouncing up and down in the saddle and closing his eyes as his mount leapt over sagebrush and gopher mounds. The horses' run eased only a little when they reached grassland in the meadow.

At last, they came to a stop at the corral. Eddie trembled as he let himself slide down from his horse's back. He was sore all over, but more especially on his backside. He looked up at the powerful animal, skin glistening and ear twitching. "Thanks for not dumping me in the cactus," he said. Junior overheard it and snickered again.

Father noted Eddie's limp and asked about it.

"Just a little sore."

"Well, it gets easier with practice, and less sore."

While the boys were riding, the men had had a vigorous discussion of politics, the course of the recent trial, and the future of human relations in general, and the women had finished preparing a ranch dinner of steak, beans, and potato salad.

Mrs. Thomas led them in after-dinner entertainment. They sang *Home on The Range* and *Git Along Little Doggies.* Then Angela sang *There's a Long Long Trail A'Winding.* It turned out she had a fine soprano voice, much like Mother's contralto, only younger. Eddie gazed in admiration. So beautiful and talented too! He could hardly contain himself.

It was late when they arrived home. A quick rinse of hands and faces and they were ready for sleep. Eddie tucked his bag full of copper cylinders under his bed. He wanted to wait to melt them when his brothers weren't around to ask where they came from. It was his treasure. Finders keepers.

Church, chores, and school took Eddie's attention over the following days. These stretched to weeks, and the copper was soon forgotten among other concerns.

Mother usually baked on Wednesdays, so Eddie was surprised one Friday to smell fresh baked bread and cake when he arrived home from school.

"Smells good," he said as he walked into the kitchen. "Can I have some?"

"No, Shirl. This isn't for us." She turned toward him. "One of our neighbors died. This is for the family, after the funeral."

"Oh. Who died?"

"The older man across the alley, Mr. Frandsen."

Eddie recalled the old man's friendly welcome to the neighborhood and his kindness and helpful attitude. "That's too bad," he said, looking down.

Just then Father came in the back door. He sniffed the air appreciatively. "Hmm! Fresh bread."

"Not for you," said Mother, reaching up to kiss him. "It's for the Frandsens."

"Ah," he replied. "I understand. Helping out, along with the other Relief Society sisters?"

"Yes." She paused. "Poor man. He was all alone the last few years. That must have been hard."

"Right," said Father. "No family here in Price."

"He has two children," added Mother. "They came in from Salt Lake for the funeral and to take care of his estate."

"What's an estate?" asked Eddie

Father answered, "His things, the house, whatever he had when he died."

"Oh." Eddie wondered "Will they move into his house?"

"No. They will sell it and most of his stuff. Just keep a few things of value, sentimental things."

"What about Mousey, his horse?"

"Old horse," said Father. "Probably end up at the glue factory."

"Oh."

Eddie did not fully understand his father's answer, but decided he did not want any more details. He pulled his coat back on and left through the back door. He petted Sheep, got a handful of carrots from the root cellar, and continued across the alley.

He found Mousey standing by the fence, head hanging low.

"Here," said Eddie, pushing a carrot into the horse's mouth. "These are for you."

He hugged the animal around the neck as it crunched the unexpected snack.

"I will miss you."

CHAPTER 31

1926, Summer.
An Explosive Close Call

When the weather improved, Mother announced that it was time for spring cleaning. Besides having to be on hand to move furniture and help scrub, the Taylor boys knew that meant they had to look through their room and remove any hidden treasures to a safe location.

Eddie only had one consistent hiding place, under his bed. There he saw the cloth sac he had filled with rocks and pieces of copper at the Thomas's ranch last fall. Peeking in first to be sure they were still there, he took the sac to the shed and put it on a shelf next to his arc furnace.

"After spring cleaning I'll melt them and make a whole bar of copper," he thought.

A long weekend of cleaning followed. Then came Monday and more after-school chores. Finally, the time came.

Eddie pulled out his little arc furnace, set it on the workbench in the shed, plugged it in, and placed the first copper cylinder in the hollowed-out brick. Slowly he brought the graphite points together. Nothing. Not even a little spark.

He checked the plug, the coil, the points, and tried again. Nothing. He sat back on the stool and scratched his head. What could have gone wrong?

Just then Gus came up to the door. "Hello. What are you doing?"

"Hi, Gus. I found some copper and want to melt it with my forge, but it won't work."

Gus looked at Eddie's apparatus, then at the cylinders on the bench. His eyes grew wide. "Don't you know what those are? Those are blasting caps! Try to melt one of those and you could blow your head off."

Eddie was stunned. He stood back. "Yeah? Really?"

His natural skepticism kicked in. "How do you know?"

"I seen 'em before. I went with my cousin to the mine in Sunnyside once and they were blasting. That's what they use to make the dynamite go off."

Eddie thought for a while. He didn't know why his furnace didn't work but was glad it didn't. Mother would have said his angels saved him. "Wow!" he exclaimed slowly.

He stared at the copper. "Say, I have some fuse left over from the Fourth. Let's go set 'em off."

"Yeah!"

They tied all twenty-nine blasting caps together and attached a fuse to the center one, fastened it with wax, then walked to the intersection of Eighth and J Streets. Looking all around to make sure no one else was around, they lifted a manhole cover, lit the fuse with a match, tossed the bundle into the storm drain, and ran for cover behind some bushes.

The boom was deafening. It was the loudest thing Eddie and Gus had ever heard. Even the ground beneath them shook. Looking out from the bush they saw the manhole cover had been thrown across the street and a cloud of smoke and dust rose from the drain.

Trying to look innocent, they stood up from the bushes and strolled away, hands in pockets. Glancing back, they saw a police car pull up with lights flashing.

Two policemen got out, looked at the drain and cover, then all around, scratching their heads and holding their hats.

Three boys emerged from behind a small house on the other side of the street. "You guys hear that?" one of them asked.

"Yeah," said Eddie. "I think it was thunder."

The boys looked up at the clear sky.

"I think you're stupid," replied one.

A fourth boy came out the front door; it was Jimmy Curtis. "I agree," he added.

It was worse than a standoff. There were just Eddie and Gus on one side of the street, and four boys on the other. "You guys are trespassing," said Jimmy.

"It's a free country," insisted Eddie.

"Yeah, well, we're the Eighth Street Gang and this is our territory."

Gus and Eddie walked back toward the west. "We'll go where we want." And at that moment they wanted to go home. A small rock flew between their heads. They broke into a run.

When out of range, Eddie commented, "So now it's the Eighth Street Gang. It used to be Little Italy we couldn't walk through."

"Those were older kids. They just care about girls now. These guys are our age. We've gotta' do something."

"It's almost summer. Let's think about it and come up with a plan. There's got to be something we can do."

Discouraged, the two boys headed toward their homes.

Summer started without any plan in mind, only the hope of pleasant, sunny days and new adventures limited by the Eighth Street Gang's territorial claim.

Eddie and Gus met in the alley early one morning to discuss the matter.

"First, we need a new name. We used to be the Flaming Circle Gang, but we can't use that anymore," said Eddie, scratching his head. "We should be the Sixth Street Gang."

"But I live on Seventh."

"That's okay. We can call my place headquarters and that's on Sixth."

"What about Frank? He's on Ninth."

"That's okay too. It means we have 'em surrounded."

"I dunno. Why can't we call it the Seventh Street Gang? Seven is kinda' in the middle between Sixth and Ninth. "

Gus had a good point.

"I suppose. And I heard seven is a lucky number. So, yeah, I guess so."

"One thing though," said Gus. "More than a new name, we need more members, 'cause there are at least four of them."

"Who else can we get?"

The boys thought, turning their heads, gazing up and down and all around, and tapping their chins with their forefingers.

"Well," said Gus at last, clearing his throat. "There is Athena."

It just did not seem right for there to be a girl in the gang. There were no girls in the Eighth Street Gang, so far as they knew. Athena had always been a tag-along, not quite a nuisance, just, there. Then again, she was a good shot, and she dressed like the boys, so unless you knew otherwise, she could just as easily be a boy.

"I suppose," Eddie mumbled at last. "In the movies, every gang has a girl. And they always call them 'sister'. Except the westerns, cowboy gangs don't have girls."

"No, but they have saloons with girls. That's almost the same."

"Yeah. I guess it is."

"And there were cowgirls too, like Calamity Jane."

So, it was decided.

Finding Frank, they explained their need for a fourth member. He readily agreed Athena should join the gang.

As for Athena, she at first wondered if this new acceptance by the boys was some sort of joke or a trick. She played along to find out which it was, then realized they really did need her, and it would be fun. They all spit in their palms and shook hands. The Seventh Street Gang was ready for action.

They did not have long to wait. Next day the four gangsters met in the Taylor backyard. They made sure they were well armed, each with a pocket full of pebbles and a flipper, their term for slingshot. Each tipped his cap at an angle and began the march to Eighth Street.

As expected, the Eighth Street Gang was loitering in the front yard of the Curtis home, two doors up from the Catholic Church. The Seventh Street Gang paused at the curb, then continued to the other side, boldly walking north past their perplexed opponents, who now stood to face them.

"Where do ya' think you're going?"

"Walkin' up Eighth Street," replied Eddie. "That's where. Anywhere we want."

"Oh yeah? We told you before. Go around. This is our street."

"No. We're the Seventh Street Gang, and we do whatever we want."

"We're gonna' teach you a lesson, snots." Everyone except Jimmy pulled out a flipper. He just stood there and grinned. "We have the cannon!"

"Huh?"

Jimmy climbed onto the porch and, reaching behind the wall, pulled out a large Y-shaped apple tree branch made into a giant slingshot. He posted it into a hole in the front yard directly in front of Eddie, put a rock the size of his fist in it, pulled back the rubber, and shouted, "Now get out!"

Eddie and his followers needed no time to discuss the matter. They were running as fast as they could back toward Sixth Street, howls of laughter echoing behind them. Jimmy did not even need to fire the cannon.

"We should go back and beat 'em all up real good," scowled Athena, holding up her flipper.

"Pipe down. We can't fight against that thing. We would get really hurt," replied Gus.

Frank and Eddie nodded in agreement.

The four sat dejected in the Taylor orchard, trying to think of a way to get back them. No good ideas came to mind.

Eddie finally spoke. "I guess we should just wait until something comes up. No good just sitting here."

He looked over at the pen. "I'm going to take care of Sheep."

The others went home while Eddie consoled himself with brushing his sheep. He had raised a new lamb each year. This was his fourth sheep and he had grown large and fat under Eddie's care. He would be sold later in the summer, like the others had been.

Sheep pushed against him with his head. Eddie reminded himself not to get too attached.

"Good Sheep," he murmured, and breathed deeply.

CHAPTER 32

1927, Winter-Spring.
Movies. Lizzie's Graduation

1926 passed uneventfully into 1927. Winter was not as harsh as in previous years, but still very cold. Grandma Mueller made Christmas cookies, there were church and club parties, schoolwork became more intricate and challenging.

In February Mrs. Johnson, Dot's mother, slipped on the ice and broke her wrist. She played the piano at the Crown movie theater and asked Mother to fill in for her. She found it very enjoyable, and Mrs. Johnson was happy to have help, so the two of them shared the job from then on.

King of Kings was a new movie about the life of Christ. Mother decided to put on a live prologue with a small choir. She dressed Eddie, Gus, Frank, Bill, and Jim as shepherds with headdresses and staffs. Eddie's sheep was the perfect addition. Mother said it "gave depth and a sense of verisimilitude to the tableau." Eddie resolved to look up those words when he had the chance.

After the prologue he tethered Sheep backstage and took his place in the audience. Later, Jesus was shown holding a lamb in his arms. As the movie lamb opened its mouth, Sheep bleated backstage. The audience applauded and afterward all agreed it was the high point of the show. Management didn't agree, though, pointing to the pile of droppings Sheep had left.

Seeing all the movies week after week seemed to change Mother. She still shared that "smile of reason" with Grandma, and was always kind and thoughtful, but she was definitely cheerier. And one day, quite to everyone's surprise, she emerged from the bathroom with short hair. Not as short as Lizzie's, but much shorter than it had been, and softly curled, not tight.

"I just thought it was time for a change. Something a little easier to take care of," she announced.

"It's like Clara Bow's," said Lizzie, referring to the beautiful red-headed star of the recently released movie, *It Girl.*

"No." Mother thought again. "If so, it is purely coincidental."

Father's eyes were wide. He had not expected this, and he figured his next few words would have great influence on his future happiness. "I love it. Very sensible, and beautiful too. Wonderful." He leaned toward her and kissed her on the cheek. "Well done."

Mother smiled knowingly. "You, too."

Between radio, movies, and newspaper, the Taylors were more and more aware of events around the world: wars in China, troubles for the British in many locations, new and "improved" governments in Germany and other countries shattered by the Great War and not fully recovered. But for them and for most Americans the biggest news besides the thriving economy and Babe Ruth was Charles Lindbergh.

"Look at that!" exclaimed Father one day, poking the paper with this finger. A picture on the front page showed a skinny, shy-looking pilot stepping down from his plane and waving, surrounded by cheering crowds. "He did it! All the way from New York to Paris without a stop. First thing you know, we'll all be doing it, just wait and see."

Eddie thought that sounded like a long time to be in the air without coming down again. He had never been in an airplane, though they flew over from time to time, usually on their way to someplace else. Junior and Johnny were very excited, though. Later that night they all crowded around the radio to hear the news reports about Lindbergh and the celebrations in Paris.

"That's what I wanna' do some day," said Johnny.

Lizzie was not so sure. "Is there enough work for all the fliers? I mean, what do they do, besides fly?"

"Sure, there's work," replied Junior. "There's mail delivery and freight and passengers, and all the machine work when you're not in the air. And there's the army."

"You can get across country faster on a train."

"But airplanes keep getting better and bigger and faster."

"Well, maybe." Lizzie sat back and sighed.

Father looked around at his children listening with varying intensity to the radio. Each so different, yet so much alike. The eldest, so like her mother, practical enough, but with a certain flamboyance. Sensible, hard-working Junior. Fun-loving Johnny, always looking for excitement. And young Shirl, smart and kind.

He had tried to be a good father with the right mix of patience and discipline, guidance and freedom. That was not always easy. He feared he had been too hard on Junior and too easy on Eddie. "Oh well," he thought. "We won't really know the answer to that until the next generation. How tough is too tough?"

The biggest events that year in the Taylor household were Lizzie's graduation from high school and Johnny's graduation from Middle School.

Lizzie's class was unusually large, sixty-four young men and women dressed in their best with black gowns and caps. Her hair was a little longer now than when she first bobbed it, but still with stylish finger curls.

Carbon County High School was known for excellence in music and in sports. Lizzie had played the clarinet in the orchestra as well as singing in the chorus of *The Belle of Barcelona*. She wiped away a tear at the end of the graduation ceremony.

"It was a really good time," she thought.

After the congratulations and farewells, the family gathered at home for tuna fish sandwiches and ice cream.

"*Ach*, Lizzie. *So schoen, so schoen*. Very proud of you," said Grandma Mueller, patting Lizzie's cheeks. "So. What you do now?"

She did not know. Everyone looked down at their bowls of ice cream and wondered what was next. The country was very prosperous, more so than ever in fact, and all the businesses were doing well. Still, hiring in Price seemed to be past the rush and opportunities for a young single girl right out of high school were limited.

Father worried the only things available would be either speculative and unreliable or in the "Gentleman's Clubs" and bars, not called by that name. He cleared his throat. "Perhaps, Lizzie, you should think of going back to Provo."

"Yes," interjected Mother. "That's just what I was thinking. I could call Vilate and ask if you could stay with her."

The thought intrigued Lizzie. She loved her friends in Price, but memories of Provo were still clear for her, the town, the college, not so very far from Salt Lake. And there were lots of men, young men, college men.

So, it was decided and the long-distance call was made. Vilate and her husband were happy to have their niece come and stay in their spare room. They would start asking around about work in town. Something would be lined up by the time she arrived.

Father turned to his oldest son and asked, "How about you, Son? What do you have for the summer?"

Junior put down his spoon. "I think I might have something at the Lyons' ranch. They need a hand. It would be tending animals and haying. I have to check back with him tomorrow."

"How much will you be paid?"

"Two dollars a week plus room and board."

"Will you be off Sundays, to come to church?" asked Mother.

"Yes, ma'am. A half day," he replied, adding apologetically, "Animals still have to be fed."

"Well," smiled Father, "That sounds like good work."

He turned to Johnny. "How about you, son?"

"Oh, uh, well," he stammered. "I don't actually have anything yet."

Father's eyebrows went up.

"But I will soon," continued Johnny. "I'll ask around downtown tomorrow to see if somebody needs a janitor or stock boy."

Father cleared his throat. "It's a little late to be starting, John. You should have been on this long before now."

"Yes, Sir. I, well, school was really hard this year, finishing up Middle School and all."

"Yes. We are proud of you, son. You graduated and that is the main thing."

In fact, Johnny failed History and barely passed the grade. The principal looked surprised to see him among the graduates.

"Thanks, Father. I'm sure I'll find something."

CHAPTER 33

1927, Early Summer.
Picking Boney on the Tipple

The Seventh Street Gang had their first meeting of the summer shortly after school let out. They met in the little Taylor orchard and debated what they should do.

"Pop says I need to go to work," said Gus. "He wants me every day in the store for at least a few hours. I can play afterward and on Mondays when the shop is closed."

"Me too," added Frank. "Some cousin or other told my pop that they can get me work at Castle Gate. I'll be staying up there with them during the week."

Eddie calculated in his mind when he would be able to play, working around chores and all.

"Say," said Frank, "Why don't you come up with me to the mine? I'm sure there will be work for you and my cousin wouldn't mind if you're there too. At least for awhile."

"I don't know. I don't think Mother would want me in the mines."

"We won't actually be in the mine. There's lots to do outside. And they don't allow kids inside anyway, only outside."

The proposition became a matter of discussion and debate that night. In the end Eddie received parental approval with a number of conditions:

1. If the work proved too hard, he should quit, but only with proper notice—he must give his employers fair work for fair pay.
2. It would only be for June, before the heat became too intense. Eddie pointed out that it wasn't that hot in the mountains, an argument which did not carry weight with Mother, who warned against heat stroke.
3. Finally, he was not to do anything dangerous. It was a little unclear to Eddie what that meant, but he assured her he would be as careful as a bee on a blossom. She had seen bees on blossoms and said he had better be a lot more careful than that.

"Yes, ma'am."

Later, with the children asleep, Father and Mother continued the discussion. She was concerned how hard the work would be, and he so young.

"It will do him good," replied Father. "Toughen him up a little. Kids today, they just aren't as tough as we were. You were out gleaning the fields younger than he is, weren't you?"

"Yes, but that was a different time. And gleaning is not so hard as . . . whatever it is the miners will have him do."

"Gleaning was hard work, wasn't it?"

"Yes." Mother thought back. "But it was fun too. Me and my sisters and friends, we all went out together after the farmers had finished, gathering what they left behind. We talked and laughed and sang a lot."

"Good times?"

"Yeah. Good times, long ago."

He put his hand on her shoulder. "He will be alright, Katherine. Really."

The touch was reassuring, though a mother's worries are never fully relieved.

Castle Gate was as pretty as Eddie had remembered, a grassy little valley between steep cliffs, with smaller canyons stretching away in all directions. Wildflowers were everywhere, and small trees grew along the river. The surrounding hills and cliffs were mostly barren rock of many colors with scattered sage and juniper. The town itself was built along the railway, with a small brick schoolhouse at town center, railroad station, mine office, store, and a couple dozen houses.

"You're too little," grunted the man at the mine office, a gruff fellow with double chin, bushy eyebrows, and stiff accent they thought was German. He paused, looked more intently down at the two boys. "You think you can work here?"

"Yes, Sir."

"*Ach*, I suppose so. You know what the tipple is?"

They shook their heads.

"I show you."

He led them to the yard in front of the mine entrance. A narrow set of rails led out of the mine to a building with a wooden frame made of railroad ties and a large cover over it. This was next to the railway, lined with coal cars. The man became animated, pointing first at one part of the structure, then another.

"*Dis* is the tipple. See. It's end of rails from mine. Tip of mine. The cars come up with coal and tip, see, they tip and dump the coal and rocks on these screens. Sift out dust and small stuff. This conveyor here carries the coal up and over there. There the coal is dumped into car to take to market.

"See? Very simple. Simple tipple. Your job is pick out rocks. Leave coal. Coal is de meat, rocks are de bones. See?

"We call it 'picking boney on the tipple'. Very important. Buyers don't want rocks, want coal. You pick boney, throw rocks in bin. See? We pay you by the bin. Fill the bin, get paid. Good?"

The man was happy with his explanation. He grimaced a smile and stalked away. Frank and Eddie looked at the other workers, older boys and some men, all picking boney or working the machines. Every once in a while, the man would come out of the office, march around the yard, and yell something at the workers, usually in German, but not like the German Eddie had heard before.

Tony, Frank's cousin, looked very much like him, dark features, narrow nose, black hair. He and his wife and baby lived in a small house on the edge of town. He chuckled when the boys told them about their first day.

"Yeah, that's the yard foreman. We call him 'Stormin' Norman, the Mormon Foreman'. I'm not sure what his real name is."

"He sounds German," suggested Eddie.

"Yeah, but he's not. He's a Bohunk, from somewhere in Eastern Europe. And don't let him fool you into thinking he's mean or something. He will make you work, but he is fair and really a nice guy."

Tony looked more serious. "I was working the tipple in '24. Everybody helped and did what they could when the mine exploded, but Norman was like a machine, looking for the men, pulling rocks out of the way, hour after hour, day after day, carrying their bodies out. And when it was over, I saw him go back of the office and cry like a baby. He's really a good man." Tony nodded to himself, looking far away, and repeated, "Good man."

Eddie did not feel like a machine. Every muscle ached each night and sleep came quickly. He and Frank worked as best they could to keep up. Over time they found they could do a good job of picking boney, though never quite so fast as the older boys and men.

Mother had been right about the heat. Not as hot in the valley, but still hot enough to work up a good sweat. Despite the river and grass in town, dust was everywhere, not just clean dirt dust, but coal dust, causing black marks on everyone and everything. The boys were glad to wash in the river at the end of each day. It was icy cold, mountain water to cool the skin and carry away the dirt. Eddie learned to sniff a little water into his nostrils and blow it out hard, otherwise they became black like a tobacco snuff user. Mother would not have liked it.

Frank had planned on staying through the summer, but when it was time to take Eddie back to Price, he decided to go too. He said it was to keep him company, but Eddie suspected that working the tipple was just as fatiguing for Frank as it was for him, though they were thrilled at having been paid real money for real work, twenty-five dollars and fifty cents each. Eddie figured that would keep him in movies and ice cream for the rest of his life.

Tony was driving. When they reached the little town of Carbonville, just outside of Price, he pulled over and stopped in front of a non-descript cinder block building with a sign out front that said 'Waterhole'. Faintly visible beneath that lettering was another name only partially wiped out, 'Saloon'.

"Getting thirsty," said Tony, who hopped out.

Frank waited a while, then turned to Eddie, "Let's take a look."

The walls inside were plain grey blocks with streaks where repairs had been made. A wooden bar with step rail was along one wall, with mirrors behind it and a variety of bottles and glasses. A calendar beside one mirror featured a brightly colored pinup girl. Three small tables with chairs were arranged along the other wall. What caught Eddie's attention was a large safe to the side of the bar with a broom leaning up against it; it seemed an odd place for a safe, but then, the whole scene was odd for him.

As his eyes adjusted to the darkness, Eddie saw that there were two other men in the room besides Tony, another customer and a man behind the bar. To his amazement, it was none other than Matt Warner.

CHAPTER 34

1927, Late Summer.
The Seventh Street Gang

"Hello boys," Warner called out.

Frank mumbled something, but Eddie replied with silence.

"Would you like a glass of cool water? Plain water is on the house."

Soon they were seated at one of the tables with glasses of water, Tony beside them with a glass of some amber colored liquid. "Flavored water," Warner had called it, of which he had several types.

"How do you know Matt?" asked Tony.

"He's a judge in Price," replied Eddie. Tony raised his eyebrows. "Well, a justice of the peace, Father says. It's a sort of judge."

"I knew that but didn't know about Warner. Kinda' interestin'."

"I didn't know he ran a bar," said Eddie.

"Not a bar. That would be like a saloon, and that would be illegal. This is a waterhole, where they serve water." He smacked his lips. "And that was mighty fine water."

"Right," replied the boys together.

"Just one thing," Tony added. "Don't tell your mothers we stopped here. Got it?"

"Right."

That did not stop Eddie from bringing it up to Father. When the rest of the family was out of earshot, he described the trip and asked if he knew Warner had a place in Carbonville.

"Yes," he said, "I did. When he's not serving as a judge or deputy sheriff, then he works at his place out there."

"I think they serve liquor."

Father smiled. "Yes, I am pretty sure they do. It used to be a saloon."

"What about Prohibition? Isn't that wrong?"

He looked at his son's eyes and chose his words carefully as he answered, "Yes, it is not exactly legal. And yes, you or I would not do it. In fact, there are a lot of places around here, right in Price, where liquor is sold under some other name, pretending it is not what it is. Those clubs and cafes on Main Street, most of them serve it, if you know how to ask or if they know you are one of their regular customers.

"You need to realize, Shirl, that there is a real question in most people's minds about whether Prohibition is a legal law or not. It may be . . . in fact, I think it is an overreach, something the Federal government should not do.

"Laws need to reflect and represent the beliefs of the people. Local laws may vary a lot from place to place. Here in Utah, or at least in those towns where most people do not drink, it might make sense to have a law against liquor, and there are many counties across the country that were 'dry' before Prohibition was passed, but a whole state? Certainly not the whole country—there are just too many who disagree."

"So, is Judge Warner right or wrong to have a bar?"

Father was silent, then said slowly, "I do not know. I do know he is not someone that I would want to judge, one way or the other."

Eddie came away undecided. He already knew life could be hard, but now it seemed more complicated than ever. Father watched him leave. The exercise in toughening up his youngest had not worked quite as expected.

Sorting out right and wrong, lawful and unlawful, was still on Eddie's mind as he went about his chores next day. In the afternoon Gus, Frank, and Athena came over so they could have an official meeting of the gang, first one since Eddie returned from Castle Gate. The July holidays were starting, and they were debating what the gang should do to celebrate. The debate was interrupted by the appearance of the Eighth Street Gang in the alley.

"What are they doing here?" asked Athena.

They all stood and took out their flippers. The other boys kept coming, carrying the cannon with them.

"You can't come here," shouted Eddie.

"We're the Eighth Street Gang. We can go anywhere we want."

The irony of hearing his own words come back to him was not lost on Eddie. His face flushed. It was wrong, just wrong.

"No, you can't," he replied angrily. "If we can't go where we want, then neither can you."

Jimmy and the others had expected this answer. They dropped the cannon and took eggs from their pockets and threw them with deadly accuracy.

"Phew. The smell!" exclaimed Frank. The eggs were rotten, which led to loud guffaws from the throwers.

This was too much!

Not waiting to wipe the eggy mess away, the Seventh Street Gang loaded their flippers and pelted their opponents with pebble after pebble. Athena's aim was excellent. And she was fast, loading the next rock before the last one hit its mark. She and the other little gangsters advanced on Jimmy and his friends, who now ran back up the alley, covering their heads.

"And don't come back!" shouted Gus.

"Hooray," said the others, exulting in their victory.

"Look what we got," added Frank, holding up the cannon. The gang had not only won, they had won a prize. They did not see the Eighth Street Gang for days after.

Frank pulled on the rubber part of the cannon, made from good bicycle tube rubber. "Let's see what this can do."

"First, let's wash," suggested Athena, wrinkling her nose. They all knelt at the irrigation ditch and splashed on the cold water, before heading toward the west for target practice.

Soon they were on a little rise of land at the base of Wood Hill. A small ranch was down below, with sheep and a couple cattle, near the Price River, just out of town. A tumble down barn was on the property, with a rusting metal roof.

"That'll make a great target!" exclaimed Gus.

They dug a hole to set the cannon base. Two of them held it while another pulled back the sling, casting the first rock. It went hurtling through the air, falling with a thud only a little short of the barn.

"My turn," said Athena, whose rock shot about the same distance.

"Now me."

It was Eddie's turn. He picked a larger rock, the size of both fists together, and pulled back as hard as he could on the rubber. "Thwang," went the cannon, and "clang," went the rock as it struck the barn roof. The gang cheered.

Frank took his place behind the giant sling shot. He picked a rock similar to Eddie's, large and a little irregular, and pulled back with all his might. "Thwang" again. This time the rock not only hit the roof, but crashed right through it.

"Wow!" exclaimed the gangsters together. A moment later a man came rushing out the barn door, looking all around. When he caught sight of the kids on the hilltop with their giant slingshot, he began waving his arms and shouting.

"Oh, my goodness," said Frank. "That's Mr. Moulin. I know him from church. He's always at mass." He stood tall and waved back.

"Sorry, Mr. Moulin," he shouted. "We didn't know anyone was there."

"Well, stop it," he called back. "And get outta' here." He waved them away.

They pulled the cannon from its hole and carried it back to the Taylor's shed. Maybe it was not such a great prize after all. Maybe best to save it for special occasions and for show.

They were still discussing potential uses for their weapon when they were interrupted by a strange buzzing sound. Gus was first to see the source, pointing overhead, "Look!"

A biplane was making its way over Price in lazy circles. It seemed the pilot was trying to attract attention, waving at the curious onlookers below. After the third pass he pointed toward the south side of town and began to descend. The gang dropped what they were doing and ran toward the visitor, joined along the way by dozens of other children and adults from every direction.

Airplanes appeared every now and then in the skies over Price, ever since the county built a small airfield in 1919. Mother said it was an unreliable and dangerous way to get around, much better to go by train or car, or even horse.

The pilot had bypassed the airfield and instead landed in an open field next to the fairground. He was a young man with a broad smile. His goggles were pulled up on his forehead and a white scarf swirled around his neck. "Hello, everyone," he cried out. "My name is Johnny, and this is my airplane, Jenny."

Some of the crowd called back, "Hello Johnny, hello Jenny!"

"Thanks. We got a little turned around. What town is this?"

"Price!" came the reply.

"Oh, okay. Which way is Salt Lake City?"

All together the crowd pointed northwest.

"Thanks again." He started to climb back into the aircraft, then turned.

"Say, anybody here want to go for a little ride?"

There was silence at first, then a little girl in front stepped forward. "I do."

"Oh, well, I think you might be a bit small." He looked up at the man behind her. Unless your father would hold you in his lap." The man looked a little reluctant, then nodded.

"Great! That'll be one dollar, plus fifty cents for the child."

"You didn't say anything about charging for it," said the man.

"Oh, well, it costs a lot of money to keep a fine machine like this running. You wouldn't expect me to do it for free, would you?'

"Hmph. I guess not." He reached into his pocket.

"Now, there's room for one more. Any takers?"

A middle-aged lady volunteered and soon they were sailing high above. Eddie and his friends watched enviously. "Well, Son, do you want to go next?" It was a familiar voice. Father had come over from the warehouse. Glancing around, it seemed to the boys that half the town was there.

"Yes sir. And I have my own dollar." He pulled a silver piece from his pocket.

"Very well."

"You know," continued Father, "this young fellow is a barnstormer and something of a huckster. He oughta' work for the circus. He knows perfectly well where he is and could have landed in the airfield. He landed here to attract attention, draw a crowd, and make some money by taking people for rides."

Eddie wrinkled his forehead. "I guess it worked," he replied. "Didn't it?"

"Yes, it did," chuckled Father. "Everybody has to make a living."

It was Eddie's turn next. Turning in lazy circles in the sky over Price, he was struck by how different everything looked from the air than it did on the ground. Things seemed a whole lot smaller and closer together, like pieces on a gameboard. He could see Carbonville and Helper, almost to Castle Gate. Whichever way he looked, from the ground below to the blue sky and white clouds above, it was all so amazing. He thought of Mother's favorite hymn. "For the beauty of the earth, For the beauty of the skies . . ."

CHAPTER 35

1928, Summer. The Slaughterhouse. Another Close Call

For a child passing thoughtlessly into his second decade, life seemed a steady routine, each season passing into another, each returning event a little more familiar with the repetition, each life's lesson fitting more clearly into the whole.

The world became larger not just because of new insights in school or information on radio and in newspapers, but larger from personal exploration, alone or in company of what now seemed lifelong friends.

In all his wanderings in the town and surrounding territory—the lumber mill, the ice plant, the car repair companies—Eddie had never gone much to the southeast where the river rushed out toward the prairie. One summer's day in 1928 he decided it was time to see what was there. Gus was working at the shop, so it was just Eddie and Frank.

Father had mentioned the slaughterhouse. He sometimes was able to get meat wholesale from one of the managers, a friend who watched for good deals to share. Most animals that were raised for meat were loaded onto rail cars and shipped away to the big meat packers in the Midwest, but small farmers and herders with animals for their own consumption or that were sold locally, if they didn't butcher them themselves, took them to Price. Father said it was better that way so other animals in the herd or flock couldn't see it.

It was a small, low building with pens at one end for steers, sheep, pigs, or goats. Skins and waste were removed somewhere on the other side, where the boys could not see, and large boxes of meat in quarters and halves exited the far end after cooling in a refrigerated room. Trucks waited to take them from there to the butchers, or home for cutting into usable pieces.

"Let's go closer," said Frank.

"I dunno. It really smells." Not good smells. Smells of decay and rot. "It smells like an outhouse, only worse."

Still, the two advanced toward a window near the middle of the building. Peering in through the grimy glass, they could make out men standing on platforms a little above the cattle. As a steer came up, one man placed a machine that looked like a pistol against the animal's head, there was a clicking sound, and it fell to the ground. It was quickly gutted, cut in half lengthwise, hung from a hook by its rear hooves, and skinned. The blood drained into a gutter on the floor. A conveyer rolled the hanging meat away while the next steer came up to the station.

The boys felt queasy and cold, despite the summer heat. It reminded Eddie of when Father came home from hunting and prepared the deer in the shed for storing and eating, only much bigger and more efficient.

On the other side of the room sheep were going through the same process, though handling the woolly skins looked more difficult. Father had taught him that when skinning a carcass, it was important not to let the skin touch the meat. It spoiled the flavor.

Eddie then became aware of the noise, the incessant mooing and bleating. "Calls farewell," he thought. It was almost mesmerizing.

"Hey kids," came a voice. "Get outta' here." It was a man in overalls, waving his arms.

"Yes Sir. Just lookin'."

"Well, there's no trespassing here. Understood?"

"Yes Sir." They wondered if they should run.

"Say." The man's voice softened. "You want something for your trouble?"

"What?"

"Wait here a minute." The man disappeared into a nearby door and returned with two soft, round, pink objects, slightly moist, each about the size of a double fist. "Here. Tie or sew off these two holes, then you can blow 'em up with air or fill 'em with water, then you tie this hole over here. They make good balls to toss around."

"What are they?"

"Pig bladders."

"Thanks, mister!" they both exclaimed.

Frank and Eddie hurried off with their new treasures, eager to tie and fill them. They were fine for playing catch, but not as good as baseballs—they leaked when batted.

Junior commented on how they used to make bladder balls when he was little. "Don't you remember?"

Eddie did not. Junior laughed and messed up Eddie's hair, adding, "Glad to see you're re-learning stuff. Maybe this time it will stick." Then he went off with Johnny to play with a real baseball.

That school year passed without too many problems. Only a few scuffles and no fights for which paddles were applied or parents called.

Eddie had begun to wonder what he would be when he grew up, what he would do for a living. Like the other boys, he had thought he would be a cowboy, but now began to realize that might not happen. It was natural at first to think of being a salesman like Father or a judge like Grandfather Alfred. After his experience picking boney on the tipple he knew working in the mines was too hard.

His teacher, Miss Maywood, told the children they should figure out what they were good at when deciding on a career. He was a good reader and enjoyed history but couldn't think of a job doing that. One day the teacher patted him on the head and said "Well done" for his drawing of an internal combustion engine. "You have a fine, inquisitive mind."

Perhaps he would become a mechanic or a scientist. He loved *Popular Science* magazine.

So, he was especially interested the following spring when trucks lined up along Sixth Street. Workmen spread first a layer of gravel followed by a thick layer of steaming black material that glistened and flowed like thick curdled cream. It looked pretty scientific to him.

"It's called asphalt," said one of the workmen when Eddie asked what it was.

Eddie took a deep breath. "It smells good," he said. "Like a really greasy fry pan."

"Hah. Not so good when you have to smell it all day."

At this point the foreman came up with a clipboard in his hand. "Beat it kid. Scram. Amscray. No time for talk."

The workman mumbled something and went back to raking the asphalt.

Eddie remembered how smooth the streets had been in Salt Lake City but had not thought about why they were that way, or why they were for the most part black. Now he realized they must have been made of this stuff.

Gus and Athena and Frank were almost as interested in this new material as he was. They sat on the sidewalk and watched as the work crews poured, raked, rolled, and pounded it into smooth new streets. When the workers had moved on and the pavement was still hot, the children crawled closer, reached out and touched it.

"It's sticky," observed Athena, pulling her thumb and forefinger apart.

"Yeah, it's sticky to hold together and so it can be rolled out. Later it'll get hard." Eddie put his blackened finger in the dust. "Look at this, how the dirt sticks to it."

At that he stood up and stepped onto the new asphalt with his bare feet, making sure to walk where some of the tar was starting to pool. Then he stepped onto the sand and dirt in the gutter, covering the soles of his feet and part way up each side.

"It's like wearing a shoe without having to wear a shoe," he proclaimed.

The others followed his example and soon all four were happily walking along the rough ground to the west, ignoring thorns and stickers and rough spots. Their wanderings led them around the other side of Wood Hill, then up to the top of the cliff, overlooking town.

Admiring the view, they noticed a group of kids at the base of the cliff, having a picnic. Another one of those irresistible urges came to Eddie. He took a pebble and tossed it down among the picnickers, quickly ducking back behind the cliff edge, then peeking again to see their reaction.

The children below had not noticed. The pebble must have fallen short. Eddie and his fellow gangsters took out their flippers and slowly, methodically began to cast pebbles, ducking back each time so they could not be seen.

Now, sometimes distance is hard to gauge, and sometimes pebbles are larger than they seem, and sometimes there is just an unaccountable power that causes a projectile to go astray. In any case, after a time one of the little rocks split in midair and pieces went flying at least two or more blocks into town. Maybe it was more than one rock.

Pretty soon a car drove up fast near the cliff base and a woman got out of the car. She looked right up at the cliff, pulled out her pistol, and began firing. The first round ricocheted off the rock a few feet from the little group of gangsters at the top.

"She's shooting at us!" exclaimed Frank.

"No kidding," replied the others in unison. "Let's get out of here."

The four gangsters hurried back the way they had come. The old saying that 'an armed society is a polite society' was not exactly true. People were still rude and thoughtless, as people are, but there were definite limits to the rudeness. And in Price, pretty much everybody was armed.

Mother was not impressed with Eddie's invention of asphalt-tar-sand-and-dirt shoes. He did not make it past the kitchen before he was directed back to the porch where he soon was soaking his feet in a washtub of warm soapy water. It took a long time to pick off all the pieces, and the skin was still dark except for where it was pink and irritated and sore from scrubbing.

Next morning dawned another beautiful, warm day. Eddie had only just finished his morning chores and started toward the alley to look for Gus and Frank when the town whistle blew and kept blowing, blast after blast. The normal 8 am whistle was past, and it was a long time until noon, so it could only be some sort of emergency. He ran toward Main Street to see what was going on.

CHAPTER 36

1928, Summer-1929, Summer. Fishing and Boy Scouts

The whistle was still sounding when he reached Main in front of the courthouse. Large numbers of men, women, and children were already there. Eddie joined a group of boys standing on the corner.

Gus soon joined them. "What's going on?" he asked.

"I dunno."

Mayor Watson was on the steps with a megaphone. When the whistle stopped, he addressed the crowd. It seemed there was a leak in the Scofield reservoir, about thirty miles away. Although Price's water was from springs in Colton near Soldier Summit, the reservoir was the main source of irrigation and drinking water for a large part of the rest of the county.

The county needed volunteers to work on moving rocks and sandbags to shore up the dam. A special train had been sent to carry the workers. Hands went up all over the crowd and men filed over to the train station.

"How about us, mister mayor?" asked Gus. "Can't we do somethin'?"

Mayor Watson spoke with the other officials, then replied, "Sure. It's going to be a hot day today. Can you kids carry clean water around to the workmen?"

Soon a dozen kids about Eddie's age were crowded onto the train, some in seats, some standing, riding to a stop near the reservoir. Once there, they were given pans and buckets and directed to collect water from a still part of the river where it eddied to the side. Though the sun was increasingly intense, the water was cold and sweet. From there they carried their refreshment to the men at the dam.

This continued for a time until Eddie noticed the fish in the water. "Hey guys," he called, "take a look."

They did not have any lines or hooks, so at first just watched the lazy trout swim between their legs. Then Gus put his hands in the water, slowly, carefully, with no sudden movements, until a fish was very close between his hands. Then he caught it and tossed it to the bank. It lay there flopping from side to side. Gus stepped over to it and put it in one of the buckets.

"Come on. It's easy."

Soon all the boys were trying hand-fishing, with varying success, for it was not always so easy. But in time they had caught several. Eddie had a particularly large and tasty looking trout in his bucket. Time has a way of slipping away when you are having fun.

"What do you think you are doing?" came a harsh, deep voice. One of the work crew supervisors was standing on the bank, hat pushed back, dripping with sweat.

"The men need water to drink. You are not here to play in the stream and catch fish. Now move your little behinds before I kick 'em in!"

They believed him and did not have to be told twice. They hurried back into their shoes and sprinted up the hill with their containers of water, trip after trip, all afternoon. It was dark by the time they arrived home. The boys kept their fish.

Mother lost her part-time job as a piano player at the movie theater that fall when it was re-fitted for the new talkies, and they did not need her anymore. The occasional silent film that was still shown could be managed by Mrs. Johnson. Mother said that, in general, it had been a good experience, but she was glad it was over. There was so much else to do after all, and a lot of the movies were really not very good. In fact, some of them were embarrassing. She was glad her children had not seen them and was sorry she had to be there for them. The new movies would be better, she hoped, even if they were not free.

1929 came bursting with optimism. The economy was humming. Sheriff Deming had retired, and Marion Bliss had been elected to take his place. He was well liked, and Father was especially pleased that he was Republican. The new president, Herbert Hoover, promised to continue the sensible policies of his predecessor, though Father and Judge Anderson were concerned that he seemed to be more of a "big government" man than Coolidge had been.

Buck Rogers, Tarzan, and Popeye all appeared for the first time in the comics; Eddie decided it was going to be a great year. He joined the Boy Scouts. Best of all, his Christmas present was a beautiful single shot 22 caliber rifle. It would not take long for him to become a fine shot and earn a marksmanship badge. Father took him hunting each year after that, but truth be told, he preferred fishing. He liked standing in the water more than hiding in the bushes.

The Scouts held a jamboree that summer in Joe's Valley, a beautiful, secluded spot in the mountains southwest of Price. The center piece of the valley was a large reservoir into which small streams and a river fed, restrained by a dam at one end. Surrounding the camp were woods of pine and juniper with open meadows of bunch grass and sage.

One of the first things Eddie noticed while exploring the camp with Gus and Frank and others in his troop were the fish. The streams and the reservoir were filled with them. Each morning while everyone else slept, he was up before dawn to fish.

"Taylor," his scoutmaster, Mr. Ackerman, said one day, "why weren't you at reveille this morning? In fact, why haven't you been at reveille any day this week?"

"Sorry Sir, I was, uh, busy."

"Busy? At sunrise? Were you sleeping in?"

"Oh, no Sir. Fact is, the fishing is great here!" Eddie smiled broadly.

"You mean you've been out fishing?"

"Yes Sir."

"Catching fish and then releasing them?"

"Yes Sir."

Ackerman thought for a moment. "Tell you what. Tomorrow, bring back all the fish you catch. We can have them for breakfast."

So next morning Eddie was up even earlier than usual. He came back a half hour after reveille with a string of fine trout. Mr. Ackerman supervised the troop as they fried them over their campfire. Gus and Frank and all the troop agreed they were the best trout ever, and other scouts passing their camp took deep, delicious, envious breaths.

Each morning and evening the scouts were all sent to the water's edge to wash in the cold, bracing water. Running back from shore, they sang an Indian song they learned at the first night's fireside, a song, they were told, that was meant to increase the corn harvest:

Keelee, keelee, keelee, keelee
Watch, watch, watch, watch
Hey, you kingkumpow-wa!
Keelee, keelee, keelee, keelee
Watch, watch, watch, watch
Hey, you kingkumpow-wa!
Hey, chah ma pah ma,
Hey chah, ma polywah-ma!
Keelee, keelee, keelee, keelee

Watch, watch, watch, watch
Hey, you kingkumpow-u-wa!

They had no idea what it meant, if it meant anything at all, but everyone sang with gusto. Eddie could not have imagined it then, but even in his old age, the song would come back to his mind from time to time, much to the delight of his children and grandchildren.

He also found himself in a new role. Rather than fighting, he became the referee. It started when he and Gus and Frank were walking along the lakeshore, killing time until dinner. Gus was talking about what he was learning in Greek School.

"Athens was the center of learning in the olden days. There were lots of schools, and rich people from all over would send their kids there to study." He glanced over at Frank. "Especially the Romans."

Frank remained silent.

"Everything the Romans did, they learned from the Greeks. Art, philosophy, history. Even law. They invented democracy."

"There you're wrong," replied Frank. "Romans invented law when they built the Roman empire."

"What do you mean, 'invented'?" said Eddie. "There have always been laws. Everybody has laws."

Gus ignored their comments and continued. "There was so much need for good teachers, the Greeks sent teachers to Italy to teach the kids who couldn't afford to come to Greece." Then he grinned. "But they only sent the crazy ones."

Frank looked annoyed. "The Romans conquered Greece because they were harder workers and better soldiers. And they had better laws. And if the Greeks sent crazies to Rome, it was because they had so many of them."

"Yeah, well, everything the Romans did they learned from the Greeks. Only they did it with a bad accent."

They stopped walking. Frank and Gus glared at each other.

"Take it back," said one.

"No, you," said the other.

Soon they pushed each other's chests, followed by more shoving and rolling around on the ground.

Eddie reached between them and pulled them apart. "Enough," he said. "It doesn't matter."

The boys stood and dusted themselves off. Before anyone else spoke, Eddie exclaimed, pointing to a nearby tree, "Oh look! A Western Meadowlark."

Over the following years he became an expert at changing the subject and helping his friends avoid ancient grudges.

CHAPTER 37

1929, Summer-Fall. Ole's Bowling Alley. The Crash

His parents listened patiently to Eddie's stories about camp and how good the fishing was and how well he had learned his knots. When those topics were exhausted Father said, "Shirl, I am proud of you. It sounds like you had a good time at camp. And I remember how well you worked last summer at the mine and how you helped out with the Scofield Dam repair.

"Now, I was talking to Ole Oleson the other day—Ole runs the bowling alley, remember him? Doesn't have any teeth, lost them all chewing tobacco, chin sticks out? Anyway, he said he's looking for a pin setter. It would be good work for you, something new."

Next day Eddie and Frank walked over to the bowling alley, a low, long building two blocks south of Main. There were six lanes, four pool tables, and a large bar with tables. It seemed every amusement hall, club, or meeting place had a bar.

Oleson was a thin man with a Swedish accent that sounded even odder than usual for lack of teeth. After a little instruction Eddie and Frank were soon hovering in the spaces between the alleys, hopping down to reset the pins, and rolling the bowling balls back along the gutters to the players.

When business on the lanes was slow, they helped clean the hall, straighten up the sticks and balls at the pool tables, and even "bus" at the bar, though that had not been part of the original job description. From the boss's standpoint, anything they could do, they should do. Eddie thought that was good enough to work as an odd job, but not something he would want to do for life; just because you could do something, that didn't mean you should.

Most of it was good, even enjoyable, except for emptying and cleaning the spittoons. Every store, bar, or meeting place had a spittoon in the corner. The tobacco chewers who used them sometimes missed, which meant cleaning more than just the spittoons.

The boys came to recognize an assortment of regular customers. One of their favorites was Bill Bianchi. Bill was a large man with very round belly. He reminded the boys of Oliver Hardy, the comedian, especially with his bowler hat and short black tie.

Bill had a talent for drinking large quantities of beer. Ole loved to tell how Bill managed to drink an entire case one night before passing out and lying on his belly. His middle was so big that his hands and feet did not touch the floor. The story was always followed by loud guffaws and knee slapping.

But Bill one evening made a comment he thought would even the story-telling score. "Ole," he said, "you're always chewing tobacco, but I never see ya spit."

Ole looked back and said in his lisping Swedish accent, "What's the use a' 'ewin' if ya don't use the 'uice?"

Ole was still one up on his large customer.

Eddie entered sixth grade that fall. He had always enjoyed school and looked forward to each new year and the things he would learn. It was different this time. Miss

Swenson was a large woman in her forties, with thick glasses, tightly curled hair, and stern demeanor. It was clear from the beginning that she viewed Eddie as a problem case, starting with his chin.

The family had been on a short drive one Sunday afternoon, enjoying the fall colors in the surrounding canyons. In his hurry to exit the vehicle, with Johnny close behind him and shoving a little, Eddie lost his footing and fell to the ground, striking his chin on the rock at the front corner of the driveway. His parents hurried him to the kitchen to wash the wound and examine it more closely. It was only a small scratch, but the bone underneath was very sore.

"I don't think it's broken," said Father after poking and prodding and having Eddie open and close his mouth. "You're lucky. Might have broken a tooth. Or your jaw."

The scratch sealed over quickly and the bruise began to subside, but it was still sore the following Thursday when Miss Swenson asked him about the capital of Rhode Island. He had not been listening because his mind was busy contemplating the number of leaves passing the window with each gust of wind.

"Mr. Taylor!"

"Yes ma'am?"

"I asked you a question."

"Yes ma'am?"

She sighed and stood next to Eddie's desk. "What is the capital of Rhode Island?"

Eddie's mind went blank. "Rhode Island?" he thought. "Did Rhode Island have a capital? Why does it matter if Rhode Island has a capital? It's an island."

Miss Swenson clicked her tongue and rolled her eyes. "I thought so. Not paying attention again. How will you ever learn? Good citizens should know the states and the capitals. How will you ever be a good citizen?"

Then she reached out and took Eddie by the chin and wiggled it back and forth. "Now pay attention!"

Eddie howled in pain.

"Hmph," she muttered as she returned to the front of the class. "As if that hurt. Such foolishness."

Eddie's friends looked at him with sympathy. Jimmy Curtis just grinned.

Fortunately, sixth grade included a special class, Music Appreciation, and that became the best part of Eddie's day. The music teacher was Mrs. Ackerman, the scoutmaster's wife. She was gentle and patient and noticed that Eddie already knew many of the great pieces of music she presented in class.

"Mother sings that around the house," he would say when she asked where he had heard it. Or he would say they heard it on the radio, or "we have that on a record."

With her encouragement he joined the choir, and from there was given roles in the plays and operettas that were an important part of each school year's activities.

Eddie already knew Angela Anderson was musical. Now he was delighted to find that she was in choir too, and had roles in many of the plays, sometimes writing or re-writing parts herself. It was another good reason to participate.

"So talented," he thought. "And so beautiful. I'm going to tell her so. Maybe next year."

It was a musical year in other ways. One Friday after school near the end of October, Eddie and Gus were walking along the east side of town, the neighborhood with nicer houses belonging to some of the leading businessmen of Price. They turned into the alley and, following their old habit, glanced into the trashcans as they passed.

"Whoa," called out Eddie, "What's this?"

There in the top of the can was a stack of records. He eagerly examined the treasure. Caruso, Rachmaninoff, Schubert, Schumann, Debussy. Some of the covers were a little scuffed, but the records themselves were pristine. "Hooray!" he exclaimed.

He could hardly wait to get home and present them to Mother and Grandma. He found them sitting at the dining table sipping their herb tea.

"For you," he said, presenting his find.

"*Ach, so schoen!*" exclaimed Grandma.

Mother's eyes were wide. "Where in the world did you get these?"

"In somebody's trash. They just threw them away."

"But why would anybody . . . ?"

"I dunno. Maybe they bought new ones or something. When I saw them, I knew you would like them."

She looked into her son's eyes. "Thank you, Eddie. That is so very sweet of you. And you know us so very well, don't you?"

Father was also pleased with the new additions to the music library.

"Where did you say you found these?" he asked when he came home that night.

"In the trash. Nobody wanted them."

"Yes. I mean, what part of town, what street?"

"Uh, other side of the courthouse, a couple blocks"

"Big house? Round pillars? Painted white?"

"Yeah. I think so. Why?"

"Ah. Well, those folks are probably moving. They will be leaving a lot behind."

Mother joined the conversation. "Why is that, dear?"

Father unrolled the newspaper and held up the front page. There, in large type were the words, *Billions Lost As Stocks Crash.*

Junior spoke up from across the room. "I heard about that. They were talking about it today in Civics Class."

"What does it mean for us?" asked Mother.

"Well," replied Father slowly, "probably not much for us directly. There was a crash back in '23, remember, not quite so bad and it did not last long. The bankers and politicians tried to get Coolidge to do something about it and he told them it was not the business of the federal government and that the market would repair itself, and it did. What happens with this will probably depend on how or whether the government responds."

"But what does that have to do with the records I found?" asked Eddie.

"The man who lives in that house is Walter Jenkins. He's a big businessman, made a lot of money on the railroad. I saw him this morning down at the warehouse. He was white as a ghost, said he had put everything in the market. Lost it all. He is going to move to California to be close to family, maybe get some help from them."

There was quiet while that soaked in.

"Do you think others will move too?" asked Junior.

"Probably not many from here. We never had money to put into the stock market, and neither did most of our neighbors. And whatever happens, people will still need groceries and warehouses, so we will do all right. There may be hard times for awhile until the businesses sort things out, but then it will be back to normal."

Things did not get back to normal for a very long time.

CHAPTER 38

1930, Summer. The Depression, a Still, and Green River Melons

Carl Junior graduated from high school in 1930. He had been working part-time at J.C. Penney's, cleaning and re-stocking. It was a good company and he had hoped to increase to full-time when school was over. Instead, he was let go. The workforce was being reduced to save money during the downturn and preference was given to heads of households. His search for work had begun.

Father wanted to hire him at the warehouse, but he was facing the same management problems as everyone else. In fact, more and more of the daily operations had to be done by him or by his assistant, Karl with a *K*.

Too many people, not enough money. Businesses couldn't keep jobs that did not generate enough revenue to pay the wages, much less make a profit. It took a few years to reach peak unemployment of 35%, but the number of unemployed was growing steadily, even in the early days of the Great Depression. Utah was hit hard and fast.

Eddie was aware of this, but at thirteen, summer still meant fun. When Fred Thomas invited him to spend the summer at the ranch again, he jumped at it, even though he would miss Gus and Frank, and even Athena. Mother would miss him too, especially his help with the chores, but Father pointed out that he would be helping a friend, working hard with horses and cattle, and Fred would be feeding him. All parents are aware of a teenage boy's appetite.

The lush meadow and surrounding mountains and canyons were as beautiful as always, their rich browns and reds, golds and greens, an intense feast for the eyes. The clean, fresh mountain air was invigorating, and the Thomas herd of horned Herefords was just as powerful as Eddie remembered. But some things had changed. There was only one hired hand now, Cal, and he was scheduled to leave mid-summer to live with family in Wyoming. Bill and Jim had taken over most of the everyday work.

There was always plenty of work. It seemed some cow or steer or a small group of them was always wandering off and had to be herded back to be with the rest; animals left alone in the canyons had a high mortality rate. The horses were more sensible in that regard, thought Eddie. They stayed close to the ranch house and corral, knowing where the hay and grain were kept. Besides chasing after strays, there were always fences that needed mending, horses that needed to be curried, and of course weeding and watering in the garden.

One afternoon he and Bill and Jim were riding out further to the east than usual, following the track of a stray steer. They had gone up a small canyon to the rolling hills beyond, past the boundaries of the Thomas ranch to sheep herding country. Large flocks and a shepherd's wagon were in the distance.

A glint of sun on metal in a gulley caught Eddie's eye. He rode down to investigate, his companions following. "Hey," he called out. "Look what I found."

There in a small clearing between the bushes were large copper and brass canisters, tubing, and pans. A couple jugs lay nearby. They had found a still. Eddie pushed the larger canister. A small amount of mash sloshed inside.

"It's almost empty," he said.

"Look at all this copper," said Bill.

"And brass," added his brother. "It's beautiful."

"And worth a lot of money." Eddie's mind was racing. "If we took this to Mr. Gordon in town, he would pay us a lot for it."

"How much?"

"Oh, maybe two, three dollars."

The boys let that sink in for a bit.

"It doesn't belong to us," Jim pointed out.

"No," replied Eddie slowly, "but look around. Nobody's here. I think they abandoned it. Maybe chased off by the cops."

"Yeah," said Bill. "Besides, 'finders keepers, losers weepers'."

"Right!"

Soon the boys were disassembling the still and loading the pieces onto the backs of their horses. They had not gotten far in this process before a loud "bang" stopped them.

"Somebody's shooting at us!" shouted Bill.

Not far from the wagon on the hillside, was a mounted man, spurring his horse toward them. The shepherd had not abandoned his still after all.

Another shot rang out, then another, the two rounds stirring up dirt to the right and to the left of the boys.

"Let's get out of here!"

They dropped their treasure, clambered onto their mounts, and galloped back the way they came, not looking back. They did not slow down until they were in the canyon on their own ranch land.

Stopping to let their horses rest, they looked at each other and began to laugh. This was not the first time Eddie had been shot at, nor would it be the last. There was something bracing about it, frightening at the time, but bracing, to be shot at, and missed.

The boys agreed it was best not to tell anyone about their experience, at least not until much later. It turned out the missing steer, a yearling, was at the mouth of the canyon. They had somehow managed to ride right past him earlier. Perhaps he was hiding in a clump of trees, or more likely, they had not been paying close enough attention.

As summer wore on it occurred to the boys that watermelons should be ripe in those places where watermelons were raised for market. Mrs. Thomas had not planted any and it was unlikely she would be going to town any time soon to shop.

"We need a watermelon," said Bill one afternoon as the boys were resting in the shade of a large pine tree planted near the bunkhouse.

"That would be nice, but how would we ever get one out here?" replied Eddie.

Bill leaned forward from the tree trunk. "Well, tomorrow Cal's goin' down to the train stop to pick up some bags of grain. We could go with him, hop the rails, and go to Green River." Green River melons were the best, sweetest, juiciest watermelons in the world.

"Won't we get in trouble for being gone?"

"Nah. Cal can handle everything for a couple days. Then we will be back. We can tell Ma we're going camping."

The boys debated the proposal only briefly before deciding. Tomorrow they would be in Green River.

Cal was skeptical at having the three boys tag along, but when they said Mrs. Thomas had approved and they would not be coming back right away, he shrugged his shoulders and let them climb in the back of the truck for the trip to the train stop.

While Cal was signing for the bags of grain and everyone's back was turned, Bill, Jim, and Eddie jumped up into an open car, carrying their little camp bags and bed rolls. To their surprise, two other passengers were already concealed there, leaning up against crates of merchandise, bound for parts eastward.

"Hello boys," came a deep, gravelly voice. The man was in the shadows, but Eddie could make out a scraggly beard, old fedora pulled down, and a work coat lying by his side. The other man did not speak.

"Hello mister." Eddie had begun to develop a sense of suspicion and at first was apprehensive of these strangers, not knowing if they were safe to be around. He soon realized they were just regular guys. A sorrowful look of loss and desperation was in their eyes, but they were still regular guys.

"Where you headed?"

"Green River. How about you?"

"Anywhere there's work. Maybe Price."

"I'm from Price," said Eddie. "Jobs are mighty scarce there. My brothers are looking for work. Not finding much, last I heard."

"Huh. Maybe we'll go further on. Maybe Colorado."

They rode in silence after that, not having much to talk about. The countryside whizzed past except for stops in Helper, Carbonville, and Price. They all held their breath, hoping they would not be found hiding behind the crates.

It was about three hours to Green River, a small town built along the river by the same name, cliffs to the north, desert to the south, but surrounded by nice farms turned green with irrigation. Once arrived at their destination, the boys made their way to the river's edge for water, then began the search for melons.

CHAPTER 39

1930, Summer. A Night in Jail and Worse

To their dismay, the fruit market was closed. All the markets were closed. The whole town was closed. Losing track of time was a common problem on the ranch; they had lost track of which day it was, and it was Sunday. Everyone was either in church or home asleep.

"What are we gonna do now?" asked Eddie, sweat gathering on his forehead.

The older boys scratched their heads. "I guess find a place to camp. Maybe down by the river."

They made their way back toward the river, passing a particularly nice farm with neat rows of watermelon plants, filled with fruit. The boys walked more slowly as the fruit seemed to call to them, pulling them closer to the field. They stopped. Their eyes were filled with watermelons and their minds were filled with flavor.

"There are so many."

"They sure look good."

"No one would miss one."

"Or two."

"Or three."

Before they could think further, they had entered the field, plucked three fine melons, and were on their way to their campground.

The boys found a grassy spot among the cottonwoods with cattails along the shore. As anticipated, the melons were sweet, juicy, flavorful, and cool, despite the sun overhead. Finishing their meal, they leaned back in the shade and fell fast asleep.

"Looks like we found yer watermelon thieves, George," came a voice.

Eddie and his companions rubbed their eyes and looked up at two men, one a farmer by his looks, with straw hat and overalls, the other a lawman with Stetson on his head, six gun at his side, and star on his chest. Pieces of watermelon rind were scattered all around the little campground.

"Sorry, mister. We, uh, we were thirsty and, uh, hungry, and . . ."

"Can it!" came the reply. "There's always an excuse, ain't there? Did ya really think nobody would see you walkin' down the road with yer arms full of melons?"

The sheriff shook his head, waved his arm, and said, "Well get up. Pick up your stuff. Get walkin'."

Soon they were in a non-descript office, giving their names, addresses, and the names of their parents. The sheriff was on the phone, glancing up every now and then to look at the prisoners in the next room, then returning to his conversation.

"Well," he said to them when he came out, "so we have some celebrity watermelon thieves here it seems.

"That was Matt Warner I was just talkin' to. He's workin' as deputy this weekend while Sheriff Bliss is out of town, and it turns out he knows you." He shook his head again. "The Thomas boys, sons of the county clerk. And young Taylor, Warner knows you too, knows your father, says he's talked to you before."

He shook his head again. "Too late for anyone to come get you tonight. And the last train has gone. I wouldn't trust you on a train anyway, desperadoes like you. So, the only place is the jail. Not much of a place, but it's what we got."

He took a large key ring from a nail on the wall and herded his charges in front of him.

A short distance out of town, well away from any houses or other buildings, stood a weathered, one room square structure of whitewashed cinder blocks with a thick wooden door and bars on its single small window. Nothing grew for acres around it.

"There you go," said the sheriff as he locked the door behind them. "My wife will be over in a little while with some soup for dinner. Mind your manners and be polite! See you in the morning."

The room had a bare dirt floor, no bed or other furniture, and no light. It did have spiders. Too hot when first they entered at the end of day, the cell cooled only a little with the night, and when darkness came, it was very dark indeed. There was a small scratching sound along the north wall. They couldn't tell if it was coming from the outside or the inside, so they crowded their bedrolls as far away as possible, which was not far in so small a room. For Eddie and his companions, it was a long night, one they would not soon forget.

Father did not arrive until noon and by then the little Green River jail was like an oven. The three boys stumbled out gratefully into what seemed like cool fresh air by comparison. Father was stone faced. He did not say a word to them, but pointed to the car door as he went around to the driver's seat.

"Thanks," he said to the sheriff.

"Sure. Good luck." He muttered quietly to himself, "'Sure wouldn't wanna be them boys when they get home."

He chuckled a little. "Come to think of it, I was them boys."

It was quiet in the car at first, then Eddie started, "Father, let me explain. It was hot and we were . . ."

"Shut up! You were supposed to be at the Thomas's helping out on the ranch." He glanced back at his passengers. "All three of you."

"But . . . "

"Shut up!"

The remainder of the trip was passed in silence. Eddie was surprised when they stopped in front of the courthouse rather than go directly home.

"Why are we here?"

There was no answer. Fred Thomas was waiting for them outside the justice of the peace's courtroom. He just shook his head and opened the door. There behind the bench was Matt Warner.

They filed in and sat quietly in front.

"Well, well, well," he started. "'Sorry to see you back here, not as spectators this time. I was wearing my deputy hat last night on the phone, but today I am a judge. Not that it matters. What you did was in Emery County and that's not my jurisdiction, but yer fathers are here, and their jurisdiction is everywhere. 'Better be glad I'm here to adjudicate the mess."

The three boys looked down at their laps. They had thought it would be over by now.

"Look up here. Keep your eyes on me." Warner paused for effect.

"I won't keep you long, then I'll turn you over to the mercy of your fathers. Now, you've all heard me tell about my life on the range. I had a lot of great times, me and Butch and Elza and the others. Once I was riding all bent for leather with a big money belt full of gold slung around my middle. My buddies and I had split up to try to shake the posse, but they kept comin' after me. The only thing between me and freedom and a life of ease with all that gold was the Columbia River.

"The Columbia, it was at high flood, more than a mile wide and raging and boiling with whirlpools and all. I didn't think my horse would go in, but he was a good'n and pretty soon we was in the middle of it. I'd throwed my guns and kit and everything heavy except the gold off to lighten the load. I look back and there's the posse on the bank, still lookin' for me."

By now the boys were on the edge of their seats. They could not look away even if they wanted to.

"I kick my horse on and he tries, but pretty soon we're under, deep in one of them whirlpools and I can't see above the edge of it, and I start gurgling in the water. Just about then I realized that would be the end of Matt Warner.

"The water surged me up a little and I see the posse is shooting and the bullets are splashing all around, with me almost dead for drowning. Well, that outraged me so, I decided I wasn't about to let the river do what no police officer or sheriff could. My pony and I forge on toward the bank. Then I see he's tiring out, can't go on, too much weight.

"I realize the gold in my money belt was too much. I starts tearing at the belt, but it won't come loose and I sees myself being dragged down to the bottom of the river, all for that gold. And I imagine it is like a snake and it's saying to me, 'you loved me more than your wife or children or anything else in the world. Now you and I will be together forever.'

"A thing like that fires yer imagination. It goes clear to the roots of a fellar. It's like the Day of Judgment. And I could hear that gold laughing all the way down. Well, I make one last try. Like a madman I tear at the belt and think to pull my knife out and cut it off. And there it goes, sinking down to the bottom and I'm promising this Judgment and Death thing that if I can only have my life back, I will do the right thing. I will never rob or gun fight again. I will prove myself.

"All this struggle helped clear my head. I look around and see my pony and I are not far from the bank now. A little more effort and we both climbed up on the sand and grass and rested, nearly done. After awhile I could see the deputies on the other side, but they had the good sense not to go into the water after me and by that time I was out of range."

The judge sat back and sighed.

"I suppose that gold is still there. And I suppose it is still laughing. Now look here, remember this. Crime doesn't pay. Not for gold. Not for watermelons."

He looked over at Carl and Fred. "I suppose they are all yours now. But . . ." Now he looked back at the boys. "I understand you spent the night in the Emery County jail."

"Yes Sir."

A faint smile came across his face. "I spent a couple nights in that little box, many years ago. Like a little oven in the summer, icebox in winter. That is quite a punishment for a couple watermelons."

"There were three," volunteered Jim.

"Three watermelons. Of course."

As they were filing out the courtroom door Eddie turned and said, "Thanks for the story, judge. How about during Prohibition? Does crime not pay then too?"

Warner did not have a chance to answer before Father swatted his son across the shoulder. "Don't be impertinent!" He pushed the boy out the door, looked across to the bench, and added, "Sorry, Matt."

"That's all right," came the reply. "Not a bad question."

Father closed the door behind him as Warner added to himself, "Wish I had a good answer."

CHAPTER 40

1930, Fall-1931, Spring.
Middle School Graduation

Father did not say anything more about Green River or Matt Warner and his stories. Eddie did not ask to go back to the ranch. The worst part for Eddie was facing Mother.

"I'm so disappointed," she said. "'So embarrassing. I did not expect this of you."

It was even worse than the night in jail. Eddie kept quiet and was careful to stay out of trouble.

Lizzie called once a week to say how much she enjoyed her job and her friends and living in Provo. Aunt Vilate confirmed all of that and added how nice Lizzie's boyfriend was, a college boy studying to be an engineer.

The odd jobs that normally went to young boys and teenagers were taken up by men who had lost their regular, except for Gus, who had dependable employment at his father's shop. Eddie and Frank and Athena and their friends consoled themselves the rest of the summer with swimming and games, especially their favorite, baseball.

There were also always plenty of chores to do around the house, cleaning and gardening and taking care of this year's sheep. Eddie did not get attached to his sheep anymore. He knew they were just animals, doing what animals do, and destined for what animals are for.

Angela had moved on to high school, so he would not see her as often as in the past, but there were lots of other girls who began to look more attractive to his eyes than they had in the past. Still, he concluded, Angela was the best. When he got to high school, he would tell her so.

All the middle school students had to take a standard test on science. It was Eddie's favorite subject and the test seemed easy. His spare moments were spent reading *Popular Science* and trying out the various projects the authors described. This was much more interesting than homework.

Mr. Howard, his teacher this year, was hands down the worst, even worse than Miss Swenson had been. Eddie was not sure at first what it was he did not like about him. He lectured well enough and seemed to know a lot. That's what a teacher needs to be good at, right?

He seemed a little cold, but it wouldn't be right to hold that against him. Many people were cold. And he couldn't help that he had a hooked nose, was skinny and bony, or that he wore wire rim glasses with small round lenses. Well, that he could change, but the rest was just the way he was.

Then one day as Mr. Howard was pointing out a student's deficiencies, it dawned on Eddie that the teacher was conceited. Yes, conceited. As if his being a teacher and knowing some fact or other made him better than a student who hadn't learned it yet. And his conceit had made him arrogant. Eddie hated arrogance.

So it was that he began to not complete homework assignments, or to not turn them in. He read the books because they actually were interesting and he still loved to learn things, but cooperating with this arrogant teacher was not in Eddie's DNA.

He knew he passed the standard test in science because he was not herded off into the remedial class that the school had organized, but it was not until spring that he saw his actual score, and that was by accident. He and Charlie Pearson, a seventh grader who thought he was bigger than he was, had gotten into a scuffle about whether Babe Ruth or Ty Cobb was the best baseball player who ever lived, and now they were waiting in the principal's office for their punishment.

The principal was in another part of the building, so Eddie quite naturally peeked onto the desk. A file folder was open with the test results and Eddie's name was at the very top. He had the highest marks in science of the whole school. "Well," he thought, "that should be worth something." It turned out not to be worth enough to avoid swats on the bottom with a paddle.

Despite the paddling, he was feeling good about himself when he returned to class and made the mistake of allowing a smile to cross his face. Mr. Howard noted it and looked down at him narrowly through his small-lensed glasses and said, "It is nothing to smile about, Mr. Taylor. Since you won't graduate anyway, you will no doubt return to have more such punishments next year."

He sneered as he added, "You are not even smart enough to get out of middle school."

Not graduating had never occurred to Eddie, nor the thought of having to repeat the eighth grade. Now he knew Mr. Howard was going to flunk him. He felt humiliated and sorry for himself for a time, then thought, "Well, I'll finish this. I'm not going to graduate but will show him I know this stuff. I am smart. Smarter than he is."

Eddie wanted to spend his spare time wandering the streets with Gus and Frank or playing ball. Instead, he plowed ahead on his assignments and finished them, one after another, and put them all together as a stack on Mr. Howard's desk, much to the teacher's surprise.

When graduation time came Eddie was not sure what to do. His parents were going to be in the audience, but he could not face the prospect of not being named among the graduates. Instead of going to school, he hiked down to the river and fished. His parents were waiting for him when he got home.

Mother spoke first. "So, Shirl, why weren't you at graduation?" There was a trembling in her face that was disconcerting to Eddie.

He thought, "What's the big deal? Just middle school graduation."

"I went fishing."

His parents looked perplexed. "Fishing? But why? We looked all around for you, then thought we would see you when they called your name, but you weren't there."

Eddie hung his head. "Because I didn't graduate."

"What do you mean?" asked Father. "Yes, you graduated. They called for you. Twice."

Then Mother added, "Only, they had your name wrong. They called for Edward Taylor. I will have to talk to the school about that, but we were so worried about you we came right home after."

"I changed it."

"Changed what?"

"My name. I changed it."

Now his parents looked even more perplexed. "You changed your name? How?"

"In first grade. I didn't like the name Shirley Edwin, so I told them my name is Edward. It's been Edward or Eddie ever since."

Mother and Father did not know what to say to that.

"Did you say that they let me graduate after all?"

They nodded.

"Huh. How about that!" A great burden seemed lifted from Eddie's shoulders.

For his parents there was nothing more to say. The interview was over. It would take some time and effort to get used to their youngest having a different name.

Their daughter's name was soon changed as well. She was no longer a teenager and had gotten on well with her life. She was married in June to her future engineer. Father decided to drive to Provo for the wedding since most of the road was paved now. Something about weddings and the open road lifted everyone's spirits. The scenery was beautiful, and they still enjoyed singing as they went.

"Oh look," cried Johnny, "a sign." There were not many road signs along the way, so when one appeared it attracted attention.

"It says, 'Tho tough'. What does that mean?"

"I don't know," replied Mother. "But look, here comes another. 'And rough.' Oh, it must be a rhyme. 'Tho tough and rough.' Look for the next."

"There it is," called Eddie, "'From wind and wave'."

"'Your cheek grows sleek'."

"'With'. That is a short one."

"Watch for it," said Father.

"'Burma-Shave!'"

A simple rhyme, but supplying significant entertainment, even for teenagers. "Tho' tough and rough, From wind and wave, Your cheek grows sleek, With Burma-Shave."

"Do you use Burma-Shave, Father?" asked Junior.

"No. Just soap. It works well enough."

Lizzie's wedding was a simple ceremony at one of the Provo churches near the BYU lower campus. Her new husband, Stephen, was a sturdy, talkative fellow with short, curly, red hair and an infectious smile. He easily won over the hearts of his new family.

Taking Junior aside at the reception afterwards, Stephen asked, "Are you still looking for work?"

"Yes. Not much out there in Price."

"You're a hard worker, aren't you?"

"Yes."

"And can follow instructions. Learn fast?"

"You bet."

"Listen, Geneva Steel is going to be hiring. My professor's brother is one of the managers out there and he told me about it. It hasn't been published yet, so nobody knows. If you want, I can give him a call."

"That would be swell."

"Okay. But the jobs will be snapped up. Big lines and all. So, you will need to get down there tomorrow first thing. I will let him know to look for you."

So, Junior stayed behind in Provo and went to work for Geneva Steel, a big mill just north of town. It seemed to Eddie that knowing someone and being ready to say 'yes' could make a big difference in your life.

With one less passenger, the car seemed bigger on the way back to Price. They were not long underway before they encountered another set of signs.

"The one horse shay, Has had its day, So has the brush, And lather way, Use Burma-Shave." They all agreed this one was not as good as the first rhyme they had seen.

CHAPTER 41

1931, Summer-Fall.
Shooting of Sheriff Bliss

"Sheriff Bliss has been shot," came a voice at the door one morning. It was Fred Thomas.

Father pulled on his jacket and grabbed his hat. "How'd it happen?"

"Don't know the details, but we're gettin' a posse together to go after them. It was those three punks they put in the jail yesterday. They stole a car and lit out of town."

The two men were hurrying to Thomas's Studebaker touring car, idling at the curb. Eddie and Johnny hurried after them. "Sorry boys. You have to stay behind."

As the car sped off toward the courthouse the brothers looked at each other and without a word set off at a run in the same direction. A couple dozen ranchers and other available men were gathering on Main, their vehicles parked at various angles. Warner and some other deputies were on the steps. One of them spoke.

"Men, the sheriff was shot straight on by these prisoners as they escaped early this morning. We don't know exactly how he will do. He's at the hospital now and the doctors will do what they can for him. We should all think of him and say a prayer or two.

"As for the hoodlums, we don't know for sure which way they went, but figure they probably headed for Colorado. Now, everyone raise your right hand and repeat after me. . . "

Eddie noticed Father raising his hand along with the other men. After the swearing in, a woman came running out of the courthouse and spoke to the deputy. He turned to address his new posse.

"We just got word that the telephone lines are out between here and Green River and points southeast. Not likely a coincidence. They must have cut them. Everybody armed?"

Most everyone was already carrying a sidearm and those who were not were issued rifles or shotguns from the sheriff's office. Soon the whole lot were streaming off toward the highway while the Taylor boys and other spectators watched and wondered.

There was not much for them to do but go home and wait. Eddie and Johnny agreed it was all wet for them not to be able to go with the posse. After all, they were nearly full grown at fourteen and seventeen years. Eddie decided he would go in search of Gus and see what he was doing. Johnny said he would see him later, said he would go for a stroll, and headed down Main.

Athena was just coming out the door of the Pappas' home with a tray full of pastries covered in tin foil. She was going to the church to help get ready for a celebration. Gus was already there. Eddie walked along with her.

The Greek Orthodox Church was a town landmark with its round dome on top. Gus was setting up chairs in the meeting hall and in the garden next to the church.

"*Ti kanis?*" Eddie called as they approached.

"*Kala,*" Gus replied.

It was the festival of the Virgin Mary's Assumption Day, one of the Greek Church's biggest holidays, and after mass there would be food, dancing, more food, singing, and more food. Eddie loved the Greeks' ability to celebrate and that they had so many holidays to do it on. Add in the Roman Catholic holidays and the Mormon ones, and there was hardly any time left for mundane worries.

Gus had not heard about the sheriff and agreed to remember him in his prayers, in fact, would mention it to the priest. More the better when it came to praying.

Prayer was all well and good, but not the same as doing, and there was not much more for Gus to do at the church. Athena stayed behind to help the ladies cook while the two boys wandered back toward Main to see if there was any news. There was none.

Father returned home next morning, tired and hungry. Most of the posse were still out, but Fred and Carl had tasks that had to be done and could not wait. The criminals had not been caught. It was not until later in the week that word came of their capture in Telluride, Colorado. The sheriff there had them and they were being transported back for trial.

"Good thing for them," said Father. "If we had caught them, they would have been so full of lead no one could carry the caskets."

It had been six years since the lynch mob had done its work. Townsfolk didn't talk about it. After the initial satisfaction with frontier justice for a murderer, the sense had grown that a serious error had been committed, one that reflected lack of thought and lack of reverence for the law. "All emotion and no brain," Warner had said about mobs. Eddie thought that was right, and though a posse was not a mob, sometimes things can get out of hand, even with the best intentions.

Life went on in the meantime. Sheriff Bliss recovered from his wound, though his arm had to be amputated. The whole town was greatly interested when the thugs were brought to trial. The large courtroom was packed. Eddie's friendship with Judge Anderson and Fred Thomas made it possible for him to bring Gus and Frank with him to sit in the audience and hear the whole story.

The three escapees were in jail for robbing a store. It was unclear how or why, but somehow, they were unguarded for a short time during which they broke loose and got hold of one of the office shotguns. When the sheriff came in, they were standing there ready for him. He told them they shouldn't get themselves into any more trouble, but they told him to put his hands up, that they were getting out of there. He knew they were going to shoot him.

"How is that? What made you think they were going to shoot you?" asked the attorney.

"The fellow with the shotgun. His eyes narrowed. They always narrow their eyes just before they shoot. So, I brought my arm down to protect my chest."

"And then he shot you?"

"Yes." He held up his still bandaged stump.

The community's love for Sheriff Bliss had always been strong. Now it was unshakeable.

Eddie started high school and was able to select some of his classes, the electives. For him they were Latin and Algebra.

"Algebra?" asked his father. "What good is that? You have to have a math class, but how about business math or accounting?"

"I need Algebra for science. And to get into college."

"College? You mean keep going after high school? I think you will need to work, Son"

"I know. I'll work part time and go to college too. Lots of people do it."

Father just shook his head and snorted. "Do what you want. Just remember, that'll be another four years or more before you actually make any headway in the world. And Latin?"

"I'll do fine." Father's doubts made Eddie more determined than ever. This will be a good year, much better than eighth grade.

The high school seniors each year repainted a large C on the Wood Hill cliff overlooking town, this year in white with blue trim. Eddie and his companions admired it from below.

"So, what shall our gang do this year?" asked Frank. The three boys were freshmen and the fights and stunts of previous years seemed juvenile. They needed something new. Athena remained silent, not wanting to draw attention to the fact that she was still in middle school.

"Say," asked Eddie, "remember when we were The Flaming Circle Gang?"

"I don't," said Athena.

"It was back when the Klan was burning crosses." Eddie glanced over at Frank. "We, uh, called ourselves that after the circle that was burned."

Changing the subject, Frank asked, "Say, whatever happened to Nick Fulcher, the electrician?"

"I heard he moved," said Gus. "He wasn't too popular."

"Well, anyway, let's do something like that, only this time it'll be a flaming 'F'. F for freshmen."

"Yeah," added Frank. "And bigger. And high up. Higher than the C."

The new freshman gang spent the day busily gathering up cans, rags, and old motor oil. That evening they made their way to the top and set it up, very large and easy to see. It could be seen for miles.

This time their activity on the hilltop attracted attention earlier than before, but not the attention they desired. Some of the seniors saw the blazing F atop their C. They raced up the hill and kicked over the cans, some of which rolled over the cliff.

"Aw, fudge!" exclaimed Gus.

"We should go up and put it back," suggested Athena.

Eddie could dimly see the numbers of young men who were undoing their handiwork. "I don't think so. Besides, this looks pretty spiffy just the way it is."

As the F became disfigured, flaming oil and rags could be seen streaming down the cliff. It was like Independence Day in reverse, with fireworks coming down from the sky to the earth beneath.

"Maybe we will have to think of something else," he added.

CHAPTER 42

1931, Fall-1932, Summer.
School and Riding the Rails

"What do you mean, you aren't going to school anymore?" Father's voice was a mixture of anger and annoyance. He sat very close to Johnny in the parlor, with Mother nearby. Eddie and Grandma Mueller sat in the dining room, eavesdropping.

"I don't need it," replied Johnny.

"What will you do for work?"

"I can find work. All kinds. Plus, I'm lucky."

"What do you mean, 'lucky'? Will luck put food on your table?"

"Yes, it will." Johnny took out his wallet and showed him a roll of bills. "I'm lucky, and I'm really good at cards and all the games."

Father rolled his eyes and sighed.

"But son," interjected Mother. "Luck doesn't last. And the atmosphere. The spirit of where you play."

"What do you know of that?" he retorted.

"Mind your manners!" said Father.

Johnny had been working at Bill's, one of the clubs on Main Street. His parents had willingly believed, or said they believed him when he claimed to be doing janitor work and waiting tables. Eddie knew differently, having peeked in. Between the clouds of cigarette and cigar smoke and scantily clad waitresses, he had seen him not waiting tables, but dealing at them. He had kept the secret, figuring it wasn't his business. Now it was coming out in the open.

"*Ach*," whispered Grandma, "such a shame."

Eddie nodded. She really did say *shame* this time. Johnny was every bit as stubborn as the rest of the family. Father and Mother knew this and shook their heads. They had little choice but to let their nearly grown son decide for himself.

That fall was the first time Eddie saw someone come to the door and ask for food. He was an older man, maybe fifty, with worn coat and cap, unshaven, with sunken eyes. He looked much like the men he saw on the train to Green River.

Mother hesitated at first, not sure what to say, then told the man to go around to the back, that he could do chores while she got him some lunch. There, she set him to work raking leaves and gathering sticks. The leaves would be burned in a barrel; the sticks would be useful for kindling in the coal stove. Soon she served him a bowl of hot soup, a roast beef sandwich, and a cup of coffee. He looked like he had not eaten in a couple days.

Soon after that first man came to the door, another came, and another. It became a regular event, every few days. Eddie realized there were many men of all ages wandering through town. They would get off the train in waves and look for work. When that failed, they would offer to do chores for food or simply beg.

Father came up behind Eddie one day as he stood on the front porch, watching a fresh group of men walking into town in the distance.

"Looks like another trainload of hoboes, son."

"Yeah. There are so many of them."

"Yes. Hard times. Hard times come to everybody eventually. Now they are coming to nearly the whole nation." He sighed. "Did you clean the curb?"

The hoboes put a chalk mark on the curb in front of houses where they were given food, to let others know it was a good, safe place to work or beg.

"Yes, but it doesn't seem to do much good."

"No. I suppose not." Father was silent for awhile, then added quietly, almost to himself, "It's alright. We have food enough to share. That could just as easily be me out there."

Eddie turned out for football. Uniforms consisted of old jerseys, whatever shoes they could round up, and leather helmets. There was no padding. Practices were held on the playing field between the schools, a dirt and gravel lot with makeshift boundaries. He learned very quickly not to land hard on the ground, especially not face first. Being a fast runner helped and he was picked as quarterback.

High school also increased the occasional glimpses of Angela, still his model of perfection. He decided to ask her out and very nearly did so one weekend, but then she was out of town with the band.

Music had always been an important part of life in Price with church choirs and bands and barber shop quartets. These resources became focused at the high school when Mr. Williams became music director. Within a short time, the bands became larger, their music better, and their precision marching more precise. That year the Carbon High School Band went to Evanston Illinois for the national competition and won first place. All who attended agreed the contest was not even close.

1932 was supposed to be graduation year for Johnny. Instead, he was working or playing full time at Bill's. For the rest of the country the depression, which should have been over by then, was reaching its worst. When summer came Eddie was at a loss to know what to do for work. He could work at the Thomas ranch, but there was no pay, just room and board. The mines were not hiring, in fact were letting people go.

He remembered what fun the circus was each year, and how the ringmaster had said he should work for him some day. He could run a booth or take care of the animals or clean or something. The schedule was on a poster outside Gus's father's shop. They weren't scheduled to come to Price until the end of summer again. Until then they were in Montana, Wyoming, and Colorado.

"June," he said to himself. "They're still in Wyoming." Another imprudent idea was forming in his mind.

He knew Mother would object, and probably Father too. It seemed like he objected to everything Eddie wanted to do, ever since he hit high school. So, he wrote a note. It read, "Have gone to work for the circus. Don't worry. Will be back by fall. Love, Eddie." Then he slipped out the back door and walked briskly to the train tracks.

He did not have long to wait. Passenger trains were infrequent, but there were many freight trains. A lot of people were riding the rails, so many that the engineers did not even bother to search the cars anymore, though they would throw you off if they stumbled on to you or you got in the way. He soon found himself with a half dozen men of various ages in an otherwise empty cattle car.

There was no talking. Not much to talk about, Eddie supposed, and when the train got up to speed it was too noisy to hear anyway, between the wind and the clanking of the wheels. He huddled in a corner, pulled down his cap, and fell asleep.

He was shivering when he woke up. "Where are we?"

One of the men answered, "Somewhere in Colorado. In the mountains."

A sinking feeling filled him. "Colorado? I want to go to Wyoming."

"Wrong train. You should have gotten the one on the other side, heading northwest. It curves around east into Wyoming. This one headed southeast, then goes east across the plains."

Peeking out between the slats, he could see the sides of mountains go by, with clumps of snow between the pines. "What now?" he thought. He reached into his bag and took out a canteen. As he put it to his lips, he could see his travelling companions looking steadily at him and realized they must be thirsty too. "Anybody want a drink?"

The canteen made its way from hand to hand, coming back nearly empty to Eddie, followed in turn with "Thanks" and accompanied by a cough or clearing of the throat.

"Wyoming, huh" said the man who had spoken first.

"Yeah," replied Eddie. "How about you?"

"Doesn't matter. Anywhere. Looking for work?"

"Yeah."

"Good luck." They rode in silence for a time. "Where abouts in Wyoming? Any particular place?"

"Yeah. Rock Springs."

"Rock Springs. That's in southeast Wyoming. You can change trains in Denver. Big station. Just find one on a north-south line instead of east-west. Make sure the engine is pointed north."

"Thanks."

"Sure. Then, when you get to Cheyenne, you gotta change trains again, heading west."

"Okay." He carefully reviewed the geography in his mind. "'Wish I had a map," he thought.

The man read his thoughts and smiled. "After a while, travellin' sorta' makes a map inside your brain."

Late in the day Eddie was greatly tempted to pull out the sandwich he had packed, or the apple, but looking around at the men in the car, he decided against it. He knew they were hungry too and it would be awful to eat with them all watching, and there wasn't enough to share. Time passed very slowly.

They did not arrive in Denver until the middle of the next day. Most of the men got off and wandered away to see what they could find. The man who gave directions grunted a goodbye, then added, pointing across the rail yard. "Over there if you still want Wyoming."

"Thanks." Eddie started to leave, then turned, reached into his bag, and tossed him the apple. "I appreciate the help."

Denver was a lot bigger than Salt Lake City, the biggest city Eddie had ever seen, though he could not see much of it from where he was. It had the biggest, busiest station he could imagine. Following the man's direction, he came to where the tracks he had been on crossed others at right angles, stepping over the switch points and watching every way to avoid the trains.

One of the engineers saw him and yelled to get out. He said he would and hurried on, ducking behind a shed, then hopping on the first open car he could find. This was not as crowded as the last one, with only two men, similar to the others with old work clothes, hats at angles, unshaven. One of them was pulling on a cigarette butt he had found.

Eddie offered a cheery, "Hello." They nodded in return. Eddie decided It would be a quiet trip. Though hunger was starting to get to him, he thought it best not to take out his sandwich.

This train was agonizingly slow, stopping in every little town along the way, or so it seemed. Boulder, Greeley, Fort Collins. Another day had passed. His corner in the car was hard and cold, but he slept anyway. When he awoke next morning the two men were gone. He eagerly reached for his bag to retrieve the sandwich. It was gone too.

CHAPTER 43

1932, *Summer.*
The School of Hard Knocks

By the time he reached Cheyenne, Eddie realized he was in a desperate situation. His first concern was water; he was absolutely parched. He stumbled out of the car and began his search. It did not take long. There were corrals and pens at the rail yard for animals going to market. And where there were animals there had to be water.

Eddie put his face into the cold, slightly discolored water of a horse trough and let it pour down his throat. It had a little more flavor than he liked in water. Catching his breath he thought, "Drinking like a horse from a trough!" he thought. If it weren't so satisfying it would have been embarrassing. He filled his canteen.

Food was another matter. He was not to the point of begging on the streets. Besides, if he hurried on his way, he would get to Rock Springs sooner, get to work, and be able to support himself. The circus fed their employees well, together in a meal tent.

This train was even slower than the last he had been on, stopping at every little town along the way. Each stop saw one or two men get off and even more get on. Eddie now followed the general pattern of not talking much. Between the bad breath, unwashed clothes, stale tobacco, and body odor, it was best to stay in his corner, not that his own smells were any better, but there was a nice little space between the slats that let in the cold fresh air.

Next day, somewhere between Elk Mountain and Fort Steele, the train made an unexpected stop. Eddie looked out. There was no town and no real station, only a camp with tents and a couple dozen soldiers and official looking men in long white coats who directed them.

"Everybody out!"

The soldiers went from car to car, rousting out the travelers and having them form lines next to the train.

"Government clean up," shouted one of the men in white coats. "Everybody has to be cleaned."

The men were directed first to an open area where they were told to strip, then given cold showers while their clothes were dusted with powder.

"What's that?" asked someone.

"DDT. Kills lice, fleas, most every creepy crawly on you."

After washing and de-lousing, Eddie and the others were herded behind another tent where the most wonderful fragrance filled the air. Cook stoves were set up and there were tables with folding chairs. Not enough, of course, so they had to eat in shifts.

Eddie could hardly wait. He was given a plate with two large pancakes and a little syrup on top. His stomach growled and even in his present dry state his mouth filled with saliva. That first bite was so delicious, he chewed quickly and swallowed. To his dismay the swallow hit with a thud at the bottom of his shrunken stomach. It felt like lead.

He took another forkful and raised it to his mouth but could not take it. The great lump in his stomach was too much. He trembled a little, put down the fork, rose, and went to the edge of the eating area. There he bent over and threw up the bite of pancake along with bile. Looking to his side, he saw that he was not alone.

Eddie had mixed feelings when the train continued its journey. He was glad to smell a little better than he did before, and he sorely wished he could have eaten, but that opportunity was gone. Things would be better at the circus.

As scheduled, the circus was still at Rock Springs. They were packing up their things to move to their next location when Eddie arrived.

"Work? You mean you came all the way from Price, Utah, to come work for us?" The ringmaster looked pained.

"All these years I've told kids they should come work for the circus. You're the first one to take me up on it."

"I'm a good worker, Sir. I'll do a good job."

The ringmaster looked pained again. "I'm sorry, Son. We don't have any jobs. Just trying to get by ourselves, working extra to get by. I'm real sorry."

Eddie did not know what to say. He was dumbfounded. All that travel, so hungry and thirsty and tired, and there was nothing to show for it.

"Tell you what, Son. The canteen tent is still up. You go over, tell the gal there that Harry sent you and you can have whatever you want to eat and drink. Okay?"

"Thank you, Sir."

Eddie had learned his lesson about eating after going without for a long time. He ate slowly and carefully, drinking a cup of tea first to soothe the system, then a little soup and bread. This time it stayed down.

What was he to do now? He had no money, no bag, no work. Nothing.

"Only one thing for it," he said to himself. "I gotta' go home." He sighed as he said it, dreading the homecoming, the criticism for how he left, the failure of returning empty handed.

The trip back was faster than the trip out, now that he knew the routes better. Standing in front of his home, he took a deep breath, and walked up the steps to open the front door.

Mother saw him first. Her eyes brightened as she threw her arms around him. "Thank heavens you are safe!"

Then she wept, which Eddie found painful. He patted her shoulders. "Yes, I'm fine. 'Sorry about being gone, Mother."

"Not another word. Just that you're safe."

Grandma Mueller, hearing the greeting, ran in from the kitchen. *"Ach, der schoene Sohn! Mein Shirl!"* She joined in the hug.

He wanted to get the hardest part over with. "Is Father at work?"

Mother sniffed. "No, it's Sunday." She paused, led him into the parlor and sat down. "But you don't know, do you? Couldn't know."

"Know what? Is Father all right?"

"Oh yes, he is fine. It's your brother, Johnny. He's gone missing and your father is out looking for him.

"We didn't think anything of it on Friday when he didn't come home at night. We thought he was out, you know. Well, then he didn't come home on Saturday and we started to worry. So, your Father went over to that club where he works, Bill's, and they said they hadn't seen him, that he had missed his shift.

"So now your father is out trying to find him. The Thomases and Johnsons and Andersons are all helping. We've called everyone we know that he might go to, everyone who has a phone, but . . . " Mother sniffed again. "And to have both of you gone. It was just too much. Thank heavens you are back." She gazed at him with wide eyes glistening with tears.

It was evening when Father returned. They had not had any luck in their searches. He hugged his youngest. "Glad to see you're home, Son. Just, so good to see you."

They sat around the dining room table. Father continued, "It seems the last anyone saw Johnny was at work on Friday evening. Manager said nothing was unusual. A few rowdies. He had to intervene to protect the girls, but nothing odd about that. A lot of gambling, some pretty high stakes."

He shook his head slowly. "I just don't know."

Later that night the household was awakened by a loud knock at the door. It was Bishop Johnson. "We found him," he said. "He's at the hospital now."

Around midnight Mother and Father and Eddie sat with Doc Williams in the waiting room of the little Price Hospital. "He'll be okay," the doctor said. "It will take some time. Broke a few ribs, a small pneumothorax—that's air around the lung, a cracked skull. That was the greatest worry, and probably why he was out for so long. But he's doing okay now, and we'll keep an eye on him for the next few days, maybe a week or two."

There was not much else to do but go home and let everyone sleep and the nurses do their job. Johnny's recovery was uneventful. He had been found in a ditch a few blocks south of Main by a janitor dumping a bucket of used grease. At first, he thought Johnny was just a drunk and he kicked him to move out of the way, but then he saw the blood. Another day in the ditch and he wouldn't have made it.

Despite repeated questioning, including very insistent questions from Sheriff Bliss, Johnny refused to say who had beat him up. Eddie wondered why he wouldn't talk about it, why he didn't want help getting back at the thugs. He guessed that some things were best left unasked and unsaid.

A few days later, Father took Eddie aside and said, "Shirl, I have a job opening for the summer. Just part-time, cleaning, moving boxes and crates around, loading. You can have it if you want."

"Yes, Sir. That would be swell. You know, I just want to be useful. And save money for college."

"I know, Son. You report tomorrow and we'll put you to work." It was not until many years later that Eddie learned there really was no job. Father simply paid him out of his own money and made do with less himself.

CHAPTER 44

1932, Summer-Fall.
The Cosmopolitan Club

The garden was very productive that year, possibly because there were fewer small children and more adults taking care of it. One afternoon Eddie, Frank, Gus, and Athena went to play catch in the playing field between the schools, but found the field already occupied by a team they did not recognize.

The gang watched them practice. They perked up their ears as they heard the strangers talking. It seemed these were professionals, a farm team, and they actually were paid to play baseball. Frank recognized one of them, a new neighbor who had moved into a small apartment.

"Which one is your neighbor?" asked Athena.

Frank pointed at the first baseman. "That's him. A real nice guy." Then he pointed over at the bleacher where some of the wives of the players were watching. "That's his wife in the first row, the pretty lady holding a baby."

Eddie thought she looked awfully thin. He thought of the men he saw on the train, how thin and hungry they were. It occurred to him that though it was great to be paid to play ball, they probably were not paid much. Then he remembered what his father had said, "That could just as well be me."

The team practiced a few more runs, then left to take a break. Eddie and his friends started onto the field. Eddie stopped and said, "Let's do something else. I have an idea."

He led his companions back toward his father's garden. They loaded up grocery bags with tomatoes, squash, and all sorts of vegetables, as well as some of the early fruit from the orchard. Then they went over to Gus's house to do the same.

Arriving at the home of Frank's new neighbor, the young woman who was watching the ball practice answered the door.

"A welcome gift," proclaimed Frank. "Welcome to Price."

The woman seemed embarrassed. "We really are not bad off," she mumbled, but received the gift gladly and thanked them. Eddie and his friends smiled broadly at each other as they walked back toward their homes.

The Taylor household settled back into a more nearly normal routine as the remainder of 1932 passed. It had been an eventful year for them, the country, and the world. The first of many big dust storms swept the Midwest. The Yankees won the pennant again. Amelia Earhart flew across the country. Governments changed in Germany, Greece, and the United States.

Except for Republican Sheriff Bliss, who was much beloved, the Democrat election sweep of the nation was matched in Carbon County. Lack of progress dealing with the depressed economy and glowing promises made by the optimism-inspiring Roosevelt, condemned the Hoover administration to a single term.

Father and Judge Anderson could only shake their heads. "The answer isn't more government," said the judge.

"No. That seems to be what the people want, though. I suppose that's what they'll get."

"You mean, in a democracy people get the government they deserve, not the one they need?"

"Something like that."

Eddie's mind was more focused on football and schoolwork, which was just as well. His adventure riding the rails made him appreciate the blessings of home life; little things like clean water, the garden, trustworthy companions. Politics seemed far removed from these things. It was thinking about these homely matters that gave Eddie his next great idea.

He loved to eat. Not just anything, which was fine enough when you are really hungry, he liked to eat different kinds of food, German or Arab with his own family, as well as Greek, Italian, or French food that other families cooked, anything that was made rich and flavorful.

That fall a trucker hit an elk out on the highway, and rather than let it go to waste, it was donated to the community. A great pit was dug, and the animal was roasted on a spit. This one was done American style, just roasted with salt and pepper. It was all good.

Eddie was chewing a piece of elk and seeing how happy and friendly everyone was with their food, Democrats and Republicans, Italians and Greeks, Orientals and Bohunks. It seemed this was one of those things that really brought people together.

"We should re-name our club," he said to Gus, Frank, and Athena.

"Do we still have a club?" asked Frank.

"Well, yeah. We pal around and do stuff, right? That's a club."

They all agreed. Eddie continued, "We should focus on good food, food from around the world." He pointed at the boys in turn. "We could eat Greek at your place, Italian at yours, and German and Arab at mine. Maybe we could expand the club and get others too."

"That sounds good," replied Gus greasily between chews. "So, what's the name? The Food Club?"

"Nah. We need something fancier than that."

"If we have all kinds of foreign food, we could call it the International Dinner Club," suggested Frank.

"That's pretty good." He thought a little longer. "That's formal and descriptive, but maybe something a little more glitzy. How about The Cosmopolitan Club? Really uptown."

"Yeah."

"Yeah."

So, The Cosmopolitan Club was born, with the help of their respective mothers, who agreed to cook. It was, they reasoned, a good way to keep the boys off the streets, and they would be cooking anyway.

One day after scrimmage Eddie was walking off the field toward the school when Jimmy Curtis stopped him. He viewed his long-time adversary apprehensively. They had not spoken to each other in years, avoided each other in the halls, and ran in different circles. Now they were face to face.

"Taylor, did you and your buddies give some bags of vegetables to a lady over on Second Street?"

"Yeah. What of it?"

Jimmy bit his lip. "That's my cousin."

"Oh no," thought Eddie as he replied, "What's the matter with that?"

Jimmy continued, "I just . . . well, I just want to say 'thank you'." He stuck out his hand.

Eddie took his hand and shook it. "Sure. I thought . . . "

Jimmy moved his head side to side. "We wanted to help, and tried, but . . . things have been kinda' tough all around. You know."

"Yeah. I know. Glad to be able to help." He shook his hand again and started to leave.

"One other thing," added Jimmy, jerking his head toward the field. "You're a really good quarterback. That game against Provo was great."

Eddie smiled. "Thanks."

"So!" thought Eddie. "That's an interesting turn of events. You just never know."

He turned again and asked, "Say Jimmy, how would you like to join our club?"

"What club?"

"The Cosmopolitan Club. We get together once a month, chip in a little for supplies, and have dinner at a different member's house. It's food from different countries, where our ancestors came from. We have Greek, Italian, all kinds. It's good fun and tastes good too."

Jimmy looked down. "We don't cook anything fancy. Just American."

"That's okay. America is a country too. Good ol' Yankee food."

"Mom is a good cook."

"Well, it's settled then. Welcome to the club."

The Cosmopolitan Club had its newest member, and Jimmy was right. His mother was a very good cook.

Eddie caught glimpses of Angela now and then, but he could not bring himself to speak to her, other than to say "hello", certainly not ask her out. "So beautiful!" he thought. "And so smart!"

Of course, Eddie realized there were other girls. Was it possible they were all pretty? Even Athena wore skirts and dresses now and had let her hair grow a little longer, long enough for finger waves. They still counted her as part of the club, even if she didn't dress or look like a boy so much anymore. There was some discussion of allowing more girls in, but that was tabled. If there were too many members, the mothers might object to cooking.

CHAPTER 45

1933, Summer-Fall.
Eddie's Third Mob

Father was shaking his head while listening to the radio. The president was speaking, vowing to put an end to the depression and saying "We have nothing to fear but fear itself."

"Nonsense," said Father. "There are lots of things to fear other than fear. And fear can be pretty healthy, a normal response to things. Otherwise, you can blunder ahead and make stupid decisions."

It seemed like each week brought a new program, a new government agency to deal with this or that part of the national condition. Not all the new administration's actions were met with disdain by the Republicans in Price. Relief was provided where state and local resources had been exhausted, and it really was needed.

"But what of the future?" asked Father rhetorically. "What happens when the relief ends? What happens if all these people become dependent on the government dole?" He shook his head a lot these days. "Handouts are not the same as pay for productive work," he said. "Productive work, mind you, not useless make-work."

There was more head shaking a few weeks later as Grandma read a letter from her cousin in Germany. She began to weep. "*Ach*," she said, "*es schmerzt*. It hurts."

Her cousin told how the government had banned any speaking or writing that disagreed with their official statements, had outlawed all political parties except the National Socialists, had paraded Jews through the streets and mocked them and hit them. They were scapegoats.

"This new fellow, the Chancellor, what's his name? Hitler." said Judge Anderson as he was visiting with Father one evening. "It seems the Germans love him, even though he's Austrian."

"Yes. He makes them feel better," replied Father. "Repudiated the debt payments from Versailles, rebuilding industry, and so forth. Likes to stand in front of big crowds and talk loudly."

"Yes. A 'big' man. Like Mussolini."

"And Stalin."

"Yes," said the judge, then added wryly, "Now don't add FDR to the list or I'll have to report you." The two men chuckled.

"I just don't understand how so many people can be swept up in this so quickly," added Father. "And the Germans of all people. They're smart, logical, traditional."

"I know. It doesn't make much sense. Then again, the world often doesn't make sense. Right?"

"Right."

Eddie, listening in, knew this must be important. His Civics teacher might ask about it, but it seemed very much something "out there" and far away, not directly connected to him and his life.

He enjoyed Civics. That early reading in McGuffy's Readers and children's history books at home served him well. Still, he was always struck by how well the Greek and Italian kids did. Gus could recite the Gettysburg Address with fewer mistakes than Eddie, even though

Eddie was raised on it and his grandfather was there when Lincoln said it.

Perhaps the children of immigrants felt a special need to study hard to fit in. Perhaps their parents, still mostly old country themselves, pushed their children to be part of their new culture. Perhaps it was just in the air. One thing was certain, their time together in school and on the playing fields had blended them better than any number of laws or special programs could have.

Eddie worked the summer of 1933 on the Thomas ranch. There were no other hired hands, just Bill and Jim and him. It was different from when he was just there as a friend—more work and harder, but with a little pocket money besides room and board. No matter, it was beautiful, and he loved the horses and cattle and countryside.

Every few weeks he returned home for the weekend. It was on one of those visits that Mother told him about Johnny. "He's gone," she said with a sniff. "He had gone back to work at Bill's, you know. 'Always seemed a little nervous, ever since he was in the hospital. Then, two weeks ago, he said he was moving to Montana. Said there's work up there."

"I think he was trying to get away from something," added Father. "Or someone. Anyway, we got this from him yesterday." Father handed him a letter. Johnny wrote that he was well and was working in a roadhouse outside of Billings. He could receive mail at the post office, General Delivery. It was a short letter and didn't say anything about his living arrangements.

"Well," said Eddie, "at least he's okay. And he found work. That's really something these days."

"Yes, it is." Father continued, "You know, Shirl, with just you at home now, the house is kind of quiet. Your mother and I were thinking of moving back to Provo, to be closer to the rest of the family."

Eddie's mind flashed to football, Gus and Frank and Athena, the club, Angela. "But school is here, and . . ." Athena?

"We know. And there's no rush of course."

"What about the warehouse?"

"Karl could take it over. Business is slow. I am sure the office would let me work out of Provo, especially now that most everyone has a phone."

There wasn't much more to say. Father watched Eddie as he left the room. He was concerned about his son. Price had been good to them, and they were surrounded by friends, but there was no substitute for family. Lizzie, Junior, and most of the rest of the family were in Provo and Spanish Fork. It would be good to be back with them, especially now, during hard times. Good for Eddie too.

Carl reached for the cigar in his breast pocket, then glanced toward the kitchen where his wife was preparing dinner. He loved her so. He loved how strong her faith was. He patted the pocket. Times were changing, the world was changing. Maybe it was time to give up smoking and become more active at church. "She would like that," he thought. "Yes, maybe it's time."

As for Eddie, he felt like a cloud was over him the rest of the summer, but they did not move that year.

The miners were increasingly discontented. Relief from the government was too slow and too little for them. Plus, union organizers were back again, led by Frank Bonnaci. By the time summer ended and school started another strike had been called. The governor recalled the violence of 1922 and acted quickly. The National Guard was sent in. Machine guns were set up again outside the courthouse.

One noon in early September the steam whistle sounded as usual. Gus and Athena headed home for lunch, while Eddie and Frank walked over to Frank's father's store to buy candy bars. It was a general store with supplies of all sorts. To their surprise there was a line at the counter.

"What's going on?" asked Frank.

"Miners coming," came the reply. "Lots of 'em."

A steady stream of men came in to buy ammunition. Townsfolk mostly, some with connections to the miners, some without. It seemed everyone was armed.

"Let's go see," said Eddie. Frank needed no prodding. Missing an afternoon of school seemed a small price to pay to watch the action, more "history in the making." The boys hurried over to the courthouse, entered the back way, and walked up to Judge Anderson's office. Bill and Jim were already there with several others. The judge was gone. No one seemed to know where.

It seemed strange to Eddie, so much like eleven years earlier. Deja vu, that was it. Machine guns, soldiers, officials looking worried and, well, official. Not much time passed before they could see cars parking at the far end of town. A large group of men and women, four, five, maybe six hundred of them, began marching twelve to fifteen abreast up Main Street. They were stopped a block from the courthouse by a row of policemen, deputies, and Sheriff Bliss.

Observers in the courthouse could not hear what was said, only low murmuring and noise from the crowd, but learned later that the sheriff had told them to disperse, that no good could come from being there, and he didn't want any trouble.

Leaders of the strike didn't care what he wanted and replied, "We're going through," and directed the mob to keep marching. The sheriff waved his hat with his good arm. Guardsmen on either side fired tear gas into the crowd while the sheriff and his deputies stepped back. The demonstrators tripped and fell as they covered their faces and tried to walk on through the gas. Some picked up the smoke grenades and threw them back at the guardsmen.

This was followed by great gusts of water from water cannons fired by the police. Men and women went sliding and slipping and falling now in every direction, striking the pavement hard. Officers plowed into the crowd, hitting the demonstrators with their rifle butts as they went and pushing them back down the street to their cars.

Eddie noticed a man with a movie camera on one of the rooftops. "Well," he thought, "I guess this mob won't soon be forgotten."

The guardsmen seemed young to Eddie, not much older than he was, and many of them were smiling, like they enjoyed what they were doing. He could not help feeling sorry for the demonstrators. They were wrong, of course, weren't they?

The union agitators were communists, after all— Bolsheviks, socialists, troublemakers. Mobsters, taking advantage of the fact that mobs have a lot of emotion and no brain. Just like Stalin, Lenin, Mussolini, and this new guy, Hitler, only on a small scale, taking advantage of a situation to gain power, to be 'big' men.

And yet, the strikers themselves, these men and women seemed so desperate, so thin, so fragile. This was different from 1922, Eddie decided. These people didn't look like a bunch of Greeks, Italians, and Bohunks. They just looked like Americans.

"I've seen enough," he said as he left.

CHAPTER 46

1933, Fall. Life and Death in Perspective. Kala.

He walked slowly back toward home, avoiding Main and going around past the tabernacle and the Catholic Church. With so much going on in the world and even here at home, perhaps it was time to get on with his life. Maybe it was time to ask Angela out, before she got too far into her senior year and made other plans. She had not been at school that day, so he decided to stop at her house. The judge and Mrs. Anderson were coming out the door when he arrived.

"Oh, I'm sorry, Eddie." said Mrs. Anderson when he asked for Angela. "She's been sick. We took her to the hospital yesterday and they just called to say they are transferring her to Salt Lake for an operation. Appendicitis. Say a prayer for her."

"I will, Mrs. Anderson."

When he got home, he wandered into the backyard. He had not raised a sheep in the last couple years; the pen stood empty. The apples and pears in the orchard were nearly ripe and the garden was still in full production, with tomatoes and squash and other vegetables. He leaned over a tomato plant and took a deep breath. How he loved that good fragrance. His eyes were filled with the green abundance of the earth, with living things of all sorts.

The next two days passed slowly for Eddie, hoping for word of Angela. He said his prayers as requested, and others in church did as well. But when the Andersons returned, they could see from their faces that it was not good news.

"We were too late," said the judge. "She didn't make it to Salt Lake, died en route."

Eddie was as devastated as if he had been a member of the family. He had thought so much about her and in the end had not even talked with her, not really. He blushed to remember the kiss he had stolen so many years ago.

He asked Mother if he could go out to the ranch for the weekend.

"Certainly, Son," she replied. "After working all summer, I would have thought you had had enough for one year."

"Yeah, I suppose. I'd like to go riding, out in the hills. You know, to think."

Mother smiled her smile of reason. She looked so much like Grandma, only younger.

The Thomas's did not expect Eddie to do much in the way of chores when he visited. It was just for the weekend, but when he quietly went about the work, they let him. They saw he was down, and besides, they were cowboys and cowboys don't talk much if they don't have to.

Saturday afternoon he rode out in the hills, said he would be back for dinner, that he wanted to go up canyon to see the sheep. He rode along quietly, enjoying the early fall color as he rose in elevation. Passing the Thomas ranch boundary, he came to the grassy rolling upland where he and the Thomas boys had been shot at a few years earlier when they found the still.

Sheep were there, several flocks scattered over the hillsides. An occasional soft clang told him the location of the bellwethers, older sheep who knew their way around the hills; the shepherds tied a bell around their necks so the rest of the flock knew where they were and could follow. He let his mount graze while he leaned up against a rock. His eyes searched over the countryside.

Why was time moving so fast now? Life was not nearly so fast when he was little; now it seemed season followed season ever more quickly, one year after another. So much had happened, he thought. So many people were gone. Angela. And earlier, Grandpa, the twins, Mr. Frandsen, Marshall, and all those men in the mine. So many coffins.

He supposed he should cry but could not. He felt sorry for those who were gone, sorry for their families, and especially sorry for himself. There were things he should have said, things he should have done. There was something else nagging at him, something he was forgetting in all this, something he did not understand. He couldn't quite put his finger on it.

As he sat thinking, a large old ram watched him from one of the flocks. He detached himself from the others and walked over, sniffing the air as he went his bell sounding softly with each step. Reaching Eddie and standing close, he nudged his shoulder.

"Go away."

The ram butted a little harder and bleated.

"Oh, can't you see I'm feelin' sorrowful? Go away." He looked up to see the intruder.

"You are a fine ram, aren't you?" He admired his long curved horns, white face, and thick wool. "And an old one, I think, from the length of your horns."

Then he noticed the small tuft of black wool on his right cheek.

"Lambie?" he asked in disbelief. "Is that you?"

Lambie bleated and pushed his face into Eddie's chest.

"You're still alive! After all this."

Eddie threw his arms around Lambie's neck and buried his face in his wool. He took a deep breath. There it was—the good smell of life.

Now he could cry. Now he wept. And now he remembered what it was he was trying to think of. Everything has a purpose. Everything is useful. Life and death, hunger and thirst, good and bad. All of it is bound up together like a book. All of it is important. All of it is part of our education and testing.

Looking into Lambie's eyes, he recited a poem he had read in a McGuffey's Reader, "All things bright and beautiful, All creatures great and small, All things wise and wonderful, The Lord God made them all." Then he stopped. "I can't remember the rest. 'Sorry.

"But I do remember Mother's favorite hymn, 'For the beauty of the earth, For the beauty of the skies, For the love that from our birth, Over and around us lies, Lord of all to thee we raise, This our hymn of grateful praise.'"

He lingered there by the rock, stroking Lambie, until the shepherd strolled up.

"You like my ram?" The man had a strong accent. Probably Basque, thought Eddie.

"Oh yes, he and I are old friends."

The shepherd looked doubtful. "Well, he's best ram in flock. See all those over there?" He pointed to a large flock. "They are all his."

"I'm really glad to hear it. You see, I raised him when he was a lamb."

The shepherd looked doubtful again.

"Really, I recognize him from the spot on his cheek. Isn't that right Lambie?" Lambie bleated. "He was a bummer."

Eddie looked up at the man and stood. "Really. The owner, the guy who bought him, his name is . . . What was it? Started with a B. Bill, right?"

"That right. Boss named Bill." He looked at Eddie a little closer. "Huh. Well, lamb turn out nice. Best old ram we got. Not stupid like other sheep. Like he knows what you think, what you want him to do."

"So, little Lambie grew up to be useful, just like he was supposed to."

The shepherd replied, "Yes. He useful. Good ram."

Lambie nuzzled Eddie's leg once more. He looked up at him and Eddie imagined he smiled, if sheep could smile, then he walked slowly back to his flock.

"That's right, Lambie, take care of your flock. Be useful for good." He looked up at the darkening sky and said goodbye to the shepherd. "I need to hurry back, or I'll be missed."

As he rode back to the ranch he thought of Mother's favorite hymn again, but now another verse came to mind and he sang it out loud, "For the joy of human love; Brother, sister, parent, child; Friends below and friends above; For all gentle thoughts and mild. Lord above, to thee we raise, this our hymn of grateful praise."

When he arrived home, Eddie first hugged his mother. "Thank you," he said.

"Thanks for what?"

"Just, thanks for being you."

"Well," she laughed. "You're welcome. And thanks for being you, too."

She was relieved to see Eddie feeling so much better. Something about being in the country, she supposed.

He realized more than ever that life could be unpredictable, and it could be short. He had wondered about why things happen the way they do in life. He did not know the answers, but he knew enough for now, enough to carry on. He knew it was not enough just to watch history in the making, to be a bystander. Sometimes you had to be the one making it, even if it was only on a small, personal scale.

He also knew that being a straight talker meant you had to talk at least some, not with many words like the politicians, but some words, right words, at the right time, because some things needed to be said. Besides, he knew Father and Mother were thinking about moving, whenever the time seemed right to them. And he might not be this way again for a long time.

Monday after school he washed up, combed his hair, and set off for Gus's. He wanted to be sure the people in his life who meant the most to him knew it, before anything else happened.

Gus's mother answered the door. "Gus, he not here. At church, Greek School."

"That's okay, Mrs. Pappas." He cleared his throat. "Is Athena here?"

Hearing her name, Athena peeked around the corner and tipped her head quizzically.

"*Ti kanis?*"

"*Kala!*"

Notes

Descriptions of many of the events told in *Growing Up Tough* are available at online history sites as well as history books about Utah, Carbon County, and the American coal mining industry. A particularly useful text is *A History of Carbon County,* by Ronald G. Watt, Carbon County Commission, 1997. Conditions in the coal camps and early 20th century medical practices are described in *Confessions of a Coal Camp Doctor,* by J. Eldon Dorman, MD, Peczuh Printing Co., 1995.

Matt Warner's stories were an important influence on the young people of Price. Wherever possible I quote or paraphrase his actual words from *Last of the Bandit Riders. . . Revisited,* by Matt Warner, updated by Joyce Warner and Dr. Steve Lacy, Big Moon Traders, 2000. The mob in Ellensburg is described in that text on pages 106ff, his fight as a youth that started him on the outlaw trail on pages 8-9, and his crossing the Columbia River and losing his gold on pages 95-98. There are numerous online sources as well. I cannot remember where I heard about the gunfight in Price, but it probably happened a few years earlier than stated in *Growing Up Tough.*

There are many books about J. Golden Kimball, and online sites devoted to his stories. One of our class assignments in a BYU college class on folklore was to collect as many such stories as we could. Our efforts could not compete with those of J. Golden's great grand-nephew, James Kimball, who has written extensively about the famous church leader. Where possible, J.

Golden's own words are used in Chapter 21 as relayed in "Living History: Mormon 'Apostle' Shoots Mouth Off, Gun Carriers Shut Up", an article in the *Salt Lake Tribune*, 28 December 2012, namely his mission call, counseling youth about carrying guns, and the KKK in the South.

The Castle Gate mine explosion of 1924 is well documented in many places. The accounts of the dream prior to the disaster and of President Grant's comments are told in "Growing Up in Carbon County, a Short Story Taken From The Journal of Lena Thorpe Wade", available online at http://www.carbon-utgenweb.com/historypage3.html. A nice summary of the Indian "war" of 1923 is given in "The Last Indian Uprising" by Robert S. McPherson at http://historytogo.utah.gov/utah_chapters/from_war_to_war/thelastindianuprising.html. Descriptions of the lynching of Robert Marshall, the Utah Ku Klux Klan, and the shooting of Sheriff Bliss are likewise readily available. Newspaper articles mentioned in the book are direct quotations or paraphrases from actual articles of the time. The testimony by Sheriff Bliss about the shooter's eyes narrowing was a recollection of my father, who, like Eddie, was present in the courtroom at the time.

Also by Roderick Saxey:

The Federalist: Excerpts with Commentary

All Enlisted: A Mormon Missionary in Austria During the Vietnam Era

Turning the Hearts: Counsel for my Distant Descendants

The Trillium Girl

Chronicle of the Lake

Coming soon:

Improve the Moment

www.ingramcontent.com/pod-product-compliance
Lightning Source LLC
Chambersburg PA
CBHW070217030726
47505CB00006B/1707